A Season to Wed

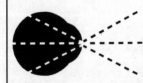

This Large Print Book carries the
Seal of Approval of N.A.V.H.

A Season to Wed

THREE WINTER LOVE STORIES

Cindy Kirk, Rachel Hauck and Cheryl Wyatt

THORNDIKE PRESS
A part of Gale, Cengage Learning

GALE
CENGAGE Learning·

Farmington Hills, Mich • San Francisco • New York • Waterville, Maine
Meriden, Conn • Mason, Ohio • Chicago

GALE
CENGAGE Learning®

LIBRARY OF CONGRESS CATALOGING-IN-PUBLICATION DATA

Names: Kirk, Cindy. Love at Mistletoe Inn. | Hauck, Rachel, 1960– A brush with love. | Wyatt, Cheryl. Serving up a sweetheart.
Title: A season to wed : three winter love stories / by Cindy Kirk, Rachel Hauck, Cheryl Wyatt.
Description: Large print edition. | Waterville, Maine : Thorndike Press, 2016. | © 2015 | Series: Thorndike Press large print Christian fiction
Identifiers: LCCN 2015047379| ISBN 9781410487841 (hardcover) | ISBN 1410487849 (hardcover)
Subjects: LCSH: Christian fiction, American. | Romance fiction, American. | Weddings—Fiction. | Large type books.
Classification: LCC PS648.C43 S43 2016 | DDC 813/.01083823—dc23
LC record available at http://lccn.loc.gov/2015047379

Published in 2016 by arrangement with The Zondervan Corporation LLC, a subsidiary of HarperCollins Christian Publishing, Inc.

Printed in Mexico
1 2 3 4 5 6 7 20 19 18 17 16

CONTENTS

■ ■ ■ ■

LOVE AT MISTLETOE INN

CINDY KIRK

■ ■ ■ ■

*To Becky Philpott and Ami McConnell,
two of my favorite editors.
I'll meet you for breakfast anytime!*

CHAPTER ONE

Although spending an entire Saturday manning a booth at the Boise Bridal Extravaganza might not be most women's idea of fun, Hope Prentiss was enjoying herself. It helped that Amity Carter had the next booth.

While Hope was at the October event promoting Harmony Creek, a popular Idaho venue for weddings and receptions, Amity specialized in helping brides plan nontraditional weddings.

Although both women were in their late twenties and were the best of friends, they couldn't have been more different. How her friend had chosen to dress for today's business event was a perfect example of her unorthodox approach. While Hope had picked black pants, a simple white shirt, and pulled her auburn hair back from her face with two silver clips, Amity breezed in looking like a windblown gypsy.

She had disheveled dark curls tumbling down her back, a boho-chic dress of purple gauzy cotton, and gladiator sandals. Amity's eyes were the color of exotic spices, and her effective use of makeup made her eyes the focal point of a striking face. Though Hope usually received compliments on her sea-green eyes, next to Amity she felt like a brown wren beside a bright peacock.

Hope sighed when Amity handed her a cup of cappuccino "borrowed" from one of the vendors touting their mobile coffee bar.

"I can't believe we're friends," Hope murmured, bringing the cup to her lips.

A sardonic smile lifted Amity's lips. "Love ya too, Chickadee."

Dragging her chair over to Hope's booth, Amity settled in with her cup of gourmet hot cocoa. The fashion show was under way in another part of the Boise Centre, which gave the vendors a chance to relax.

Hope took a long drink and let the caffeine jolt her mind. "I meant you're adorable and so much fun."

"All true." Amity flashed a grin, then blew on the steaming cocoa. "Though I prefer mysterious to adorable."

"You're beautiful and mysterious while I'm average and forgettable." Hope's lips lifted in a self-deprecating smile.

"Oh, I don't know," Amity drawled. "You have a few redeeming qualities. You're a nice person. And a most excellent friend."

"I'm not exactly spontaneous."

"Are you referring to the incident last week when you refused to go to a concert with me so you could stay home and watch your pears grow?"

"I needed to *pick* pears," Hope clarified. "Anyway, the cost of the ticket for that show was out of my price range."

Amity's eyes twinkled. "What range is that?"

"You know. Under twenty."

Amity's laugh sounded like the tinkling of a hundred mini wedding bells. "Darlin', those prices went out in the last century."

"I believe in being careful with my money."

"A word from the unwise to the wise." Amity took another sip of cocoa. "Can't take it with you."

Hope lifted one shoulder in a slight shrug. Even after all these years, the memories of her parents arguing over money, the worry over almost losing the only home she'd known, remained with her. So she was conservative — being fiscally responsible wasn't a crime. But she wouldn't win this argument. Not with spendthrift Amity.

"I brought you something." Hope rummaged around and found the box she'd stashed under the table. "Asian pears from my aunt's orchard."

"These look fabulous. They almost make me forgive you for the concert thing." Her friend snatched the box, mouthed a quick 'thank you,' then abruptly narrowed her gaze. "Are you still hanging with Chester the molester?"

"He's not a molester and his name is Chet," Hope reminded her friend for the zillionth time.

Gold nails glimmered as Amity waved a dismissive hand. "Some names just seem to conjure up certain words. Hannah . . . banana. Fatty . . . Patty. Dirty . . . Debbie."

"Hey, my mother's name was Debbie."

Amity only smirked. "Last, but certainly not least, Chester the molester."

"Chester, er, Chet Tuttle, is from one of the most prominent families in Harmony," Hope said, alluding to the small town just outside Boise where they resided. "He'd never molest anybody. He's as upright as they come. The guy has never even had a parking ticket."

"Am I supposed to applaud?"

Hope had to chuckle at her friend's dry tone before her smile faded. "Chet would

14

like for us to be exclusive. But I'm not ready to make that commitment to him."

"Smart girl." Amity nodded. "Why tie yourself to Mr. Super Boring?"

"Chet isn't boring." Hope rushed to defend the conservative banker. "He's sensible."

"A.k.a. bo-ring." The response came in a singsong tone.

Hope lifted her chin. "If he is, then I like boring."

"Face it, Chickadee, you wouldn't know how to handle a red-blooded male. Wouldn't have a clue what to do with a real man." Before Hope could protest, Amity jumped up as if the seat of her metal chair had suddenly turned red-hot. "Yikes! I just remembered I promised Sylvie in the Mad Batter booth I'd drop off a few of my business cards. Since she does nontrad stuff like me, she said she'd hand them out. Back in five."

Hope had seen Sylvie's cakes. They were definitely "nontrad." The wedding cake displayed in the Mad Batter booth today was a perfect example. The multilayer concoction designed for a Christmas wedding sported red-and-white vertical stripes, black flowers, pearls, and . . . two prettily decorated fondant skulls. The words " 'Til death us do part" flowed in elegant script across the front.

While Hope thought the cake was more than a little creepy, Amity had squealed and raved. Hope liked to think she grounded Amity and made her fun-loving friend think twice before she jumped into some new venture.

As for Amity, well, listening to her friend's tales of exploits allowed Hope to live vicariously in a world she would never again embrace.

Ten years ago Hope had ignored common sense and allowed herself to be swept from the safety of the shoreline into rocky waters where she was immediately in over her head.

Amity was wrong. Even ten years ago, Hope had known what to do when she was confronted with a red-blooded male. She'd . . . married him.

She'd been eighteen when she and John Burke had skipped their high-school prom and headed to Boise to elope. She couldn't even console herself that it had been an impulsive, "hey, let's get married tonight" kind of thing.

They'd planned it out, getting a license and finding a minister to marry them. The preacher — and she used that term loosely, as the guy had been ordained online — had been in it for the cash.

They'd said their vows, exchanged rings, and been pronounced husband and wife. Then the minister, "Buddy," had demanded fifty dollars. John had balked, insisting they'd agreed on twenty and he didn't have the extra thirty.

A cold chill had traveled down her spine, just as it did now, remembering. Hope had been struck by the enormity of what she'd just done. She'd tied her future to someone who didn't even have enough money to pay the preacher.

Hope was embarrassed to recall how she'd fallen apart and cried like a baby, insisting she'd made a mistake and didn't want to be married. John had tried to comfort and reassure her, but she'd been inconsolable.

Buddy had taken pity on her. Though he was supposed to file the license within thirty days to make the marriage official, the college-student-turned-minister told her not to worry. He simply wouldn't send in the forms. It'd be as if the marriage had never taken place.

She and John returned to Harmony that night. On the ride back, John tried to talk to her, but she shut him out. For the next six weeks he tried repeatedly to breach the wall she'd erected.

But when John gave up and hopped on

his motorcycle the day after graduation to make his fortune, Hope felt as if her best friend had deserted her. Which made no sense at all.

"Botheration!" The words came out on a groan.

Hope blinked back to the present and realized the sound had come from Amity. "What's the matter?"

"They're coming this way," Amity hissed.

"Who?"

"Brooke Hauder and her mother." Amity busied herself arranging brochures on her table, as if not making eye contact would cause the two to walk on by. "Brooke's wedding plans are solid but she's convinced something will go wrong. Crazy high-maintenance."

The two women were definitely sauntering their direction. The girl was whippet-thin with a pale complexion common to gingers. The mother was short and stout and reminded Hope of a fireplug.

Amity turned and offered a bright smile as the two stopped in front of her booth. "Hey, gals. What brings you here today?"

Hope knew she shouldn't eavesdrop, but she couldn't remember ever seeing Amity attempt to avoid speaking with someone. Crouching down, Hope pretended to be

18

sorting through a box of pamphlets.

The older woman placed a supportive hand on her daughter's back. "Brooke has gotten herself all worked up over something. I hope speaking with you will reassure her."

"Of course." Amity spoke in a surprisingly soothing tone. "What's got you stressed, sweetie?"

The girl toyed with the button on her coat. "Mom thinks I'm being silly —"

"Now, Brookie, I never said that." The mother laughed lightly and shot Amity a conspiratorial glance.

"You thought it." The girl narrowed her eyes at her mother. "I know you —"

"Tell me the problem." Amity interrupted in a firm tone that silenced the two women.

"It's Pete's uncle. The one who is going to marry us."

From her vantage point, Hope could see Amity nod.

"You know he's not a real minister. I mean, he got ordained on one of those online sites, but he doesn't have a church or anything."

"I assure you, his online ordination means he can legally marry in the state of Idaho," Amity said calmly.

"Pete and I were at his house last night. He said he hoped he didn't forget to send in the marriage certificate after the ceremony because then we'd be living in sin. He laughed as if it was some big joke. I told him he'd better not forget. Now I'm worried he will."

"He was teasing you, Brooke."

Brooke continued as if her mother hadn't spoken. "I told him if he didn't send in those forms, Pete and I won't be legally married."

"And *I* told *you,*" Mrs. Hauder interrupted, "that the marriage would still be legal."

Hope's knees began to tremble. She rested a hand on the nearby chair for support.

"Your mother is correct," Amity said to Brooke. "Even if the forms aren't sent in, the marriage is legal."

"Are you certain?" Brooke fixed her gaze on Amity.

"One hundred percent positive. This issue has come up before. I verified it myself with the county recorder."

"See, I told you." The older woman's tone turned chiding. "Do you ever listen to me? No."

Cold fear stole Hope's breath. As mother and daughter continued to bicker, a dull roaring filled her ears. She couldn't move.

"You can come out now," Amity said

good-naturedly. "Troll Bird and Spawn have departed."

Slowly, Hope rose to her feet.

"Did you ever hear anything so silly?" Amity chuckled and refilled the bowl on the vintage scale decorating her booth with more chocolate mints. "Thinking that just because the forms didn't get sent the marriage wouldn't be legal."

A shaky laugh was all Hope could manage, while inside her thoughts raced.

On a sunny Saturday in early October, John Burke rode into Harmony on the back of his new Harley. The sights and smells of early autumn surrounded him. While most of the lawns were still green, the leaves had already morphed into vibrant shades of red and yellow and orange. There was a pleasant earthy fragrance to the air, as if it had recently rained. John inhaled deeply.

He'd been back many times, but those had mostly been quick trips around the holidays. This was different.

He reached the business district and continued to drive slowly, admiring the town square. A three-story stone city hall anchored the middle of the square, while shops lined the perimeter. Old-fashioned gas lamps stood like sentinels at the edge of the brick streets, ready to cast their light on the canopied storefronts.

In no particular hurry, John circled the square several times, taking note of businesses that were new since his last visit. The names were displayed on colorful awnings over storefront windows: The Coffee Pot, Petal Creations, and Carly's Cut and Curl. The only business not showing any action on a lazy Saturday afternoon was the Thirsty Buffalo, a popular local bar.

Though John had loved working and living in Portland for the past ten years, Harmony was home. When he'd left after high school, he'd vowed to return when he was a success.

Against all odds, he'd reached that goal. But along that circuitous route with its peaks and valleys, John had discovered an undeniable truth. Success was more than a healthy bank account, more than following your passion; it was putting God and family first. Now he was coming home to put that belief into action.

John never knew his grandparents. His father had taken off when he was ten, shortly after his mother had been diagnosed with cancer. When he was sixteen, she'd died of the disease. The only family he had was Aunt Verna, who wasn't really his aunt.

Verna had been his mother's childhood friend. When his mom passed away and John was tossed into the foster care system, Verna had taken classes to become a foster parent and brought him into her home. She was his family now. As she aged, he wanted to be there for her. But Verna wasn't the only reason he'd returned to Harmony.

John turned his cycle onto a brick street where older homes sat far back with huge expanses of lawns draped before them like green carpets. Except for one barking beagle and a boy on a bike, the neighborhood was quiet.

At the far end of the road, he caught sight of his destination. The two-story home, with its wraparound porch, stained-glass window panels, and abundance of gingerbread molding, stood big and white against the brilliant blue of the sky. The ornate wrought-iron fence surrounding the main yard only added to its charm.

Seeing it now, John was filled with a sense of coming home. He pulled the Harley into the drive. Almost immediately Verna appeared on the porch, a willowy woman with hair the color of champagne. When she raised her hand in greeting and he saw her broad smile, his fingers relaxed on the bike's handlebar grips. He was home.

This time for good.

Hope saw the motorcycle sitting in front of the carriage house when she pulled into the driveway. Idly, she wondered who Verna was showing through the barn. Though her aunt hadn't had any late afternoon appointments scheduled when Hope left for the bridal fair that morning, it wasn't unusual for prospective clients to drop by without an appointment.

Despite Amity's remarks looming over her like a dark cloud, Hope felt good about what she'd accomplished today. The booth had been worth every penny of the premium price they'd paid. Barn weddings were all the rage, and her booth displayed a slideshow of their gleaming red barn with its arched roof and remodeled interior. A number of brides and their mothers had set up times to visit Harmony Creek.

After they'd torn down their booths, Amity had urged Hope to join her and some friends for dinner. But Hope was in no mood to socialize. Thankfully, Chet had called off their date for tonight. The man who would be his campaign manager had scheduled a meeting with business leaders about a possible state senate run.

Just as well. Hope had too much on her

mind, none of which she was ready to discuss with Amity or Chet.

What if I am still married to John?

Hope stepped from the car, closing her eyes against the sudden stab in her heart. She knew God wouldn't give her more than she could bear.

It will be okay, she told herself. *It will all be okay.*

She entered the house, where she lived with her aunt, via the back door. Aunt Verna stood at the stove stirring a pot of soup and speaking with a man whose back was to Hope. He was tall and lanky, his wavy dark hair almost as long as hers. Hope had never seen her aunt cook in front of a potential client.

Obviously Verna knew this man and felt comfortable around him. Still, since her aunt seemed so determined to get dinner on the table, Hope would be a good niece and offer to show him around.

Before she could make the offer, the man turned. Her heart dropped to her toes. She didn't know whether to laugh hysterically or cry. Not more than she could bear? God apparently had more faith in her than was warranted.

"Hello, Hope," she heard John say. "It's good to see you again."

CHAPTER TWO

Dinner in the Prentiss household was always served family style. Tonight was no exception. A large platter held pieces of fried chicken, John's favorite. Bowls of whipped potatoes, green beans, and carrots sat in the middle of the farmhouse table.

Hope's appetite had vanished, but she was determined to get through the meal if it killed her. It would be the best way to find out exactly what had brought John back to Harmony . . . and how long he planned to stay.

She'd been tempted to ask earlier, when she'd first seen him in the kitchen. But when he drew her to him in a quick embrace, she'd lost the ability to form a single word. Though she'd seen him at various holidays, he hadn't touched her since the night they'd . . . married.

By the time he released her and she'd regained her power of speech, John was out

of the house, promising to be back by din-
nertime. Now here he was, sitting across
from her.

If he was uncomfortable in her presence,
it didn't show.

"I didn't get a chance to ask you earlier."
Hope passed him the gravy boat and spoke
in what she hoped was a casual tone. "How
long will you stay this time?"

Other than Christmas or Thanksgiving,
his visits had only lasted a day or two before
he was back on the road again for Portland.
He was an artist, specializing in sculpting.
Hope had to admit the piece he'd given
Verna last Mother's Day — a figure of a
woman with arms outstretched toward the
sky made out of steel, data cables, and ten-
inch-long nails — was impressive. Almost as
impressive as the man himself.

Hope watched John add to the whipped
potatoes some of the white chicken gravy
that Verna claimed was a special recipe.
Actually, what made it different — and so
delicious — was the addition of bacon drip-
pings that Verna saved in a jar.

Meeting her gaze, John smiled. Hope was
ashamed to admit her traitorous heart flut-
tered. When she was a teenager, she'd been
convinced that he was the handsomest boy
on the planet. With his jet-black hair, pierc-

ing blue eyes, and features that could have come from a Roman warrior, John had been every young girl's fantasy. He was even handsomer now.

He'd let his hair grow long until the dark strands brushed his shoulders. The extra twenty pounds of muscle he'd put on for high-school sports had disappeared, leaving a leaner frame and even more pronounced cheekbones. But his lashes were still long and those perfectly sculpted lips just as tempting.

Hope couldn't take her eyes off his mouth, recalling how he used to trail kisses down her neck while whispering sweet words of love. She wondered suddenly what it'd feel like to kiss him again.

The mere thought had her lips tingling.

"What did you ask me?" His eyes remained fixed on her.

Hope blinked, confused.

"She asked how long you planned to stay." Verna resumed her seat at the table after removing perfectly formed biscuits from a cast-iron skillet and dropping them into a heated bread basket.

Hope had been convinced she wouldn't be able to eat a bite, but then Verna handed the basket to her. The wonderful aroma teased her nostrils. She took a biscuit and began to butter it, conscious that John was still looking at her.

"How long?" she repeated when he didn't answer but continued to stare.

"Didn't Verna tell you?" John cast a curious glance in his foster mother's direction. He appeared to relax at Verna's encouraging smile. "I'm moving back to Harmony."

The biscuit Hope had been buttering slipped from her fingers onto the bread plate. "Why, that's . . . wonderful."

She picked up the biscuit and tried to gather her thoughts. It seemed like a quirk of fate that, on the day she discovered they might still be married, John showed up in Harmony.

Consoling herself that John's proximity would only make getting an annulment — if it proved necessary — that much easier, Hope bit into the biscuit.

Verna nudged Hope's hand with the bowl of carrots and persisted until Hope added a few to her plate, then passed the bowl to John.

His fingers brushed hers, and a sizzle of heat traveled up her arm.

Hope inhaled sharply. Her reaction made no sense. She was reacting to him as if their connection had never been severed.

Botheration, nothing was making any

sense. Hope put a hand to her head and closed her eyes for a second.

"Are you okay?" Concern filled John's voice.

She opened her eyes and forced a wan smile. "Just a little headache. It was a long day."

"Tell me about the bridal fair," Verna urged. "I've been so busy getting dinner made that we haven't had a chance to talk."

"John's decision to move back is so much more interesting." Hope shifted her attention to him. "What made you leave Portland? I thought you liked it there."

"I did." He added carrots to his plate. "But Harmony has always felt like home. And I can work from anywhere."

He hadn't really answered her question, but to press further might appear as if she was hounding him . . . or was overly interested.

"You and Verna have a great thing going with Harmony Creek," he said, bouncing the conversational ball back to her. "I'd think that'd be enough to keep you busy, but she tells me you're doing payroll for the Tuttle banks as well as some tax work in the spring."

It appeared Verna had done quite a stellar job updating John on her life. Too bad her

30

aunt hadn't done quite so well keeping Hope informed of *his* activities.

"I like to stay busy." She stabbed a carrot with her fork. "And I'm in the critical years of building my portfolio. I put most of the money from my accounting work into the market. So far, so good."

"I'd have expected you to be more conservative in your investments. Perhaps a CD or maybe a money-market account."

Hope narrowed her eyes. Was he making fun of her? His stoic expression made it difficult to tell. "The return on a CD or money market wouldn't even keep up with inflation."

"But no risk," he said, a tiny smile hovering on the corners of his lips. "From what I remember, you're averse to risk taking, for any reason."

The heat rose up Hope's neck like a fire in dry kindling, reaching her cheeks in seconds. She wasn't fooled by his innocent expression. No, sirree.

She slammed the glass she'd brought to her mouth back on the table with such force the milk sloshed in the air. Placing her hands on the edge of the table, Hope leaned forward. When she spoke, her voice was razor-sharp. "What I'm not willing to take are foolish risks."

"I believe this time together around the table is the perfect opportunity to let you in on my latest brilliant plan," Verna interrupted, her tone cheerful but determined. "I'm going to call it Mistletoe Inn."

Hope sat back, suddenly confused. "Call what Mistletoe Inn?"

"The house, of course."

"What house?" John asked.

"The one you're sitting in, silly." Verna's lips lifted in a pleased smile, as if knowing she now had their full attention. "I've decided to open my home for weddings — initially, during the month of December only. We'll offer small wedding packages. Couples can marry in the parlor and use the entire main level for the reception. We'll make a few rooms on the upper level available for the wedding couple and their guests."

"When did you decide this?" Hope couldn't hide her confusion.

"I've been considering it for some time." Verna added a dollop of honey to her biscuit.

"I thought" — John spoke slowly, as if maneuvering his way through a minefield — "that you enjoyed your privacy and liked having friends and family over for holiday decorating and activities. How are you going to do that if you have people in your home for weddings?"

"I agree." Hope exchanged a look with John. She had mixed emotions about their shared solidarity in opposing this venture.

"It would only be for a select few." Verna carelessly waved a hand. "It wouldn't be one of those 'come one, come all' kind of things."

"Do you have a couple in mind?" Hope asked. "Is that what prompted your decision?"

"No." Verna took a bite of chicken, then delicately wiped the edges of her mouth with a linen napkin. "But I'd like to start this year."

What was her aunt thinking? December was two months away. If they wanted to do this right, that didn't give them much time.

Now wasn't the time to go into the particulars, but Hope intended to speak with her aunt about this scheme soon.

She lifted a piece of chicken that had somehow found its way onto her plate and took a bite. As the delicious blend of spices melded with the succulent meat, she realized she hadn't asked John where he planned to live.

"Have you given any thought to where you'll live?" Hope asked. "I'm sure you'll want your privacy."

She recalled that much about him. That meant there was zero chance of him wanting to live under Verna's roof for more than the few days it would take him to get settled.

"I wanted John to stay in the house with us," Verna said. "It would be wonderful having him here again. Despite my begging, he said no."

A smile began to form on Hope's lips.

"So I offered him the carriage house."

They'd renovated the apartment over the carriage house last year when Verna had thought about renting it out. But then she'd reconsidered, not sure if she wanted someone she didn't know living so close.

"It's perfect." Verna's voice reverberated with excitement. "All that space was going to waste. And John will be able to use the carriage house for his art."

"The space isn't that large." Hope knew she was grasping at straws, but a sick panic had begun to rise from her belly.

"True," John admitted. "But it'll be big enough."

Hope's eyes met his and she couldn't look away. It was as if his eyes were the ocean and she was once again being drawn from the shore to that spot where she would be in over her head. "What are you saying?"

"I'm taking Verna up on her offer. I'll be moving into the carriage house. Like I said before . . ." Those brilliant blue eyes held a hint of challenge. "I'm here to stay."

Hope was grateful John didn't accompany her and Aunt Verna to Sunday services. The moving van hauling his work equipment and a few personal items had arrived shortly after the family dinner last night, and he'd been "busy" getting settled.

Though John had always prayed with them before meals and usually attended church services with them around the holidays, Hope wasn't certain where he was on his faith journey. Frankly, she didn't care.

Perhaps that wasn't very Christian of her, but right now the only thing she had to be thankful for was that he wasn't going to be staying in a bedroom down the hall. On the same property was bad enough.

For now she was determined to keep her distance. She wasn't ready to talk about their 'maybe' marriage yet. That's why, when John had turned down Aunt Verna's invitation to the soup supper this evening, she'd abandoned her plan to spend a quiet evening at home.

"Earth to Hope."

Hope blinked and realized Chet had

maneuvered them into the soup line while she'd been lost in her thoughts. The event in the church basement was to raise money for a youth mission trip. "I'm sorry, what did you say?"

"You look especially lovely." Actually, with his stylishly cut blond hair and all-American good looks, Chet was the lovely one. He had a face made for campaign posters.

"Thank you," Hope said, surprised by the compliment. "I love your new shoes."

"Ferragamos," he said with a pleased smile, and she felt her heart warm.

Chet had been extra charming today. As if trying to make up for breaking their Saturday night date, he'd sat with her and Verna during church this morning, then asked if she'd sit with him at the soup supper this evening.

At the time, she'd told him she didn't think she would make it. That was before she knew John was staying home. She wasn't surprised Chet planned to attend. Such an event was prime campaigning territory.

"I'm happy you decided not to wear jeans." His palm rested lightly against the small of her back. "It's important for a woman to look like a lady."

It wasn't the first time Chet had said

something like that, and she'd always let it slide. "You have something against women wearing pants?"

She could see he'd caught the slight edge to her voice and that it had surprised him. Well, his archaic attitude rubbed her wrong.

"I'm simply saying it's important to me that you always look your best when we're out together. If I decide to run for office, and it's looking that way, your attire and actions will be a direct reflection on me."

"First, if you do decide to be a candidate, you'll be running for the state legislature, not for President of the United States." Though she considered the whole conversation ridiculous, she kept her voice low in deference to his position in the community. "Second, I'm not your steady girlfriend or your wife."

She didn't get a chance to say more because Tom Coffey, Chet's political advisor, appeared. "The photographer I brought along wants to speak with you. I think he'd like to get some shots of you mingling with the churchgoing crowd."

Tom, a slender man with a receding hairline, shot Hope an apologetic look. "I'm afraid I have to steal him away for a while."

Hope simply smiled. She remained in line, chatting with an older couple standing next to her. She was nearing the long, rectangular tables holding large Crock-Pots filled with soups when Amity strolled up.

"You don't mind if I join my friend, do you?" She shot the couple in line behind Hope a blinding smile.

"Certainly not, young lady." The portly older man appeared enchanted by Amity, who looked angelic in a surprisingly demure white cotton eyelet dress. "We'll all reach the same place. As long as you don't take all the chili, I'll be happy."

"We'll make sure to leave plenty," Hope assured him.

"Unless I'm unable to resist temptation." Amity gave the man a teasing wink.

He cackled.

Amity smiled, then shifted her attention back to Hope. "Surprised to see me?"

"I am," Hope said. "What are you doing here?"

"Verna mentioned this little shindig when I ran into her in the market this afternoon." Amity's smile flashed. "She sold me a ticket while I was a captive audience in the checkout lane."

"I bet she got you to toss in a little more for the youth group's trip to Haiti."

"She's a salesperson, your aunt. She's always got her fingers in some pie."

Hope opened her mouth, prepared to tell Amity about Aunt Verna's Mistletoe Inn idea, when John entered the room. Dressed in jeans and a long-sleeved henley, he fit in with the casually attired crowd more than Chet did in his dress shirt, trousers, and Ferragamo loafers.

Amity followed the direction of Hope's gaze and let out a low whistle. "Ooh la la. He's a real hottie. Do you know him?"

"That's John Burke, Verna's foster son." Hope fought to keep her voice casual as John's eyes met hers and he started across the room. "I've mentioned him to you. He just moved back to Harmony."

Since Amity had only recently moved to town, it wasn't surprising she'd never met John.

When he reached them, Hope performed quick introductions, then decided to be polite. "Will you join us?"

He hesitated. "I don't want to intrude."

"You won't be intruding. Hope and I are best friends." Amity offered him a brilliant smile. "Since you two are already friends, that means I should know you too."

John looked amused. "Is that how it works?"

"Absolutely," Amity said with a decisive nod. "Hope said you just moved back. But

39

she didn't tell me much else. Are you an accountant too?"

"Hardly." As John began to explain his work as an artist, Hope was impressed he'd been able to support himself by doing something so unusual.

"I'd love to see your work sometime," Amity said. "I'm a big fan of Boris Kramer's art."

"Really?" John appeared surprised by her knowledge. "My stuff is more along the lines of Karen Cusolito. She and I both do a lot of work with mixed media, but mine is on a much smaller scale. Her sculptures weigh tons and often need to be set by a crane. I'm not quite at that point yet."

"What is mixed media?" Hope found herself drawn into the conversation despite her desire to keep her distance.

"Just how it sounds," John said, appearing pleased by her interest. "An artist uses a variety of media — for example, metal and wood — on a project."

"I'd love to see what you're working on now," Hope said without thinking.

He smiled at her. "I'd love to show you."

Amity asked several more questions before John was hailed by a friend from high school and left to speak with him and his wife.

Amity's gaze followed him for several

seconds, then she turned to Hope. "You've been holding out on me, Chickadee."

Hope stared after the man who might still be her husband and sighed. "You have no idea."

CHAPTER THREE

The next morning, John was unpacking boxes in the downstairs "carriage area" of his new home when Hope appeared. The distressed look on her face had him rising and crossing to her in several long strides. "What's wrong? Is it Verna?"

The older woman had appeared to be in good health at breakfast, but Hope's expression told him something was wrong.

"No. Not Verna." Hope shook her head but her assurance didn't tamp down his unease. Her voice quavered and two lines of worry sat between her brows. "Something else."

He took her hand, wanting to soothe her. To his surprise, she didn't pull away. Whatever was troubling her had to be major.

"Tell me," John demanded.

She glanced around the dusty work area as if searching for a place to sit.

"We'll go upstairs." He tugged her to the

staircase. "It'll be more comfortable and private."

Hope's protest seemed to die in her throat. He had the feeling it wasn't the comfort part but the promise of privacy that convinced her.

As the stairs leading to his new apartment were narrow, John followed her up the steps. *A mistake,* he thought. The light, sultry scent of Hope's perfume wafted behind her. Worse yet, he had the perfect view of her backside. Her jeans hugged her curves and accentuated her long legs.

John felt eighteen again. Though Hope remained the only woman who could make his heart beat faster simply by walking into a room, his feelings for her weren't just physical.

She was intelligent. She was strong-willed and that was just the beginning. He loved every part of her. When he'd left Harmony, he'd hoped the hole in his heart would fill. It hadn't.

He never stopped thinking of her as his wife.

Looking back, John couldn't believe a night that had started out so positive had gone so bad. He'd never forget the look in Hope's eyes when he'd been forced to admit he didn't have the extra money Buddy, the "minister," had demanded.

All of his extra cash had been spent on the special engraving inside Hope's wedding band. A ring that had been on her finger less than five minutes before she'd tugged it off and told Buddy she'd changed her mind.

The gesture had crushed him. But that was the past. He was home and determined to capture her heart.

Hope grabbed the knob and pushed open the door. He followed her inside.

She moved to the middle of the living room and turned in a circle. "I still think this is the loveliest room. Verna gave me carte blanche in decorating it. I hope you don't find it too girly."

Verna hadn't mentioned Hope's role in the renovation. Though when the older woman had shown him the space, she'd waxed poetic about everything from the overstuffed sofa upholstered in a sunny garden pattern and plaid slipper chairs in a coordinating fabric to the crown molding topping a whimsical wallpaper pattern of vines and branches. She'd pointed out how the leaves on the Tiffany accent lamp continued the theme.

According to Verna, the rag rugs scattered on the hardwood floors coupled with several ancestral wall portraits added a homey touch and saved the room from being too perfectly coordinated.

"*Lovely* isn't a word I normally like to use." John grinned. "But it's a nice space. I like it."

The style of the furniture had a warm, comfortable feel. Wooden shutters had been pulled back, allowing the outside light to fill the room with a golden glow.

The scent of cinnamon hovering in the air from a basket of Verna's scented pinecones brought calm to the atmosphere. Though the frown remained, he saw Hope's shoulders were no longer stiff.

"May I get you something to drink?" he asked politely. "A glass of water?"

She shook her head. "I'd like to sit down."

He gestured to the sofa. Instead of taking a seat in a nearby chair, he sat beside her.

"It's good to see you again, Hope. It's been too long."

Her laugh held a nervous edge. "You were just here in May for Verna's birthday."

"We didn't have much of a chance to talk." This wasn't surprising considering they'd both worked to keep a distance between them since he'd left Harmony.

Not this time.

"There's something we need to discuss."

45

Her voice cracked when he took her hand.

Using his thumb, John rubbed slow circles in her palm. He had a good idea what she wanted to discuss. She wanted him to know that she'd moved on, that she and Chet —

"We're still married."

His thumb stilled. The words may have been softly spoken, but he'd heard them clearly. That didn't mean he understood. "Did Buddy send in the paperwork after all?"

"No. He kept his word." Hope pulled her hand from his and placed it in her lap. "I confirmed this morning with the county recorder's office that even if the license and certificate aren't sent in, the marriage is still legal."

John collapsed back against the sofa. Hope was his wife? Indescribable joy rushed through him. He'd prayed for a second chance. For the opportunity to show her he could be the husband she deserved. Now, through a bureaucratic loophole and God's providence, he'd received that chance.

"You're probably as upset as I am," he heard Hope say.

John tamped down his jubilation and schooled his features.

Her face was bleached white, those stunning green eyes wide with worry.

46

Sensing this wasn't the time to tell her how thrilled he was, he forced a grave expression. "This is quite a surprise."

"I'm so angry at Buddy," she blurted out. "He assured us if he didn't send in those papers that it was as if the wedding had never taken place. I suppose we shouldn't have taken the word of a college guy who'd gotten his ordination online and had only performed one wedding before ours."

Hope stopped and pressed her lips together as if realizing she was chattering. Taking a deep breath, she let it out slowly. "The bottom line is — we're still married."

There was a beat of silence.

He drew air slowly into his lungs. "You're certain?"

"Positive. The person I spoke with at the county recorder's office said if we had the license, the minister met the qualifications in Idaho — which Buddy did — and the marriage took place, it was legal, just not on record."

John forced a nonchalant tone. "If we don't say anything, who would know?" He had to bring up the option before he got too jazzed.

"Don't think I didn't consider that already." Hope gave a humorless laugh. She didn't appear to notice when he placed his

47

arm on the top of the sofa. "But you know how I am about rules. I can't simply close my eyes and pretend it didn't happen or isn't legal just because to do so would be more convenient."

"You always were a stickler for following rules," John murmured, rubbing a strand of her hair between his fingers. It was soft, like the finest silk. How long had it been since he'd touched her hair, her face, since his mouth had closed over hers?

Hope lifted her face to his.

His heart clenched at the tears swimming in the green depths.

"I'm s-sorry."

With the tip of a finger, he gently brushed a tear that slipped down her cheek. "For what? This isn't your fault."

"For me not being able to pr-pretend it didn't happen."

"Ah, sweetheart," he said softly. "If you could do that, you wouldn't be you."

"But it would b-be so much easier." Her voice broke and she covered her face with her hands.

"It appears, my darling Hope, that you and I are married." Tenderly he separated her hands and gazed into eyes blurred with tears. "In the sight of God and man."

Though he kept his tone mild, it produced

more tears.

John shifted and gathered her close. Hope was his wife.

His heart was a sweet, heavy mass in his chest.

As he kissed a tear on her cheek, her arms wound around his neck and he touched her lips with his.

When her fingers slid into his hair, he folded her more fully into his arms, anchoring her against his chest as his mouth covered hers in a deep kiss. She fit perfectly against him. She always had.

This was the woman who held his heart. Whether she wanted it or not, she had it for all eternity.

John had always felt connected to her. He'd never forgotten the vows they'd made and the promise given. In this moment, he saw those same sentiments in her expression.

Several hours later, Hope left John's bed and headed downtown for an appointment she'd made after speaking with the county recorder. At Reid Mueller's office, she received the news that her actions that morning made getting the marriage annulled impossible. The family law attorney had been adamant that even if she or John were willing to swear they were of unsound mind at the time they married, the fact that they'd slept together made divorce the only option.

She'd known what Reid would say, but she had to hear it from his own lips. She couldn't believe she'd been so foolish, but being in John's arms again had brought all her buried emotions to the surface. It felt as if they'd just stood in front of the minister, had just said their vows. In one minute, all her years of denying her feelings for John had been swept away.

Divorce.

Filing for an annulment, effectively saying that a marriage had never taken place, was one thing. But a divorce . . .

Every part of her being railed at the thought. Still, she wondered if it might not be better to call it quits before they ended up hating each other. As attracted as she was to John, she needed a responsible man, one who took life — and his finances — seriously.

A sense of melancholy filled Hope. She paused at the top of the stairs leading down from the second floor of the law office on Market Street. She gripped the railing but couldn't make herself walk back into the real world.

If only she hadn't kissed John back . . .

What had happened in his apartment had been as much her fault as his. When his arms had closed around her in comfort, she hadn't pulled away. Hadn't wanted to pull away. She'd wanted him to hold her, to love her.

Kissing him again had felt so natural, so right. He'd been so gentle with her, taking his time, not rushing. The experience had been worth the wait. Slipping out of his bed when he'd hopped into the shower had been hard. She'd much rather have kept him company in the steaming water.

Hope told herself she shouldn't feel guilty over making love to John. He *was* her husband. But for how much longer?

The attorney had been blunt. If she wanted out of her marriage to John Burke, she would have to file for divorce.

Hope straightened her shoulders. She'd get through this challenge as she had all the other trials in her life, by putting one foot in front of the other.

She must speak with John. Her phone dinged with a text. Hope glanced down and rubbed the bridge of her nose. Chet had already called her twice today. Now he'd sent her a text while she'd been speaking with the attorney. He probably thought she

51

was playing hard to get when the truth was, she was simply busy.

Okay, so perhaps she was avoiding him. Though she and Chet's relationship had never been exclusive, she did need to tell him about John. The trouble was, she wasn't sure what to say.

She stepped out of the building onto the sidewalk and was horrified when her stomach growled so loudly a woman walking by turned to stare. Impulsively, Hope crossed the street to All Ground Up, a popular coffee and sandwich shop.

She'd just ordered a tuna salad to go when she saw Chet at a table by the window. By the way he and Tom were intently studying a laptop screen, it appeared to be some sort of business meeting or strategy session.

Hope willed Chet to keep his eyes focused on the screen. She would speak with him soon, but now wasn't the time.

She paid the college-aged clerk and offered him a sunny smile that was at odds with her stormy insides. Taking the brown bag, Hope dropped money into the tip jar and turned toward the door. She'd almost reached it when she glanced over at Chet's table and . . . caught his eye.

His smile of obvious pleasure had guilt rushing through her and her feet skidding to a stop. How could she even consider walking out without speaking to the man she'd been casually dating?

What would he think when he discovered she was married? And had slept with John? The situation reminded her of a scene from one of Verna's favorite TV soaps.

Hope waited for Chet to cross the dining area.

"I've been trying to reach you all day." He smiled appreciatively at the conservative dark suit she'd chosen for her trip to the attorney.

"I've been super busy." She lifted the brown bag. "Then I got hungry."

"I saw you coming out of Reid Mueller's office."

Even if she'd been tempted to evade, there was no point. "Oh, Chet."

"Is something wrong?" Concern deepened his voice. "Is that why you haven't returned my calls?"

"What's going on is complicated." She forced a smile but felt her lips quiver. "I promise I'll tell you all about it. Soon. You're busy now."

"Actually, Tom and I have concluded our business." Chet took her arm firmly. "As I don't like puzzles, I prefer you tell me now."

When they reached the table, Chet dismissed Tom — who didn't appear to realize the meeting had ended — then pulled out a chair for her. It was close to 2:00 p.m. and most of the lunch crowd had already headed back to work. Their table was far enough from any of the other occupied ones to afford them some privacy.

Perhaps it was best, Hope concluded, to simply get this out in the open. If Chet had discovered *he* was married, she'd expect him to tell her immediately.

He took her hand. "Tell me what's wrong and what I can do to help."

Hope sat back, the move extricating her hand from his. Like it or not, she was a married woman. As long as she was married, even such simple intimacy with another man wasn't appropriate.

"I'll tell you." She looked him in the eye. "But there's nothing you can do."

"You might be surprised. We Tuttle men are expert problem solvers."

Hope smiled. The supreme confidence underlying his declaration came from decades of Tuttle privilege.

As quickly and concisely as she could manage, she told Chet the story. She began with the impulsive wedding and ended with why she'd consulted with the attorney.

Chet sat back in his chair, his blue eyes

simply astonished. "You're married?"

"Yes." She stared down at her hands. "At this point, staying married or getting a divorce are our only options."

"What about an annulment? You were so young and —"

"We were eighteen. No parental consent required."

"Couldn't you say you weren't thinking clearly?"

Hope's lips twisted in a humorless smile. "That only works if the marriage has never been consummated."

Chet's brows pulled together. "You said you realized your mistake right away and had him take you straight home."

Okay, so perhaps she hadn't told Chet *everything*.

Heat rose up her neck. She cleared her throat. "It didn't happen that night."

"Ah . . ." Chet let out a long breath.

Hope wanted to tell him she wasn't a hypocrite. She'd meant what she'd said to him about not sleeping with a man until she was married.

She hadn't abandoned her morals. She hadn't given in to her desire for John until she'd known they were married. But that piece of information seemed far too personal to share.

"It's a certainty we won't be able to go out again until your divorce is final. Even then I —"

"Ending a marriage is a serious step." Hope found herself irritated he just assumed she'd quickly jump into a divorce.

Shock skittered across his face. "Don't tell me you're thinking of staying with him? That would be crazy."

Hope lifted one shoulder in a casual shrug. "I'd say everything about this situation is crazy. Wouldn't you?"

CHAPTER FOUR

After her stressful encounter with Chet, Hope drove home with her thoughts whirling. She and John had lots to discuss.

If she hadn't been so reckless this morning, ending their marriage would be easy. Still, she couldn't place the blame on John. From the first time she met him, she'd been mesmerized. She'd never experienced a similar reaction to any other man, including Chet. When she and John had gone their separate ways, Hope had tried to tell herself it was simply a chemistry thing.

Deep down she'd known the attraction went beyond the physical. There was so much that drew her to John — his sense of humor, his intelligence, and his playfulness.

Unfortunately, his irresponsibility and inability to take life seriously made him totally wrong for her. For most of the past ten years he'd lived a hand-to-mouth existence pursuing his dreams of an art career. Her dad had a lot of dreams too. But his disregard for financial matters had made her home life a living hell.

Still, a divorce . . .

Marriage was a sacred institution. Not that she'd shown much respect for that institution thus far. Choosing to be married by a college student, rather than a man of God, had been her first mistake. But certainly not her last.

Yet, what would be the point in continuing a union that would eventually break apart anyway?

With a heavy heart, Hope climbed the steps to the wraparound porch. Instead of going inside, she took a seat on the porch swing, hoping the sunny and unseasonably warm October day would boost her spirits.

She closed her eyes. *Dear God, please help me. I've made such a mess of everything.*

"Want some company?"

Hope's lids flew open. Though John's lips curved upward, there was a wariness in his gaze.

Impulsively, she patted a spot beside her on the white lacquered swing. Even if her actions in the past twenty-four hours gave no evidence of maturity, there was no reason they couldn't handle this situation like adults. "Please. Join me."

John ambled to the swing, looking more attractive than any man had a right to in jeans and a white T-shirt. When he took a seat beside her and she inhaled the clean, fresh scent of him — soap, shampoo, and that indefinable male scent that was uniquely his — she was tempted to close the few inches that separated them.

But it was that desire for closeness that had gotten her into this situation in the first place.

His gaze met hers. "I was surprised when I came out of the shower to discover you'd left."

"I needed time to think." She attempted to banish a sudden image of how he'd look with beads of water dotting his sleek muscles. Her lips twisted in a wry smile. "I thought I'd stand a better chance of thinking clearly with my clothes on."

His low, rumbling laugh had her smile widening into a reluctant grin.

John's gaze turned thoughtful. "Did you?"

She tilted her head.

"Do some thinking?" he clarified.

When Hope shifted to face him, her leg bumped his. Warmth flowed from his body into hers. She told herself even if she wanted to move out of reach, there wasn't room.

A crow cawed overhead and the scent of

basil and rosemary teased her nostrils. From where Hope sat, she could see pumpkins in the garden, almost ready to be put on the porch with bound sheaves of wheat. It all looked so normal. Yet she felt as if her life would never be normal again.

"I went to see Reid Mueller this morning. He's an attorney on Market Street. Very well regarded," she added when she saw his brows draw together. "Specializes in family law."

John's foot pushed off the wooden floorboards and the swing moved back and forth. "What did you and Mr. Mueller discuss?"

Unexpected tears pushed at the backs of Hope's eyes. She blinked rapidly and took a moment to steady her breath. "Annulment. Divorce."

John's face looked as if it had been carved from granite. He reached out, then pulled his hand back as if rethinking the movement. "Those were the only options you discussed?"

This time, *she* drew her brows together. "What others are there?"

"Oh, I don't know," he began, his tone holding a hint of sarcasm. "Perhaps —"

"I didn't realize the two of you were out here." Aunt Verna stepped out onto the porch, a smile lighting her face.

John started to get up but she motioned him down. "You stay right where you are. I'll pull over a chair and we can all sit and visit. It'll be like old times."

Aunt Verna took a potted plant from the seat of a lightweight wicker chair and moved it close to the swing. She wore a skirt of teal and brown with a distinctive southwestern flavor.

This was the woman Hope had known and loved for as long as she could remember. The friend and comforter who'd always been interested in what she had to say and who'd always had her back.

She saw the question in her aunt's eyes and knew the time had come to tell her everything. Verna would be disappointed in her behavior, but she was family. And family stuck together.

"Verna, John and I have something to tell you."

A half smile formed on the older woman's lips. Interest sparked in those pale blue eyes. "Sounds intriguing."

"The night of our senior prom, Hope and I got dressed up but we didn't go to the high school." John spoke while Hope was still trying to push the confession past her lips. "Instead, we drove to Boise and got married. We were in love and didn't want to wait."

Aunt Verna's eyes widened. Her astonished gaze shifted from John to Hope, then back to John. "Married?"

"We thought it wasn't legal," Hope said quickly. "We just found out it was."

With the words tumbling out, Hope did her best to give her aunt the condensed version of what had occurred. "We planned to rent an apartment in Boise and attend college in the fall. The way we saw it, two could live as cheaply as one."

"Hope had second thoughts shortly after we'd said our vows," John interjected when she paused for breath. "Buddy said as long as he didn't send in the license and marriage certificate to the courthouse, it wouldn't be legal. We recently discovered that was incorrect information."

"Oh, my dear ones. What were you thinking? Getting married by a man who was ordained online? Even if you wanted a simple ceremony, you should have at least gotten a proper minister."

A proper minister?

Hope swallowed a nervous giggle. She'd just confessed that she'd skipped her high-school prom to get married at eighteen, and the only concern her aunt expressed was about the *minister*? Though Hope had to admit that a proper minister would have known it was legal the moment he'd pronounced them husband and wife.

"All these years we've gone on as if the events of that night never happened," Hope continued, ignoring her aunt's comment. "Then, on Saturday, I overheard Amity speaking to a woman about a similar issue. Amity insisted that even if the forms weren't sent in, the marriage would still be legal. I called this morning and discovered she was correct and Buddy was wrong. That's when I went to speak with an attorney."

"First, you told me," John corrected.

Disappointment filled Aunt Verna's eyes when she turned and looked at him. "You urged her to see an attorney."

"We both believe it's good to have all the relevant information," was all John said.

"I met with Reid Mueller." Hope didn't need to say anything further about the man or his reputation. Her aunt had mentioned on more than one occasion that Reid had been in her Sunday school class when he was in third grade. Apparently the prominent attorney had been what her aunt kindly referred to as a "handful."

"He told me we'd have to get a divorce."

Verna raised a brow. "Not an annulment?"

Once again, Hope felt heat begin a slow but steady rise up her neck. "No, ah, an annulment isn't a possibility."

"The marriage has been consummated."

Was that satisfaction she heard in the woman's voice?

"That's correct," John said when the silence lengthened.

"Do you want a divorce?" Aunt Verna's gaze shifted between them, and it wasn't clear which one of them she'd asked.

Hope straightened. "Of course I don't *want* a divorce, but we didn't really plan to be married, and —"

Verna raised a hand, silencing her. "I seem to be confused about some parts of the story. Let me clarify. At eighteen, when you were both considered legal adults, you and John went to the courthouse and obtained a marriage license. Is that correct?"

Hope flushed, experiencing the full impact of her aunt's unblinking gaze. The look was the same one she'd given her when Hope had insisted it wasn't her fault that the horses had gotten out because the latch was defective.

The excuse hadn't worked then, and Hope had no doubt she was about to go down in flames again.

Hope moistened her suddenly dry lips

with the tip of her tongue. "That's correct."

"You secured the services of a minister, and I use that term very loosely in this case, and drove to Boise where you said your vows." Verna's gaze narrowed on John as if letting him know Hope wasn't alone on the hot seat. "Is that correct?"

John nodded.

"Tell me, how is that not planning to get married?"

Hope chewed on her lower lip.

"And you consummated the marriage even though you believed it wasn't legal."

"No. No," Hope said quickly. "It was only after we knew we were married that we —"

She stopped, but it was already too late.

"You confirmed this morning the marriage was legal." Verna nodded her head sagely. "Which means it was just today that you —"

"I believe you've got a good grasp of the timeline," John interrupted, and Hope shot him a grateful look. "This has been a stressful day for Hope. I see no purpose in more questions."

Verna's gaze settled on John and something that almost looked like approval lit her eyes. "I see no need to hurry into a decision. You've both seen what can happen when you rush. Though I must admit, I always thought you'd be good together."

"You did?" John's voice held a note of shock.

Confusion made Hope's voice soft. "You never told me."

Aunt Verna waved a dismissive hand. "I encourage you both to speak with Pastor Dan and to give this decision time and a lot of prayer. Divorce doesn't need to be your first choice. Take time to get to know each other. Give your marriage a chance. You spoke vows. Consummated the union. Shouldn't you at least see if you can make the marriage work?"

"I don't think —" Hope began.

"John is right. We've talked enough about this issue for today." Verna gazed thoughtfully at the two of them. Her lips curved. "Besides, I have some exciting news of my own. I have the perfect couple for Pastor Dan to marry at Mistletoe Inn this Christmas."

"Wow, that didn't take you long." John pounced on the change in topic with the enthusiasm of a man about to go under for the third time.

"They're lucky to have Pastor Dan officiate." Hope's expression turned dreamy. "His sermon on love always brings tears to my eyes."

"This will be a small wedding but a lovely one officiated by a true man of God." Her gaze lingered on Hope. "Every woman deserves to have that special day."

"Who's the couple?" John asked. "Anyone I know?"

Hope knew he didn't give a fig; he was probably just as glad as she was that Verna's attention was now focused on a different couple.

"Names?" Aunt Verna asked, seeming oddly perplexed at the simple question.

"The names of the couple who'll be married at Mistletoe Inn?" Hope prompted.

"Oh." Her aunt's lips lifted in a slight smile. "Luke and Laura," she said, then repeated the names with more surety. "Luke and Laura."

"That's funny."

Verna lifted a brow.

Hope grinned. "Don't you remember? That's the couple from *General Hospital,* the soap you used to watch every afternoon."

"What a coincidence." Verna gave a little trill of a laugh. "They, ah, won't be around much so I'm going to require both of you to be involved in the preparations."

Hope narrowed her eyes. "Why won't they be around?"

"They're . . . deployed," Verna announced. "But they'll be back at Christmas."

"I should hope so," John said with a wry chuckle. "If they're getting married it would probably be a good idea for them to show up."

Aunt Verna nodded, her smile appearing overly bright. "Exactly so."

"What kind of help will you need with the preparations?" Hope asked.

"Oh, little things like picking out the wedding dress and the tuxedo. We can go tomorrow if you're both free."

"You want us to choose what they're going to wear to their wedding?" John asked. "Don't they have family for that?"

"I'm afraid there's no one except us." Verna's gaze shifted between John and Hope. "I'm counting on both of you to help me. I want this to be as special as if we were doing it for ourselves."

CHAPTER FIVE

Boise Bride and Groom was a full-service shop on West Emerald Street that catered to both sides of the wedding party. When they reached the front door of the shop, John stopped and held up a hand, his gaze focused on Verna.

This was his last chance to get out of this ridiculous errand. "Since you have Luke's clothing and shoe size, you don't really need me. I'll pick you up when you're finished. Just call —"

"I don't believe I've ever asked much of you." Verna spoke in a quiet tone that gave him pause. "I want this wedding to be something very special for these two young people. Picking out a tux or a suit from a brochure isn't the same as seeing it on a person. As I stated on our way here, you and Luke are the same size and build."

While John had been speaking, Hope's mouth had opened as if to second his comments. She closed it without saying a word. Since she'd tossed out the D word on the porch last evening, Hope hadn't said much, even during dinner that evening.

The conversation at the table had been like a trip down memory lane. Verna had kept the conversation flowing as she brought up adventures the three of them had shared over the years.

Emotions had flooded back as Verna recounted biking trips along the Boise River Greenbelt, excursions to the World Center for Birds of Prey, and visits to the Old Idaho Penitentiary, including one at night, just before Halloween their senior year.

John realized that while he and Hope had never run out of things to say, they'd rarely spoken of anything substantial, including past heartaches and dreams for the future. They'd been too focused on simply being in love. Just like now, the air practically sizzled when they were in the same room. But Hope had been determined back then to wait until they were married to make love, and he'd respected that decision.

A part of him wondered if that's why she'd been so eager to marry him . . . just so she could have her way with him. The thought made him smile. She'd certainly wasted no time embracing the benefits of married life yesterday.

"Well?" he heard Verna ask.

John grinned. "Let's do it."

"That's what I like to see," Verna said in satisfaction. "A positive attitude."

As they strode into the elegant shop, John realized that by running off the way they did, not only had Hope been cheated out of all this, Verna had been cheated too. The knowledge that he hadn't considered anyone's feelings but his own was sobering.

Though they'd both felt mature and ready to take that step, looking at the situation now, John could see just how immature they'd been. He'd loved Hope and that hadn't changed. But back then he hadn't known what he wanted to do with his life, hadn't even begun to become the man he was now.

If they'd stayed together, would she have become a CPA? Would he have discovered his talent for metal sculpture?

He liked to think if they'd stayed together they would have found a way to make it work. He really wanted to believe that . . .

"Instead of explaining everything to the clerk, let's let them assume you and Hope are the bridal couple," Verna suggested.

Hope frowned. "Why would we do that?"

"Perhaps because I don't want to hear all

the *General Hospital* comments," Verna said in a lighthearted tone. "I also don't feel like going into a lengthy explanation with one store clerk after another about Luke and Laura's deployment."

"I don't like to lie —" Hope began hesitantly.

"I hoped this could be fun." Verna's expression had taken on that pinched look that usually indicated a migraine was on its way.

"We'll do it your way," John said in a soothing tone. He shot a glance at Hope. "It'll be faster."

Something passed between them. It was the way it used to be when they could practically read each other's minds.

Hope looped her arm through her aunt's. "This will be fun. I mean, what woman doesn't like to try on a bunch of pretty dresses?"

They decided to pick out the tux first since that would go more quickly. Separate from the bridal salon, the tuxedo shop had a more masculine feel with dark-stained wood and fewer indoor plants. No one raised an eyebrow when Verna and Hope began pointing to various tuxedos they liked.

John drew the line at white tuxes, brightly

colored vests, and bow ties. Once those were eliminated, he tried on a variety.

After fifteen minutes, he stepped out of the dressing room in a black mirage tuxedo, Abboud fullback vest, and black Windsor tie. The look of awe on Hope's face told him this was the one.

"Oh my." Hope glanced at Verna. "He looks incredible."

"Very handsome." Verna gave a decisive nod. Then she surprised him by stepping forward and resting her hand on his cheek. "I wish your mother could be here now."

"Yeah, it'd be a proud moment." John swallowed past the unexpected lump in his throat and forced a tone of levity. "To see her son shopping for wedding clothes for another guy."

Verna ignored the comment. "She'd have been proud of the man you've become."

"Thank you, th—" John cleared his throat and began again. "That means a lot."

"Since we have John's, I mean Luke's, attire decided," Hope said with a little smile, "I believe it's my turn to play dress-up."

"Are you really . . . excited?" John asked Hope in a low tone as Verna finalized this part of the order with the clerk.

Hope looked slightly embarrassed. "Let's just say I've decided to embrace the moment. I must confess that when I was a little girl, my friends and I often played wedding dress-up. I'd imagine myself in a beautiful white gown . . ."

The light from her eyes faded but a hint of a smile remained on her lips. "Kid stuff."

He wondered if a high-school prom dress in red had ever been part of her wedding fantasies. He'd guess running away in the darkness, lying to family and friends, and being married by a guy with a goatee named Buddy had never played a part . . .

Strange he'd never considered any of that at the time. Proof that he hadn't been as mature as he thought.

John returned to the dressing room to change. As he tugged off the shirt and vest, he found himself wishing that he could give Hope the wedding of her dreams.

But it was too late now. Ten years too late.

Stacee, the salesclerk on the bridal side, was a pretty young woman in her midtwenties with light brown hair and big blue eyes. She stared at John with a horrified expression. "You — you're going to help her pick out the dress?"

John angled his head. "Is there any reason I shouldn't?"

The young woman hesitated and cleared

her throat. "Some consider it bad luck for the groom to see the bride in her wedding dress before the ceremony."

"I'm not —" Hope saw John pause as Aunt Verna leveled a long, pointed look in his direction. "— superstitious."

"Me either," Hope chimed in.

Stacee's smile froze on her face. "Well, then let's get started."

Hope tried on so many dresses that after a while they began to blend together. Still, she had to admit she was having fun. Verna's mood was upbeat and she insisted on helping Hope into the gowns. John played the part of Luke-the-attentive-groom to perfection.

He sat in a comfortably stuffed gray chair, with a glass of iced tea, and watched her parade in and out of the dressing room in her finery. Hope felt like a princess in all the dresses. But when she strolled out and John gave a low whistle, she knew she'd found THE ONE.

The strapless lace dress in a circular tea length had a timeless, classic feel. The short satin gloves only added to the allure.

"I love this." Hope fingered the flower and feather attached to the silk cummerbund around her waist, then cast a worried glance at her aunt. "But what if Laura would prefer a long gown with a train?"

"What do you want?" Aunt Verna asked.

"This dress," Hope said, puzzled by her aunt's seeming disregard for Laura's wishes. "But I'm not the bri—"

"I have been given carte blanche on all decisions," Verna announced.

"You or John could take a picture of me in the dress, then text it to her," Hope said. "See what she thinks. This is, after all, her special day."

"But if this *were* your special day, you'd be happy with this one?" Verna pressed, her expression intense.

"Absolutely." Hope gently stroked the skirt of the beautiful dress, her smile wistful. "I envy Laura getting married at Christmas. To me, that's the most wonderful time of the year for a wedding."

"I remember you once telling me that," her aunt said with a little smile.

John rose from the chair and pulled out his phone. "Smile pretty," he said to Hope.

After considering where she should put her hands, Hope settled for resting them at her sides and smiling as John snapped pictures of her from all angles. He even took several pictures of her and Verna.

Finally, Hope laughingly held up a hand. "Enough. We should have at least one good picture for Laura in all of those."

He smiled back at her, making her heart skip a beat, then pocketed the phone. Pausing, he cocked his head. "Do you think we should have taken some shots of me in the tux?"

"I don't think Luke will care," Verna said dismissively. "Now, if you'd chosen something flashy, I'd say yes. But I believe we're okay."

"It's a great tux," he said. "I liked it."

"It looked as if it were designed for you," Hope said, then flushed when he gave her a sardonic smile.

She wondered if he'd choose something similar whenever he married in the future. The thought was so disturbing, she cast it aside.

"I've had a wonderful time," Aunt Verna said.

Hope glanced at her aunt's flushed cheeks and love swamped her. In many ways, Aunt Verna had been more of a mother to her than her own.

No, she wouldn't ruin the day by focusing her thoughts on the future. She would have plenty of time for that later.

That night Hope's dreams were filled with images of her wearing the dress they'd chosen for Laura. John stood in the parlor by the ornate marble fireplace. He wore the dark tux and she saw love in his eyes as she walked toward him, clutching a gorgeous bouquet of red roses.

His hand reached for hers and she quickened her step. Only inches separated them when he vanished and was replaced by Chet. Horrified, she stopped midstride.

"Where's John?" she demanded.

Chet's laugh was an ugly sound that made her cringe. "Forget him. He's your past. I'm your future."

"No-ooo!" The word tore from her throat and Hope jerked upright, her heart galloping.

It took several seconds for Hope to realize it was only a dream. She looked around her bedroom — not the parlor — and took several deep breaths. Sunlight streamed in through the lace curtains and a robin chirped happily outside her window.

Finally calm, Hope began the morning as she did every day by thanking God for all His blessings, including good friends and an aunt she loved dearly. Though her personal life right now was fraught with challenges, she had no doubt that God would walk this path with her.

Still, didn't everyone say that God helped

those who helped themselves? She was going to go with that. And for her, organization was critical to figuring out what to do about her marriage.

Hope's spirits lifted. Nothing cleared her mind like making a list.

After meeting with the representative of JPK Wealth Management to discuss the sculpture for the lobby of the company's new office in Boise, John returned to Harmony. On his way home he stopped by the church to speak with Pastor Dan. Other than impressions John had gleaned from listening to his sermons, he didn't know the young minister. But after an hour of one-to-one, John left feeling not only at peace, but as if he'd found a new friend.

He wanted to make a go of his marriage to Hope, but at the same time, he didn't want to be selfish and tie her to him because of some technicality. When he'd said the same to Dan, the pastor had smiled and said something about God working in mysterious ways.

Because there was no one John trusted more than the Lord, he decided for now to simply have faith that his being married to Hope was part of some larger master plan. Because of the vows he'd made, he would give this marriage his all and try to convince Hope to do the same.

After all, as Verna had said, what did they have to lose?

Feeling more cheerful, John returned home to finish unpacking.

CHAPTER SIX

After praying for the strength and wisdom to do what was right, Hope sat at her desk and began to compile a list. Asking the Lord to help her do what was right felt a bit odd. Did she really believe God was going to say, "Hope, I want you to walk away from your marriage, from those vows you made, without even attempting to make it work"?

Still, when she thought about her parents and those fights over money . . . When she thought how John hadn't even been able to scrounge up enough money to pay the guy who'd married them . . . When she thought about how he'd left town before the ink was dry on his diploma and without even saying good-bye . . .

Why should she try? How could she trust him? Why should she willingly put her heart on the line knowing it could be easily shattered? Wouldn't it make sense to simply walk away before either of them got hurt?

Sleeping with him had been a huge mistake. Not only because it had made getting an annulment impossible, but because it dredged up all those old feelings. The truth was, whenever he touched her, emotions and desires made rational thought nearly impossible.

If they did decide to try to make their marriage work, they would need to establish some rules and guidelines for their interactions. She had to protect her heart.

Forty minutes later, Hope put down her pen and glanced at the list that now spilled from one page onto the next. If she had more time, she'd key it in, organize, and color-code the various requirements.

But first she had a group of seniors to take through the barn. They were planning a large fund-raising dance in the spring to raise money for an airlift of Idaho Korean War vets to Washington, DC, next summer.

Hope had just finished showing six chattering women and one long-suffering man through the barn. She was waving good-bye when John rode up on his Harley. Drat. Speaking with him about their marriage had been at the top of her list. But seeing him dressed in all black and looking so sexy drove all the items she'd so carefully composed from her brain.

Instead of rabbiting for the house as was her inclination, Hope waited by the driveway while John pulled to a stop and removed his helmet. "You were out and about early."

His lazy grin did strange things to her insides. "I had some business in Boise. What about you?"

"I just booked the barn for a Spring Fling fundraiser," she said, then, remembering the list, added, "and did some thinking."

He studied her. "That sounds serious."

"It was," she said before amending, "it is."

"It's much too nice a day to be serious." He gestured to the sunny sky. "Take a ride with me."

"I don't have a helmet."

"I have an extra one."

"I really should stick around here." She made a vague gesture with one hand.

"Do you have an appointment?"

"Someone might stop by."

"If they do, I'll handle them," Hope heard Aunt Verna say as the older woman walked up from the orchard with a basket of pears. "Go and have fun. While it's beautiful today, it is October and the weather we've been enjoying lately could disappear in a snap."

Hope chewed on her lip, stalling. No doubt John would want to discuss their situation. She hadn't had time to fine-tune her list, to prioritize, to practice the exact words to use. "I'm sure John needs to work."

"I do," he admitted. "But I'm still waiting on a couple pieces of equipment. They're supposed to arrive later today. Until they do . . ."

"While you're out, I'd really appreciate it if you'd stop by Petal Creations. Take a few minutes to pick out the flowers for the wedding." Verna's tone implied everything was settled. "If you get hungry, I'd love it if you'd check out Fatbellies, a new place that opened on Elm. My bridge club is thinking of meeting there, but I'd like an unbiased review of the food first."

Hope cocked her head, her spidey-sense tingling. It was almost as if her aunt were sending them off on a date. "What about your dinner?"

"Don't worry about me." Verna tossed John a pear. "I have book club this evening and it's Mexican night. I'm bringing my guacamole salad."

John caught the fruit easily and glanced at Hope. "Looks like it's just you and me, babe."

Chet would never call her "babe" or have such a devilish twinkle in his eye. Hope discovered there was something about being the focus of all that male energy that had

84

blood sliding through her veins like warm honey.

In her mind she'd assumed their talk — whenever it occurred — would take place in the parlor. Still, if the bistro wasn't too crowded and they could chat without being overheard, a public place might be better than having her aunt in the next room.

She turned to John and smiled. "Where's my helmet?"

Hope had to admit that riding on the back of a motorcycle was an experience. Before they left home, she changed into jeans and boots. Worried she might get chilled, she'd slipped a jacket over her long-sleeved shirt.

When John told her to put her arms around his waist and hold on, Hope was unprepared for the intimacy of the action. After a few minutes she relaxed and let herself enjoy the closeness. They'd almost reached the business district when her thoughts drifted to the list, the one she'd left sitting on her dresser.

Drat. Drat. Drat.

She desperately tried to recall what she'd written down. Perhaps when they stopped to look at flowers she'd have a chance to jot down a few quick notes and put them in some semblance of order.

But when they reached Petal Creations, there was no time for notes. The clerk looked confused when they explained they were picking out flowers for the wedding of "friends," but quickly rallied.

They agreed Laura would carry a cone-shaped bouquet of deep red amaryllis blossoms interspersed with ruby berries of hypericum and delicate bits of arborvitae. What did it matter they'd have been Hope's first choice if she'd been the bride? The colors were perfect for a Christmas wedding. Vases scattered throughout the parlor would contain other seasonal favorites. Hope was sure Laura would be pleased with arrangements overflowing with blooms of hydrangeas and cattleya orchids in icy white.

John agreed the combination was "lovely" and "festive." She decided she may have gone a bit overboard with her effusiveness over the arrangements when she found him staring at her with an odd expression.

"I wish every couple could agree so easily on flowers for their wedding." The pretty young clerk smiled as she wrote up the order.

Hope thought about reminding the clerk the flowers weren't for their wedding, a fact that the girl seemed determined to forget, but didn't see the point.

"Hope and I share similar tastes," John told the girl. "And interests."

Hope nodded. He'd spoken the truth. While she'd never been as adventurous as John, they both enjoyed hiking and movies and dancing.

Unlike with Chet, who was happiest entertaining a houseful of people or socializing with a group, it had been the dates with other couples or quiet evenings at home watching movies that she and John had cherished.

Hope signed the order form and frowned. How had she forgotten everything they had in common?

"Is there something wrong with the price?" the clerk asked, two lines creasing her brow. "I gave you the standard discount since Harmony Creek sends business our way."

Hope shook her head. "No, no. I was thinking of something else."

"I'm getting hungry," John said when they exited the shop. "Shall we check out Fatbellies? It's just down the street."

Hope wrinkled her nose. "I can't imagine why Verna would want to take her bridge club to a place with a name like that."

He laughed and took her arm. It felt so natural to walk beside him on the sidewalks of the town square. Almost like old times when they'd spent most evenings and weekends together. She liked it. Liked it a bit too much.

Hope brought a hand to her head. She was so confused.

Her heart gave a lurch just as her heel caught on an uneven piece of concrete.

John's hand tightened on her arm and he steadied her. "Whoa. Are you okay?"

"I'm not sure," she said honestly. "I don't know what to do about everything that's happened between us."

They reached the café, but he kept walking.

"You're referring to us being married."

"I'm referring to everything. Finding out we're still married, sleeping together, how I feel when I'm with you."

She hadn't meant to include that last part, but it was definitely part of the picture.

They strolled in silence for several long seconds.

"When I spoke with Dan Sullivan —"

"You spoke with Pastor Dan?"

"Like you, I've been doing a lot of thinking."

Hope remembered her aunt suggesting they visit with the pastor but hadn't given it serious consideration. While she liked and admired the minister, she was embarrassed to talk about how irresponsible she'd been. Or maybe, she admitted, to have him say things she didn't want — or wasn't ready — to hear.

"What did you think of him?"

"I'd met Dan before on a few occasions, but I didn't really know him." John paused near an ornate wrought-iron bench at the edge of the sidewalk. "I like the guy. Oddly enough, he went to seminary with the pastor of the church I attended in Portland. Just goes to show it's a small world."

"You had a church you attended?"

"That surprises you?"

"It does."

"We used to go to church together back in high school," he reminded her.

It was another thing she'd forgotten.

"The pastor and I talked about there being a time or a season for everything. Back when we got married might not have been our time. We needed to grow up, to mature, to become the people we were meant to be."

Hope considered, nodded.

"But this is a different season in our lives. And, while it's impossible to know why, we find ourselves still married. Is this part of some eternal plan? While it may not fit into our goals, it may be part of God's plan for us."

"Dan thinks we should stay married, give it a shot." Hope emitted a dry chuckle. "It doesn't surprise me. I can't imagine him pushing for divorce."

"I want to make our marriage work." John stopped and turned to face her on the sidewalk. "I meant the vows I said to you that day. I meant every word inscribed in this ring."

John reached into his pocket and held out the vintage band in white gold.

He'd kept it. The ring he'd placed on her finger, the one she insisted he take back on the drive home. She didn't need to look at the inscription. Every word was etched on her heart.

From every valley to every summit, faithfully yours forever

She stared down at the ring. Tried unsuccessfully again to think of the list she'd methodically composed that morning.

"I-I made up a list this morning." She forced the words past her dry throat. "With some rules and an implementation plan should we decide to consider taking this route."

"I know you're a planner and very detail-oriented." A slight smile lifted the corners of his lips. "Those are wonderful qualities, especially for a CPA. But this time, I propose we simply take it a day at a time. No list to follow. No formal plan. No rules. Just get to know each other again and make the success of our marriage a priority. I believe it will be worth the effort."

His eyes held a questioning glint.

"If we do this," she said, "this time I won't say 'I love you' until I'm certain that I do. I won't put this ring on my finger until I know I want to be with you forever."

She'd offered the words of love so freely last time. Too freely. It had led to their getting married before either had been ready for such a commitment. All this pain and heartache might have been avoided if she'd kept her emotions under control until she'd been absolutely sure of her feelings.

"Understood." John slipped the ring back in his pocket. "But I promise you, I'm going to do everything in my power to make you fall in love with me again."

CHAPTER SEVEN

Hope studied the menu at Fatbellies. Because of the name, she'd anticipated mostly high-calorie, high-fat entrées. Surprisingly, the bistro menu held a number of relatively healthy options.

The waitress had just brought their drinks when Amity sauntered in. Her friend's eyes lit up when she spotted Hope and John.

"Amity is headed this way," Hope said to John, then lifted her hand in a friendly wave.

John put down his menu and stood when Amity reached the table.

"This is a treat. I didn't expect to see you here," Amity exclaimed. She cast a friendly glance in John's direction. "Always a pleasure to see a handsome guy."

John grinned. "Won't you join us?"

"I don't want to intrude." Amity brought a long nail to her lips, the hot pink perfectly matching one of the colors in the fringed kimono top she wore over black leggings.

"Everyone has been raving about the Belly-burgers here so I thought I'd pop by and get one to go."

"Stay," Hope urged. "Eat with us."

If she and John were going to try to make their marriage work, socializing with friends would be part of the plan.

"Since you insist." Amity slid into a chair across from Hope and cast John a curious glance, and Hope began to fill her friend in on the details of her wedding. When Hope told her about their teenage elopement, Amity sat slack-jawed and demanded to know every "scandalous" detail.

The waitress had just brought Amity a menu and a glass of iced tea when Pastor Dan strolled through the door.

Interest flared in Amity's eyes when the minister caught sight of them and started over. "Who's Mr. Hunky? He looks familiar. Was he at the soup supper?"

Hope didn't have time to reply before Dan was at the table.

John rose to shake his hand. "Good to see you."

"I decided it was time to check out the Bellyburgers everyone is talking about," the pastor said.

"That's why I'm here too." Amity gazed at Dan through lowered lashes. "Will you be taking one home to your wife?"

Hope recognized the predatory gleam in her friend's eyes. She stifled a groan. The pastor might not know it yet, but he was in Amity's crosshairs.

"I'm not married," Dan said with an easy smile.

"In that case" — Amity gestured to the empty chair — "join us."

"I don't want to intrude —"

"Don't worry your gorgeous head about that," Amity told him. "I already intruded on Hope and John's little tête-à-tête. What's one more interloper?"

Dan laughed. "When you put it that way . . ."

The minister — looking very un-ministerial in jeans and a chambray shirt — took a seat, and this time it was John who performed the introductions. Hope wondered if the omission of "pastor" was deliberate or an oversight.

The waitress took their orders, and Amity's gaze remained focused on Dan. She tilted her head. "I was certain I knew every handsome man in this town. How did you escape my notice?"

"I thought I knew every beautiful woman," Dan returned. "How did *you* escape my notice?"

"I like your style." Amity batted her long, dark lashes at him. "Do you like to dance?"

"I do."

"There's a street dance this coming Saturday night," she told him. "Part of the Harvest Festival. I think it'd be fun if the four of us went together. Unless you have a girlfriend. Five would definitely be a crowd."

"No girlfriend." Dan cocked a brow. "What about you?"

Amity laughed. "No girlfriend for me, either."

"What about a boyfriend?"

Hope's friend tossed her head, sending those dark curls cascading down her back. "I know you'll find this impossible to believe, but I'm completely unencumbered at the moment."

"Lucky for me," Dan murmured.

"Totally lucky for you," Amity agreed. She shifted her gaze to Hope.

Hope could see the question in her gaze.

"Sounds like fun." She turned toward John.

"It's a date," John said.

The waitress delivered the food and Amity was halfway through her burger when a thought seemed to strike her. She ignored the question Hope had just asked about an upcoming wedding she was planning and fixed her gaze on Dan.

"I don't believe you told me what you do for a living."

He smiled, dipped a fry into a mound of ketchup. "I don't believe you asked."

"You're going to make me guess." A smile crossed her lips. "I love guessing games. I'm really good at them."

Hope and John exchanged a quick, significant glance and smiled.

Amity went through a number of occupations, then scowled in frustration. "Okay, I give up. Tell me."

"I'm a minister."

"Har-har." Amity rolled her eyes and stole one of his fries.

"He's giving it to you straight," Hope told her friend. "Dan is the minister at my church."

"Get out of here." Amity's startled look changed to amusement. "I've never had the hots for a preacher before."

Hope wished she could clap her hand over Amity's mouth before she dug herself into a deeper hole, but Dan only grinned.

John leaned close to Hope's ear. "Something tells me Saturday night will be an experience we won't soon forget."

John had barely pulled the Harley into the

driveway and was feeling pretty jazzed about the day when Hope casually mentioned needing to cancel her date with Chet. Apparently they'd discussed attending the Harvest Festival together.

Chet had been a few years ahead of him in school, and while they'd been on several sports teams together, they'd never been friends. John could see where that kind of man might appeal to Hope.

Financially secure. Stable. Conservative.

The perfect trifecta.

But Hope was married to *him.* There was no doubt in John's mind that he loved Hope more than Chet ever could. But that didn't mean their marriage was out of the woods yet.

Hope had made it clear she didn't want to love him. He had the feeling she didn't trust him either. How could she? He'd taken off as soon as things got tough.

One thing was certain. He wouldn't make that mistake again.

Hope's conversation with Chet was unraveling, as she'd expected. When she told him she was committed to making her marriage work, which meant they wouldn't be able to see each other anymore, there'd been stunned silence on the phone.

"Do you love him?" Chet asked.

"I did ten years ago, but we've been apart ever since," Hope reminded him. "I don't know what I feel."

"You were a child when you married him. At that age you're still trying to discover who you are." He spoke in that dismissive tone he used when her opinion differed from his. "Now you're an intelligent woman with a lot going for you. You could have any man you wanted."

Hope gave a little laugh. While flattering, it wasn't necessarily true. Besides, it didn't matter. "John and I are legally married. We spoke vows. I have to try to make the marriage succeed."

"You're smarter than this," Chet said softly, reverting to his persuasive tone. "Simply because you chose unwisely when you were eighteen doesn't mean you should compound the mistake by sticking with someone you don't love now."

Hope noticed he'd automatically assumed she didn't love John. Irritation bubbled up. How could Chet know what she felt? While she preferred not to delve too deep into her emotions right now, she'd always had feelings for John, she'd simply buried them.

With a calm she didn't feel, Hope attempted to explain that John was a fine man

98

and they had much in common. But she'd barely started to make her point when Chet interrupted.

"Staying shackled to this man makes no sense at all." Chet's voice rose with each word. "How can you even think of tossing over someone like me, who might one day be a U.S. senator, whose family is one of the most influential in the state, for a guy who welds metal? You won't be happy with him. How can you be? He's inferior to you in every way."

"Tread carefully here," Hope warned. "You're speaking about my husband."

"I'm so much more than him."

Hope suddenly understood why she'd never wanted Chet as a steady boyfriend. Chet thought more of himself than he did her. While she believed he liked her and genuinely enjoyed her company, deep down it had always been about him. What he wanted. What he thought.

Chet was competitive. The fact that she hadn't been interested in an exclusive relationship with him had only fueled his desire for her. For him, it was all about winning. Her reluctance to tie herself to him had been an obstacle for him to overcome.

Her choosing John over him was like throwing a red flag in front of a bull. He wanted her even more now, simply because he couldn't have her.

Hope let him rant for several more seconds, then abruptly ended the call, wishing him only the best in the future, but making it clear she wasn't interested in hearing from him again.

For a minute, she remained seated, waiting for the tiniest hint of sadness to surface. She felt nothing but relief. She stood and moved to her closet.

Excitement coursed through her as she stared at the clothes and contemplated what she would wear to the Harvest Festival and her date with John.

CHAPTER EIGHT

On Saturday, Hope dressed carefully in skinny jeans, heeled boots, and a fluffy sweater the color of mint. Expert use of the curling iron had her normally straight hair falling in gentle waves. She knew from past experience the soft curls wouldn't last. Fifteen minutes in a light breeze was all it would take to undo her work. Still, she wanted to look good when John first saw her.

With that thought in mind, she took extra time with her makeup. She applied smoky gray eye shadow and three coats of mascara with a deft hand. Then, in seconds, her lips became a glossy sheen of coral.

When she was satisfied she looked her best, Hope grabbed her brown peacoat. She scooped up a cashmere scarf in autumn shades of gold, pumpkin, and russet before heading downstairs. She found Aunt Verna and John at the kitchen table.

John had gone casual, in jeans and a navy sweater that made his eyes look the color of the ocean. Normally she'd compare them to the sky, but it had been cloudy and overcast all day and the afternoon had felt more like true fall than the Indian summer weather they'd been enjoying.

Hope loved the slight bite to the air. While Aunt Verna dreaded the approach of winter, Hope looked forward to it. She couldn't wait to sit in front of a roaring fire, a cup of hot cocoa in one hand, with snow falling gently outside the window.

Both John and Verna looked up when she entered.

John's eyes widened in appreciation. "Hey, beautiful."

Yes, the time with the curling iron had been worth the effort. Hope smiled, unable to stop the ripple of pleasure. Feeling smug, she crossed to the table, to the open laptop Aunt Verna and John had been studying.

"What are you two working on?" she asked, peering over her aunt's shoulder.

"Invitations to Luke and Laura's wedding," John said.

Hope looked at the date Verna had plugged in and pulled her brows together. "The wedding is less than two months away.

The invitations should already be in the mail."

"I had to confirm the date with Pastor Dan first." Verna gave a little shrug. "This will be a small ceremony, so it's not as essential they go out so far in advance."

"Even after you order," Hope began, "it will take time to get them, then address —"

"Under control." Verna patted Hope's hand. "I'll get expedited shipping. Trust me. Everything is proceeding exactly as I hoped."

Hope wished she shared her aunt's faith.

"What kind of invitations do Luke and Laura want?" Hope glanced at the choices on the website. "Vintage? Modern? Artistic? Classic? Whimsical?"

"Once again, they've given me carte blanche."

"I can't believe neither of them have a preference." Hope frowned. "They don't seem at all interested in their own wedding."

"They're in a war zone. They may be more focused on staying alive," John offered.

"Good point." Reluctantly, Hope acknowledged she may have been too quick to judge.

"You're in your late twenties." Verna settled her gaze on her niece. "What would you prefer?"

"I'm not into classic." Hope studied the

103

screen, paused, considered. "Whimsical is too cutesy. I'd say somewhere in between."

Verna glanced at John, which led Hope to conclude Luke must be in the same age range.

"I agree with Hope." John shot her a wink. "We're on the same page again."

"You guys are making this easy." There was satisfaction in the words. Verna tapped the screen. "What about something like this?"

Hope glanced at the simple design. Clusters of pinecones edged the invitation. Their deep brown was a perfect foil for the white center where the wording was displayed. Shaped like a snowflake, the center boasted strategically placed swirls of burgundy. A single sprig of mistletoe near the date and time added a festive touch. She cocked her head, nodded. "I like it."

"We have a winner," John announced.

"But the wording needs some tweaking," Hope said quickly when Verna selected the image.

"What's wrong with the words?" Verna asked.

"If this were for me, I'd want something more personal," Hope told her aunt.

"Like what?"

As Hope chewed on her lip and thought,

John took the ball and ran with it.

"For instance, if Luke is having something personal inscribed on Laura's band, you could get rid of this wording" — John pointed at the screen — "and substitute the inscription at the top."

"You're right," Hope said, loving the suggestion. "That would be a great touch."

"Why don't you give me an example?" Verna asked John.

"In Hope's ring, I had inscribed the words 'From every valley to every summit, faithfully yours forever.' "

Hope didn't know what to think when Verna began to key in the inscription. "John isn't saying to have them use that — he's just giving an example."

"I understand that." Verna continued to hunt-and-peck the letters. "If Luke hasn't had anything inscribed in her band, I want him to see how many words would fit."

"Oh," Hope said. "That makes sense."

"Where is it?" Aunt Verna asked.

Hope inclined her head.

"Your wedding ring." Verna looked pointedly at her hand. "John is now wearing his wedding band, but your finger is still bare."

For a second, Hope almost thrust her hand into her pocket, but that wouldn't solve anything. Verna had already seen the bare ring finger. She lifted her chin. "I'm not quite ready to put it on."

"I thought you'd decided to embrace your marriage." Verna spoke as if John wasn't even in the room.

"I have." Hope shifted from one foot to the other, not sure how much to divulge. Some things needed to stay between her and John. Unfortunately, her decision not to wear the ring until she was sure they were going to stay together made it look as if she wasn't invested in their marriage. Especially since John had chosen to wear his.

She chewed on her lip and tried to think of an appropriate response.

"Hope's ring is a special symbol between us. When I put it on her finger the next time, we will both know that's where it's going to stay." John stood up and laid an arm casually around Hope's shoulders. There was no mistaking the gesture. He was telling Verna he stood with his wife.

Hope experienced a rush of pleasure at his support and understanding. How had she forgotten how kind he could be? He'd been like this even as a boy. She leaned into him, taking in his warmth.

"There's another comment I have about the invitations." John pulled her even closer and absently kissed her hair. "Or rather, a question."

Verna lifted a brow.

Hope wasn't sure if the gesture was in response to his comment or his increasingly easy show of affection.

"Why aren't the names of the parents listed on the invitation?" he asked.

"I chose one that didn't include the names," Verna said casually. "I find the practice a bit old-fashioned."

Hope exchanged a surprised glance with John.

"I like the practice," Hope said hesitantly. "I don't find it old-fashioned at all."

"I don't either," John echoed.

"If we were the ones getting married, I'd want your name on the invitation. You're our family and we'd want you to be part of this special day."

John's gaze focused on the screen, his expression sober. "We didn't think of anyone but ourselves when we ran off to get married."

"You were too busy thinking how much you loved each other," Verna said softly, her tone one of understanding rather than condemnation. "Love should be at the base of any marriage. Other things are nice, but in the end, they aren't what matters."

Impulsively, Hope reached over and

hugged her aunt, tears springing to her eyes. "I love you. I couldn't have asked for a better mother after my own died."

John's arms encircled them both. "I agree, you're the best."

Verna blinked back tears and swatted them away. "I love you both too. Now get out of here and let me work."

Hope straightened and grinned. "Yeah, we wouldn't want Luke and Laura's guests not to show up at their wedding because the invitations didn't get sent out in enough time."

"Once again, I appreciate your comments and insights." Though Verna's eyes still held a sheen of tears, she smiled.

"Are you certain you don't want to come to the festival with us?" John held his hand out to his foster mother. "We're taking Hope's car, so there's plenty of room."

"I'm looking forward to enjoying a cup of hot tea and getting these invitations ordered." Her aunt's gaze shifted between Hope and John. "Besides, there's a full moon tonight. A night for romance and love."

Aunt Verna blew them a kiss.

When John linked fingers with hers, Hope knew the only thing he needed to do for the night to be absolutely perfect was to keep holding her hand.

"What do you mean you don't like Mexican hot chocolate?" Amity looked at Dan as if he'd suddenly grown horns.

"Chili pepper belongs in chili," he insisted. "Not in cocoa."

The two had been sparring since they'd met up in front of the church. It was really quite cute. Hope hid a smile and pretended to refocus on the parade.

The parade down Market Street was typical for a small town. There were eight or ten decorated tractors that would later be competing in the "best-dressed" tractor competition, several antique cars, a couple of clowns tossing candy to the kids.

"There's the queen," Hope announced, gesturing to a Chevy 4×4 pulling a flatbed trailer. The Harvest queen sat on bales of hay, surrounded by her court.

The queen was always a senior at the local high school, so the pretty blonde couldn't have been more than seventeen or eighteen. Staring at her, Hope couldn't believe she'd been married at that age.

Amity cast the girl an appraising glance. "She's cute."

"Not as cute as you."

Dan's comment appeared to render Amity

momentarily speechless.

Amity had obviously decided to go cowgirl for the evening. She wore a western-cut shirt with pearl snaps, tight Wrangler jeans, and cowboy boots with a swath of teal across the sides. Her dark, messy hair had been pulled back in a flouncy tail, which oddly suited her just as well as the boho-chic attire she normally preferred.

"That should have been you in high school," John murmured.

Hope looked at him in surprise. "Who?"

"The Harvest queen. Back in high school you were the most beautiful girl I'd ever seen."

Out of the corner of her eye, Hope saw Dan and Amity exchange a quick, significant glance.

Heat rose up Hope's neck. "Yeah, right."

"You still are," John said earnestly.

"Well, thank you."

"The dance won't start until seven," Dan remarked as the last antique car drove past. "Anyone interested in walking through the Arts and Crafts tent?"

Amity's hand shot up in the air. "If there's food, count me in. Especially if they have pumpkin sage polenta."

Dan grimaced at the mere thought of the dish. "Who are you?"

"Amity Carter." Amity's expression was solemn but her eyes danced. "I'm surprised you can be an effective minister if you have such difficulty with names."

Hope tried not to laugh at Dan's perplexed expression. "I want a pumpkin scone."

John looped an arm around her shoulders as they walked to the tent. "Give me a caramel apple over a scone any day."

For a second Hope almost stepped away from him, then she remembered there was no need to keep her distance. With Chet, any public display of affection had been strictly verboten. Which was fine with her because she hadn't really been attracted to him physically. John's closeness made her feel all warm and tingly inside.

Since the temperature outside had dipped into the forties and the tent was heated, the aisles were packed with people. Hope soon lost sight of Amity and Dan in the crowd but knew their paths would cross again eventually.

John picked up caramel-apple bites at one booth and Hope got her pumpkin scone at another. She'd eaten about half of it when they paused at a small booth with stunning black-and-white photographs.

"Ty," John said when a broad-shouldered

man with a thatch of brown hair asked if he could help them. He extended his hand. "It's John Burke. And, of course, you know Hope Prentiss."

"I was glad to hear you were back." Ty Rowen shook John's hand, then he turned to Hope. "And I swear you get prettier every time I see you."

Though the smile remained on his lips, Hope could feel John stiffen beside her at the warmth in Ty's voice.

"How's Katie?" she asked.

"Doing well." Ty grinned at John. "My wife and I are expecting our first child this summer."

"Congratulations." John's shoulders seemed to relax and he gestured to the pictures. "These are fantastic."

"Thanks. Photography is my thing. I feel blessed to be able to make a living doing something I love." Ty turned to Hope. "I spoke with your aunt yesterday. I'll be taking wedding photos at your place in December. I'm not sure who's getting hitched. Verna was kind of vague about the details but we locked down the date and time."

"It's going to be a small ceremony." Hope thought about mentioning Luke and Laura's names but she knew Ty's mother had been a big *General Hospital* fan. She didn't feel like hearing the jokes just now.

They chatted with Ty for a few more minutes, with John buying a photograph that Hope admired of McGown Peak over Stanley Lake. She and John had once talked of camping in that area. Perhaps now they'd get the chance.

"I'll carry it." John lifted the protective container from the counter. "But the photo is yours to keep."

"You didn't need to buy it for me," Hope said. She'd seen the price and couldn't justify spending the money on such a luxury.

"While I like making you happy, I admit I have an ulterior motive," John said with a wicked smile. "I'm hoping every time you look at it, you'll think of me . . . fondly."

"I will." Hope threw her arms around his neck and kissed him. "Thank you."

When she released him, he grinned and rocked back on his heels.

"I'm sorry." Hope felt her face redden as she caught a couple of people staring. "I probably shouldn't do that with everyone around."

"Darlin'," he slung an arm over her shoulder. "Let me make something perfectly clear. You can kiss me anytime, anywhere."

Chapter Nine

The next month flew by. John saw Hope every day. Their intimacy remained confined to good-night kisses. Though she still refused to sleep with him or say she loved him, he felt them growing closer. They spent hours sitting in front of the fire talking about what their lives had been like the past ten years and sharing future dreams.

"I don't understand why you work so much. If you're not on your laptop doing payroll, you're busy with Harmony Creek stuff," John told her one evening in early November as they sat on his living room sofa, a blazing fire in the hearth. Outside, two inches of fluffy white snow blanketed the lawn. The onset of cold weather apparently made Hope think of tax season. Only seconds earlier she'd mentioned again how much she dreaded its start. "I'd think working for Verna and doing payroll for the banks would keep you busy enough. You can't need the money. Especially when you factor in my income."

They may not have combined their assets yet, but John wanted to reinforce that they were a team and whatever he had was hers.

Because his arm was around her shoulders, he felt her stiffen.

"I have a strong work ethic." She lifted her chin, the gesture warning him this was a hot spot for her. "People think they have all this money, then it's gone and they're left with nothing."

John carefully considered his response. Several weeks ago, during a late-night discussion, Hope had mentioned that her parents had spent money they didn't have and were deeply in debt when they died. Because her voice had begun to shake at the memory, he hadn't pushed for details. Still, it was clear their spending habits had profoundly impacted her attitude toward money.

"If you continue to work all those jobs" — he spoke slowly, keeping his tone conversational — "how will you have time for what's really important?"

Hope's head snapped back. Her scowl warned that once again he'd hit a nerve. "Are you complaining?"

"I'm saying —"

"Because when you got a sudden urge to go for pizza at three o'clock today, I went with you." Hope shoved aside the cotton throw he'd draped across her lap moments earlier when she'd complained of being cold. "We both should have been working."

John raised a brow.

"Responsible people work. They pay bills on time. They put money away for a rainy day."

"Responsible people also take time for those who are important in their life," he said mildly. "One of the benefits of being your own boss is you set your own hours. If I'm not hungry when lunchtime rolls around or I'm in the middle of creating something, I keep working. Conversely, if I want to take a midafternoon break, that's my privilege. I don't see why it should be any different for you."

"We're not talking about me." Two bright swaths of red cut across her cheeks. "We're talking about you."

"Okay." John shoved his hands into his pockets. "Let's talk about me."

"I have serious concerns about your work habits and how you handle your money."

His cheek stung as if she'd slapped him hard. Despite everything they'd shared in the last weeks, it appeared Hope still didn't trust him to be a responsible partner. The only consolation was he now understood why she'd been unwilling to fully commit to him and their marriage.

"Let's start with work habits. I've never been late with a project." John met her gaze steadily. "I may not work eight to five Monday through Friday, but creating art is different than a typical day job. When a design is percolating in my brain, sometimes performing mundane duties around the house or going for pizza helps me get clarity."

"I suppose I can see that," she grudgingly admitted.

Hardly a ringing endorsement. John rubbed his neck. It was time to get to the bottom of the deeper issue looming between them. "Tell me why you believe I'm not good with money."

She squirmed under his penetrating gaze.

"One example." His voice sounded flat, even to his ears.

"Okay." Hope surged to her feet and blew out a breath. "Today at the pizza place."

John cocked his head, puzzled by her return to a subject they'd just discussed.

"You gave the waitress a huge tip." She began to pace. "The rule is fifteen percent unless the service is stellar, then bump it to

117

twenty percent. Our service was mediocre at best. I saw what you left her."

Her accusatory tone rubbed like a pair of too-tight shoes. An image of the gray-haired waitress with tired eyes flashed before him. "I left twenty dollars. Not a big deal in the grand scheme of things."

"She didn't deserve that much." Hope tossed the judgment out there, coupling the careless words with an equally careless shrug.

John thought of his mother and the long hours she'd spent on her feet in a similar café. After his dad took off, her tips often made the difference between eating or not. He recalled her joy when someone left more than she expected and likely more than she *deserved.*

He set his jaw and held on to his temper. "Who are you to say what someone deserves or doesn't deserve?"

The quiet vehemence in his tone had her eyes widening.

"I may not know everything," she insisted stubbornly, "but I know money. I'm telling you right now, I won't be with someone who plays fast and loose with it."

The words hung in the air.

The implication snaked around his heart, compressing it like a tight, unyielding cobra.

She wasn't threatening to end their marriage because of a generous tip; she was using the incident as an excuse to push him away.

Facts didn't matter.

He didn't matter.

John's anger re-fired on all circuits. "You think you have all the answers, but you don't. You —"

The loud ring of her phone cut off his words. To his surprise, she took the call.

Hope listened for a second. "We'll be right there."

When she turned to him, her face was as white as her shirt. "It's Verna. She's fallen."

Dr. Eli Webster put a hand on Hope's arm, but addressed his comments to both her and John. "Your aunt sustained an intramuscular bruise to her left shoulder. Otherwise, she's fit and healthy, which is a good thing."

John blew out a breath. "What do we need to do for the bruise?"

He took charge, just as he had when they'd first responded to Verna's call. When Hope had seen her aunt sprawled at the bottom of the stairs, laundry scattered everywhere, John had been the one to spring into action. After a quick assessment, he'd made the decision to call Verna's local physician instead of taking her to the emergency room in Boise.

Hope had no doubt they'd still be sitting in some overcrowded ER waiting for Verna to be seen. Dr. Webster's son Eli had arrived minutes after the call, black bag in hand. They'd gone to high school with him. Currently in the process of finishing his residency, he told them he planned to return to Harmony next summer to join his father's practice.

"Apply ice to the front and back of the shoulder for ten minutes. Remove it for thirty minutes, then put it back on for ten," Eli told them. "That will help with the swelling in the first twenty-four hours. Keep the injured shoulder elevated above the heart, including when she's sleeping."

"What about pain?" Hope asked.

"Pain? What pain?" Eli's lips twitched, making him look like the mischievous young boy he'd once been. "She looks pretty dog-gone happy to me."

Hope felt her cheeks warm. "After we'd gotten her comfortable and John pulled out his phone to call you, she asked for her purse and a glass of water. I thought she was taking a couple of Advil. Before I could stop her, she'd swallowed one of those narcotic tablets her dentist had given her after her oral surgery last week."

"I believe that level of pain management is a bit excessive." Eli grinned. "Tylenol or Advil every four hours should be more than adequate for the injury she sustained."

John extended his hand. "Thank you for coming so quickly."

"My dad will be sorry he missed tending to Verna. She's a favorite."

"Where is he?" Hope asked.

Eli had mentioned earlier that his father was out of town and he was covering for him.

"He and my mother are on a cruise. I'm filling in until they return on Saturday." Eli's gaze shifted between her and John. "Please don't hesitate to contact me if you have any concerns."

Hope threw her arms around him in a heartfelt hug. "Thank you."

"It was good to see you again." Eli's gaze encompassed the two of them. "Once things settle down, let's set a time to meet up at the Thirsty Buffalo. It'll give us an opportunity to catch up."

"I'd like that," John said.

Hope let a simple smile be her answer.

Minutes later, she and John stood in the open doorway, shoulder-to-shoulder, silently watching the taillights of Eli's Prius disappear from view. Before John even shut the door, tension rushed in like a tsunami, adding a stifling weight to the air. Hope could only hope John would set aside their personal issues for now so they could focus on Verna.

She got her wish. Without speaking, John followed her up the stairs. Verna looked old, frail, and as white as the sheets of her canopied bed. Still, her eyes flashed open when they entered the room.

The rueful smile that touched her aunt's lips was like a balm to Hope's frightened spirit. She quickly moved to the bedside and clasped Verna's hand. "You gave us quite a scare."

"I'm sorry, honey. I was trying to get all the laundry put away before I got ready for the Chamber of Commerce ceremony at seven." Verna's forehead puckered into a frown. "What time is it anyway?"

Hope glanced at the old-fashioned bedside clock. "Six thirty."

"One of you has to attend the meeting." Verna's voice held an edge of panic. "Harmony Creek is getting the Horizon award. Someone has to be there to accept."

"Don't worry about that now." John reached over and calmly repositioned the ice bag.

"I don't want to leave you," Hope said softly.

Verna's desperate gaze swung to John and she struggled to sit up. Despite the narcotic's influence, she was becoming agitated.

"I'll go." John answered the question in her eyes, stroking her arm in a soothing gesture. "If it means that much to you, I'm happy to attend."

"Thank you. You're a good boy." Verna collapsed back into the pillow. Though her pale blue eyes remained half open, they slowly lost focus and turned cloudy.

"Rest." John brushed back a strand of hair from her face, then kissed her wrinkled cheek. "I'll be back soon with the award in hand."

"My Tommy," Verna murmured. "He was so like you."

It was high praise indeed. Verna rarely spoke of the fiancé who'd gone off to war and had never come back.

"I loved him so much." Her aunt's fingers tightened around Hope's hand as her voice broke. "We didn't get a second chance. Vietnam didn't give second chances."

"It's okay." Hope's heart ached at the pain in Verna's voice. "Sleep now."

"But the Lord didn't forsake me. I'd always wanted children. After Tommy . . . I never thought I'd have a child. No husband. No child. Then God sent me you and John . . . such a great gift." Verna was rambling now, her words slurred from the narcotic. "That's why . . . I only want you to have . . . forgive me for meddling."

Hope shot John a questioning glance. When he lifted a shoulder in a slight shrug, she looked back at her aunt. Verna's eyes had fully closed and her breathing was slow and steady.

"You better go," she told John, glancing once again at the clock. "The ceremony will begin in twenty minutes."

"Call if you need anything." He shifted from one foot to the other. "As soon as the awards are presented, I'll cut out and head back."

"Don't rush." Hope lifted a hand in a dismissive wave. "I'll take good care of her."

Actually she wished he wouldn't hurry back. She needed to sort through her tumbled thoughts, bring some order to them, then plan where they went from here.

"Hope."

She looked up and found him staring. His blue eyes were clear and very blue. A sudden look of tenderness crossed his face. "Verna will be okay."

Hope stole a quick, worried glance at her aunt.

"I'll be a phone call away."

She started to nod when, in one deft move, John shifted and gathered her close against him.

"I love you so much," he whispered against her hair.

Her head fit perfectly against his chest, just under his chin. For several heartbeats, Hope let the warmth of his body embrace her, imparting strength, giving comfort. Words of love rose from deep inside her and threatened to spill out.

At the last second, she clamped her lips together. She would not say the words until she was absolutely sure the marriage would work. Slowly and deliberately, she stepped back. "Drive carefully."

He stared at her for a long moment, as if she were a puzzle he couldn't quite put together. Then he turned on his heel and strode from the room.

Not until Hope heard the door close behind him did she allow the tears to fall.

CHAPTER TEN

Hope kept the lights in Verna's bedroom on low. While snow continued to fall, she reviewed her calendar and pondered the earlier conversation with John.

In the glow of the bedside lamp, Hope admitted to herself what she'd been unwilling to admit to him. She didn't need the money from her tax work, especially when she factored in the aggravation and impact to her personal life.

She abhorred the added pressure during a time of the year when Harmony Creek was at its busiest. Last tax season she and Verna had joked they'd seen so little of each other they'd forgotten what the other looked like.

Was that the kind of life she wanted? The kind of life God wanted her to live? If she and John combined their incomes, they could still put a healthy amount of money away and have a richer personal life.

Last week, John had shown her his tax

statements. She hadn't asked. He'd just pulled them out, saying he didn't want any secrets between them. She'd been shocked at his income, which was significant and appeared to be steadily rising.

Of course, everyone knew a substantial income didn't matter when expenditures surpassed revenues. Her father had been a successful businessman and her mother had enjoyed a flourishing career as an interior designer. Money had flowed in. The problem was it flowed out even faster. Their home had been filled with constant bickering and tension, all over money.

From the time Hope was old enough to understand what was going on, she swore once she was grown she'd never put herself — or her children — in that situation.

She'd work hard and save her money. If she married, she would choose a man with similar views on money. She wouldn't take his word on his spending habits; she would watch and observe. That way she would know for sure.

When John had encouraged her to play hooky from her duties to grab some pizza, her antennae had started to quiver. Yet Hope admitted that his point about not working a regular eight-to-five job, as well as the need to be flexible, had validity.

Tossing a twenty-dollar bill on the table for an eight-dollar tab had red flags popping up all over. She'd be a fool to ignore such a blatant warning. Hope leaned back in her chair and shut her eyes. Tears stung the backs of her eyelids and slipped down her cheeks.

"Hope."

Verna's soft voice had her blinking rapidly and straightening in the antique rocker.

"You're awake." Hope cleared her throat and swiped at her eyes, hoping the light in the room was dim enough that Verna couldn't see she'd been crying. "How are you feeling?"

"My shoulder is a little sore," Verna admitted. "But I'm hanging in there."

"That's the spirit." Hope pasted a bright smile on her lips. "Can I get you anything?"

Verna glanced around. "Where's John?"

"He's not back yet."

"Ah, yes. He went to pick up the award." Verna nodded, then winced.

Hope's heart twisted. "You're hurting."

"Just a bit. Would you mind repositioning my pillow?" Verna asked. "It seems to have slipped."

"Of course." Hope leaned over her aunt and made the adjustment.

"Why the tears?" Verna asked in a low voice.

Too late, Hope realized that bending close to adjust the pillow had given her aunt a good view of her reddened eyes. "I'm just tired."

Worry furrowed Verna's brows. "What's wrong?"

Hope averted her gaze and took several long strides toward the door. "I'll get you some Advil."

She'd almost reached the door when Verna's voice sliced the air. "Not one more step, Hope Anne."

Her aunt's use of her middle name had her skidding to a stop. Hope turned and strove for a matter-of-fact tone. "I don't like seeing you in pain."

"My pain isn't in my shoulder, it's in my heart." Verna's gaze softened with compassion. "Tell me what's wrong, honey. We've always been able to talk about things that matter. I know John matters to you."

Heaving a resigned sigh, Hope crossed to her aunt's bedside. "I love John, but I don't see how we can be together."

Verna patted a spot on the bed. "Tell me why you feel that way."

After grabbing a tissue, Hope sat and did as her aunt requested.

Verna listened attentively, without commenting, until Hope stopped, not knowing how to make her position any clearer.

"Did you ask John why he gave the woman twenty dollars?"

Hope shrugged. "Does the why matter?"

"Oh, dearest . . ."

She bristled at the underlying hint of reproach in the words. "Our tab was eight dollars. The service was mediocre at best."

"Do you know how John's mother supported the two of them after his dad took off?"

"He told me she worked a lot of part-time jobs."

"She was primarily a waitress." Verna's eyes took on a distant look. "Caroline worked extremely hard to provide for her and her son."

A tight band encircled Hope's chest. "You think John left such a generous tip because his mother once waited tables?"

"It's possible."

"He should have told me," she insisted. "He —"

Hope's voice trailed off. He *had* tried to tell her. She'd just been too stubborn to listen. She recalled his words and the accusation in his eyes — *You think you have all the answers, but you don't.*

Though shame flooded her, fear remained, like a pebble in her shoe she couldn't ignore.

"I'm scared." Her laugh held a desperate quality. "I'm terrified of staying with John and building a life with him and then regretting it. I don't want the kind of life my parents had. I'd rather be alone. I started to make a pros and cons list while you were sleep—"

"Have you prayed?"

Hope chuckled. "I've prayed so much I'm sure God is sick of hearing my voice."

"Have you tried quiet?"

"I'm not sure I understand."

"When you're confronted with a problem, your first impulse is to make a list of pertinent factors so you can arrive at a logical solution. Correct?"

Hope nodded.

"I'm suggesting you try a different approach." Verna met Hope's confused gaze with a steady one of her own. "Forget the lists. Make room for God's presence by being still. Trust in Him. He will guide you down the right path."

Hope opened her mouth, but shut it without speaking.

"We listen and wait." Verna's bony hand curved around hers in a comforting gesture as they sat in the quiet, the only sound the steady *tick-tick-tick* of the old clock.

Hope wasn't sure how long she sat there, listening in the silence. And it was in the silence she understood that instead of accepting all the ways she and John were so perfectly matched, instead of admiring him for being a generous, thoughtful man, she'd looked for reasons their relationship wouldn't work.

He'd given her no reason to fear or doubt him — unless you counted a generous tip — yet she'd continued to worry. Worse yet, she'd withheld her love. She'd refused to tell him she loved him even though she did . . . totally, completely, desperately.

Hope looked at her aunt's sweet face and thought of Verna and her Tommy. They hadn't been given the opportunity to build a life together. She and John had that chance.

It was time to commit to her marriage, to John, and to the life they would build together. Full in. No second guesses, just faith. The rightness of the decision brought both joy and peace.

Hope continued to sit motionless in the silence until she heard Verna's soft snore. Only then did Hope slip down the hall to her bedroom, to the small drawer in her jewelry box.

John had made her keep the ring. She'd told him she wouldn't put it on until she knew she loved him and was ready to be his wife for eternity.

Hope slipped the band on her finger.

In a roomful of suits and silky dresses, John accepted the Horizon award on behalf of Harmony Creek in jeans and a ski sweater. The Chamber members didn't seem to mind, especially once he told them of Verna's fall.

Every person in the room expressed their concern and urged him to take Verna their wishes for a speedy recovery. John skipped the dinner after the ceremony. He was eager to get home to Verna. To Hope.

He was out the courthouse door and headed to Verna's car when Chet fell into step beside him.

"Bad news about Verna." Chet's tone seemed more conversational than concerned. "Be sure and give her my best."

"Thanks. I'll do that." John picked up his pace. He wanted to call Hope and see how everything was going, but he didn't want to risk waking Verna.

"You need to let her go."

John realized with a start that Chet had continued to walk across the lot with him.

"You need to let her go," Chet repeated.

"Verna?"

"Hope." Chet swiped at the snow dusting his cashmere coat. "You need to go away quietly and not put her through a messy divorce."

"What are you talking about?" John frowned, feeling as if he'd suddenly dropped into some alternate reality. "Hope and I aren't getting a divorce."

"She was eighteen, impulsive. She made a mistake," Chet said, as if that explained everything.

John ignored him and pulled out his keys, clicked the door unlocked.

"You know how loyal Hope is." Chet might have been leaning casually against the Buick, but his eyes glowed with an intensity that was anything but casual. "Because of a sense of duty, she's honoring something that never should have been. Do the right thing and give her a chance at the life she wants, the one she deserves. Be man enough to walk away."

"You don't know anything about Hope." John jerked open the car door. "Or about our marriage."

He slid behind the wheel and shut the door, almost clipping Chet's fingers in the process.

The banker yelped and jumped back.

"You know I'm right," Chet yelled.

John hit the gas and sped from the lot. He drove several blocks before wheeling the car to the curb. He sat there while the engine idled. *Was* he being selfish? Tying Hope to a vow made when she was only a girl? Would it be better for her if he simply walked away?

She didn't trust him. From her lack of response when he left, she might not even love him. Maybe she never had. Maybe she never would . . .

He could take the car home, pack a few items, and jump on his bike. Hope would be free to start her life with a man who was more what she wanted. Since he would be the one to break it off, the guilt would be all his.

But even as the plan began to take shape, John thought of the promises he'd made — to God, to Verna, to Hope.

In his heart John knew if he ran, it wouldn't be because he thought it'd be best for Hope. Regardless of what Chet seemed to think, Hope was a strong woman who had no trouble making her own decisions. No, if he left it'd be because he was worried Hope would *never* love him, that she would never feel about him the way he felt about her.

John realized fear had been the reason he hadn't stayed and fought for Hope all those years ago. He'd thought he wasn't someone worth loving. His dad had walked out without a backward glance. His mom had died and left him alone.

But he wasn't a scared boy anymore. What had Dan said in last week's sermon . . . that God doesn't give us a spirit of fear?

God never breaks promises, and neither would John. He wouldn't walk away from the woman he loved. He would stay. He would fight for their marriage and Hope's love.

And he would comfort himself with the belief that one day she would love him.

Hope hurried to the stairwell when she heard the front door open.

John looked up from where he stood in the foyer as she descended the steps, his expression unreadable.

"How'd the ceremony go?" It was an inane thing to say but the best she could muster. Seeing him, she felt suddenly shy and unsure.

John lifted a block of etched glass in the shape of Idaho on a wooden base.

"It's a beauty." His smile flashed briefly. "Everyone sends their best. They were all

upset about Verna's accident. Except for
Chet Tuttle. He's more upset you and I are
still together."

Hope frowned.

"Are we still together?"

The question said in a flat tone sent icy
fear slithering up her spine. "Of course. Why
would you think otherwise?"

"Our argument earlier."

Though his posture remained relaxed,
Hope noticed a flicker of something that
looked like fear hidden deep in his eyes. She
forced a light tone. "Oh, you're referring to
our *discussion*."

He leveled a long look at her.

"I'm pretty sure I was being unreason-
able," she admitted, offering a rueful smile.
"In fact, I'm certain of it."

"My mom used to be a waitress," he told
her as if their earlier conversation had never
been interrupted. "Sometimes, after my dad
left, the extra money she earned from tips
bought our food."

While she considered a response that
would convey she truly did understand,
Hope lifted the award from his hand and
placed it on the side table. This brought her
close to him, which was right where she
wanted to be.

"When I see someone waiting tables who

appears to be struggling, I like to help them out." He met her gaze. "That's not going to change."

"I don't want you to change." Hope rested her hand on his arm, her gaze remaining on his.

"I just thought you should know."

"And you should know I'm not going to do taxes anymore," Hope announced and saw surprise skitter across his face. "You were right. Financially, there's no need and I don't enjoy it. What I do enjoy is spending time with you and Verna. I like having the option of going for pizza at three in the afternoon if the mood strikes me or my husband."

A light flared in his eyes. Though he hadn't yet noticed she was wearing her wedding ring, she knew he hadn't missed the significance of her use of the word *husband.*

"Chet stopped me when I was leaving the courthouse. He said I was holding you back, that I needed to let you go. But I won't just walk away from you. You have to tell me to go and mean it."

"Chet Tuttle doesn't have a clue how I feel about you." Hope closed the last few inches that separated them. She wrapped her arms around his neck and gazed into those amazing blue eyes. "If he did, he'd know I'm hopelessly in love with my husband. I'm only sorry it took me this long to say it."

John drew her to him and held her close, not saying a word.

"I love you." Her voice cracked with emotion. "I never stopped."

His lips brushed her cheek. "It's the same for me."

"Look." She stepped back and lifted her ring hand. "It's on and it's staying there."

His smile flashed as bright as a bolt of sunshine. He bent to kiss her, but as she melted against him her foot hit something on the floor. John's arms tightened around her as she stumbled.

"What in the —" Hope glanced at her feet. She narrowed her eyes. "How did that end up on the floor?"

Always the gentleman, John retrieved the box and handed it to her.

She smiled at the return address. "I bet these are Luke and Laura's wedding invitations. I wonder which ones Verna ended up ordering."

John nuzzled her neck. "If you're curious, open it."

She giggled as he continued to scatter kisses against her throat. Grasping the front of his coat, Hope pressed a hard kiss against his mouth before releasing him and focusing on the box.

Lifting out one of the invitations, she read for a second, then gasped.

John's fingers, which had been toying with a strand of her hair, stilled. "Surely they can't be that bad."

Words failed her. Hope could only gesture mutely at the invitation in her hand.

John took the embossed paper from her. As he read aloud, his lips curved.

From every valley to every summit,
faithfully yours forever
Miss Verna Prentiss
Asks you to join her in honoring
Hope Anne Prentiss
and
John William Burke
As they celebrate the beginning of their
lives together
and exchange vows of commitment
December twentieth at five o'clock
Mistletoe Inn at Harmony Creek
Two lives, two hearts united forever in
love

Hope glanced at John. "You know what this means?"

"We're Luke and Laura." He grinned.

"And we're about to have a proper wedding."

EPILOGUE

Hope stood outside the parlor of Mistletoe Inn, which had been transformed into a Christmas bridal chapel. Garlands of evergreen, pinecones, and white lights adorned the window ledges. Chairs covered with sheer red fabric and ruffles added a festive air, as did the large urns filled with red roses, white calla lilies, and eucalyptus decorating the small platform at the front where they'd soon repeat their vows. Every chair in the room was filled. Despite all the holiday festivities and the lateness of the invitations, every guest had showed up.

Resplendent in his dark tux, John waited with Pastor Dan at the edge of the platform.

The dress Hope had picked out in the bridal shop two months earlier fit perfectly. Verna had given her a blue garter to wear that she'd bought long ago for her own wedding. Hope was touched. Not only by the offer of something so precious, but by everything her aunt had continued to do to make this day special.

Amity stood beside Hope in a tea-length black satin dress that hugged her curvy figure like a glove. With her hair pulled back in a waterfall braid, she somehow managed to look elegant yet adorable.

The two women stood just outside the entrance to the room waiting for the piano to switch from the fifteen-minute set of romantic songs to the processional, Canon in D. That would signal it was time for her trip down the aisle.

After giving Pastor Dan a jaunty wave and flirty smile, Amity shifted her attention back to Hope. "What did you think of Sylvie calling your aunt and offering to make the cake?"

Hope froze. Had she and Verna even discussed the cake? "Sylvie, the Mad Batter?"

"There's only one."

Hope closed her eyes briefly.

"Don't worry." Amity placed a gloved hand on Hope's arm. "Syl knows exactly the kind of cake you prefer. She told your aunt how you'd raved over the one she displayed at the Bridal Expo. Verna said that's the one she should make."

Swallowing hard, Hope offered a faint

smile. "Would that be the striped one with the . . . skulls?"

Fairly quivering with excitement, Amity nodded. "It's amazing."

"Fabulous." As she said the word, Hope realized it was true. What was a couple of skulls between friends? And knowing Sylvie's baking skills, the cake would be melt-in-her-mouth delicious.

Amity searched her face as the processional music began. "Ready for this, Chickadee?"

"I love him, Am." Hope's heart swelled. "I can't wait to say my vows again, in front of friends and family. I want everyone to know just how much John means to me and how committed I am to this marriage."

Verna hurried over, her eyes shining with excitement and pride.

As Hope followed Amity down the red carpet runner with her arm linked through Verna's, her eyes met John's.

Every emotion was there. The love, the promise, the " 'Til death us do part." Thinking of all the adventures they would share in the future, Hope hurried down the aisle to her husband to begin the next stage of their lives together.

DISCUSSION QUESTIONS

1. Harmony Creek's barn is used for weddings and receptions. Tell us about the last time you attended a wedding that wasn't held in a church.
2. The book begins at a wedding fair. If you've attended one in the past, what part of the event did you enjoy the most?
3. Sylvie, the "Mad Batter," specializes in nontraditional wedding cakes. What is the strangest wedding cake you've seen?
4. What did you think about Chet encouraging Hope to divorce John?
5. Verna encourages Hope to stay silent and listen for God to speak to her. Give an example where you've used this in your own life.

ABOUT THE AUTHOR

Cindy Kirk sold her first book in 1999 as a result of a contest win, which garnered a critique of the entire manuscript. She's been writing — and selling — ever since. Cindy has been a Booksellers' Best Award winner, a finalist for the National Readers' Choice Awards, and a *Publishers Weekly* bestseller. Cindy has served on the board of directors of the Romance Writers of America (RWA) since 2007. In November 2014, she began serving as president of the 10,000+ member organization. She's a frequent speaker at not only the national RWA conferences, but large regional writing conferences. She has also presented at smaller retreats and conferences across the country. She lives on an acreage in Nebraska with her high school sweetheart husband of too-many-years-to-count and their three "boys" (a shih tzu, a blue heeler, and a dorkie). Their daughter lives close by with her wonderful husband

and their two little girls.

Cindy invites you to check out her website,
www.cindykirk.com.
Twitter: @CindyKirkAuth

■ ■ ■ ■

A Brush with Love

RACHEL HAUCK

■ ■ ■ ■

To
Susie Warren
Beth Vogt
Alena Tauriainen
For being there . . .

CHAPTER ONE

The crazy January day it snowed in Rosebud, Alabama, Ginger Winters sensed a shift
in her soul.

In the distance, pealing church bells
clashed with the moan of the wind cutting
down Main Street.

"Have you ever?" Ruby-Jane, Ginger's
receptionist, best friend, and all-around girl
Friday, opened the front door, letting the
warmth out and the cold in. "Snow in
Rosebud. Two hours from the Florida coast
and we have snow." She breathed deep.
"Glorious." Then she frowned. "Are those
the church bells?"

"For the wedding . . . this weekend."
Ginger joined Ruby-Jane by the door, folding her arms, hugging herself. "If you're
Bridgett Maynard, even the wedding bells
get rehearsed."

Ruby-Jane glanced at Ginger. "I thought
they were getting married at her grand-

parents' plantation."

"They are, but at four o'clock, when the wedding starts at the Magnolia House, the bells of Applewood Church will be ringing."

"Disturbing all of us who didn't get an invite." Ruby-Jane made a face. "It's a sad thing when your friend from kindergarten turns on you in junior high and ignores you the rest of your life."

"Look at it this way. Bridgett dropped you and you found me." Ginger gave her a wide-eyed, isn't-that-grand expression, tapping the appointment book tucked under RJ's arm. "What's up with the day's appointments?"

"Mrs. Davenport pitched a fit but I told her we were moving appointments around since you didn't want anyone driving in this mess. And you know Mrs. Carney wanted you to come out to the house but I told her you weren't driving either."

"Sweet Mrs. Carney."

"Demanding Mrs. Carney."

"Come on, RJ, she's been coming to this very shop, with its various owners, since after the Second World War. She's a beauty shop faithful."

"Either way, she can go a day without you blowing out her hair. Maggie never catered to these blue hairs."

"Because Maggie was one of them. I'm still earning their respect."

"You have their respect. Maggie wouldn't have sold you this shop unless she believed in you. So they *have* to believe in you."

The wind rattled the window and skirted tiny snowflakes across the threshold. "Brrr, it's cold, Rubes. Shut the door." Ginger crossed the salon. "I think today . . ." She pointed at the walls. "We paint."

"Paint?" Ruby-Jane walked the appointment book back to the reservation desk. "How about this? We lock up, go home, sit in front of the TV, and mourn the fact that *All My Children* is off the air."

"Or, how about we paint?" Ginger motioned to the back room and shoved up her sleeves, a rare move, but since the doors were shut, the shop was closed, and snow was falling, she didn't mind exposing her puckered, relief-map skin. "We can use the old smocks to cover our clothes."

Ruby-Jane had been the first person outside of Mama and Grandpa to ever see the hideous wounds left on her body after the trailer fire.

At the age of twelve, *everything* changed for Ginger Winters. But out of the pain, one good thing emerged: her superpower to see and display the beauty in her friends.

Despite her own ugly marring, she was *the* go-to girl in high school for hair and makeup.

It was how she survived. How she found purpose. Her ability took her to amazing places. But now she was back in Rosebud after twelve years, starting a new season with her own shop.

She'd left home to become a known stylist, fleeing her "burn victim" image.

And she'd succeeded, or so she thought, landing top salon jobs in New York, Atlanta, and finally Nashville, traveling the world as personal stylist to country music sensation Tracie Blue.

But the truth remained, even among her success. Ginger was *that* girl, ugly and scarred, forever on the outside looking in.

Face it, some things would never change. If she hoped different, all she had to do was look at her role in her old "friend's" wedding. The hired help.

Ginger tugged the paint cans from the storage closet. Six months ago, when she returned to Rosebud and signed the papers for the shop, she ran out to Lowe's and purchased a pinkish-beige paint to roll on the walls, giving the old shop a fresh look and a new smell, adding her touch to the historic downtown storefront.

But Maggie kept a full appointment book and Ginger hit the ground running, with only enough time to paint and decorate her above-shop apartment.

Then the two long-time stylists who had worked for Maggie retired. And ten-hour days turned to fifteen until Ginger hired Michele and Casey, part-time stylists and full-time moms.

Painting had to wait.

"Can we at least order lunch?" Ruby-Jane tugged open the doors of the supply closet, the long-handle roller brushes toppling down on her. With a sigh, she collected them, settling them against the wall.

"Yes, pizza. On me."

"Ah, I love you, Ginger Winters. You're speaking my language."

Kneeling beside the paint can, Ginger pried off the lid and filled the paint trays, then moved to the shop and dragged the styling stations toward the center, covering the old hardwood floor around the perimeter with paper and visqueen.

"Have to admit, I love this old shop," RJ said, pausing between the shop and the back room.

"Me too." Ginger raised her gaze, glancing about the timeworn, much-loved room. "Don't you wish these walls could talk?"

Ruby-Jane laughed. "Yes, because I'd like to hear some of the old stories. No, because talking walls would really freak me out." She eyed Ginger, pointing. "But one day these walls will tell *our* stories."

"Can we go back to talking walls freaking you out?" Ginger laughed with a huff as she pulled the last station away from the wall. "I don't want any stories going around about me."

She'd heard them already. *Freak. Ugly. She gives me the creeps.*

"I think the walls will tell lovely stories: *Ginger Winters made women feel good about themselves.*"

She smiled at Ruby-Jane, the eternal optimist. "Okay, then I can go with the talking walls. Okay . . . painting. Shoo wee, this is a big wall. Let's do the right side first. Then, as time allows, we'll finish the rest. With the right side done, we'll be more motivated to get the rest done."

"You're the boss."

Adjusting the scarf around her neck, Ginger smoothed her hair over her right shoulder, further covering herself. While she had the courage to shove up her sleeve and expose her scarred arm, she wasn't brazen enough to expose her neck and the horrible skin graft debacle.

Two infections and three surgeries later, Mama had given up on doctors and decided to "leave well enough alone."

Ginger had cried herself to sleep at night, her hand pressed over the most hideous wrinkled, puckered skin patch at the base of her neck.

She knew then she'd never be beautiful.

"You can have a social life if you want," RJ said, helping her with the last station.

"Who said I wanted one?" Ginger headed for the storeroom. "Let's get painting."

Five minutes later, their rollers thick with paint, Ginger and Ruby-Jane covered the wall with fresh color, their beloved country tunes filling the air pockets with twang.

"You ready?" RJ said. "For this weekend? One bride, seven bridesmaids, two mothers, three grandmothers —"

"Yep. Just a walk in the park, Kazansky."

"I still can't believe she didn't invite me. We were good friends until high school."

"Maybe because you dated Eric for awhile after they broke up."

"Well, there's that." *Sigh.* After graduation, when Bridgett and Eric went their separate ways, Ruby-Jane was more than eager to be the new future Mrs. Eric James.

"As for dropping you in high school, I don't know, but her loss was my gain."

There were no truer words in this moment. With an exhale, Ginger relaxed into the repeating motion of rolling on paint.

The shop was warm and merry with the occasional ting of crystalline flakes pinging against the glass.

"Well, that's true, but I like to think we'd have become friends anyway."

Ginger glanced over at her tall, lithe friend. "You can come to the wedding as my assistant."

"And flaunt my shame in front of everyone as the help of the help? No thanks."

Ginger laughed. "Good point. You can get Victor Reynolds to take you to a romantic dinner instead."

"Ha! Haven't heard from him in weeks."

Ginger lowered her paint roller. "Really? Why didn't you say something?"

"Oh, I don't know . . . I'm twenty-nine, divorced, living in my hometown with my parents, in my old bedroom, and when all is said and done, I can't keep the interest of Victor Reynolds." Ruby-Jane's expression soured. "Victor Reynolds . . . who couldn't get a date to save his life in high school."

"You and me . . ." Ginger rolled paint against the wall. "The single sisters in solidarity."

"Ugh, so depressing. At least you have a

life calling. A skill." Ruby-Jane loaded her roller with paint. "You can take an ordinary woman and make her extraordinarily beautiful."

"I love what I do." Ginger glanced around the shop. "And I want to make this the best place in the county for hair, makeup, and all things beautiful. Next year, I hope to have an esthetician on staff."

She stepped back to admire the beige-pink covering the dull yellow wall. Beautiful. She loved it.

Making things — women — beautiful was her calling, *her* duty in life. She channeled every ounce of her heart and soul into her work because the truth was, she could *never* do it for herself.

And this weekend Ginger would play her role as a behind-the-scenes stylist, or as Tracie Blue called her, "the beauty-maker," for the Alabama society wedding of the year, if not the decade.

Socialite Bridgett Maynard was marrying the governor's son, Eric James. A pair of Rosebud High sweethearts, the beautiful people, united under their umbrellas of success and wealth.

While Ginger was looking forward to working with Bridgett, she did not look forward to the weekend. She'd have to live

161

among *them* at the old plantation.

"Well, if anyone can make this place a success, it's you, Ginger. Last time I saw Mrs. Henderson, she was still smiling over how you styled her hair."

"Grandpa was the first to tell me I could see the beauty in everyone else." She saw it that day Mrs. Henderson sat in her chair, with her wilting, over-dyed, over-permed hair. "I believed him. He'd buy me a new baby doll every month because I'd cut the hair off the old one. Right down to their plastic scalps." Ginger's heart laughed. "Mama would get mad. 'Daddy, stop wasting your money. She's just going to destroy this one.' And he'd say, 'She's becoming who she's meant to be.' " Ginger added paint to her roller and started a slow roll along the wall, the blue sparkle of her grandpa's eyes making her warm and sentimental.

She missed Gramps, a stable force in her trailer park life, always making her feel safe. Especially when Daddy left. And again after the fire.

Then came Tom Wells. Ginger shook his name free from her thoughts. He didn't deserve any part of her memories. Handsome high school boy who disappeared on her and broke her heart.

She'd pushed him out of her mind until she moved back to Rosebud. Until Bridgett walked into the shop three months ago, begging Ginger to be her wedding stylist, and the boxed memories of her youth in Rosebud, of her high school days, busted out.

"Can I ask you something?" Ruby-Jane said, pressing the last bit of paint in her brush against the wall. "Why did you leave Tracie Blue? Really. Not because Maggie called you about this place."

"It was time."

"Did something happen? It wasn't because of your scars —"

"Nope."

"Because that would be crazy, you know. You were on the road with her for three years. Your scars weren't a factor."

Oh, but they were.

Tears blurred Ginger's eyes as she covered the old wall with a thick swath of paint. Goodbye old. Hello new. She hated lying to RJ, but talking about her departure from Tracie Blue sliced through the wounds no one could really see.

Ugly. That's what one tabloid called her. She'd found an article on the Internet one day last year naming the ugliest stylists to the stars. And Ginger Winters was number one.

Where they found that odd picture of her with her neck exposed, she'd never know.

Ginger swallowed a rise of bitter bile, inhaling, wrestling to shove the accusation out of her mind.

Yet she wasn't sure how to get it out of her heart. The words formed wounds and scars beneath her skin, creating tentacles of shame no long sleeves or colorful scarves could cover.

Ginger stepped back once again to admire her portion of the wall. "What do you think?"

"I like it," Ruby-Jane said. "A lot."

"Me too." The shop was starting to really feel like hers.

The top-of-the-hour news came on the radio. Ginger peeked at the wall clock. Eleven. "Hungry? Let's order lunch from Antony's," she said, cradling the brush handle against her shoulder, tugging her phone from her jeans pocket. "I'm thinking a large cheese pizza."

"You're singing my song. Oh, order some cheese bread too." Ruby-Jane stepped back, inspecting her work. "Love this color, Ginger. The shop is going to look amazing."

"I was searching online for new light fixtures last night and . . . Hey, Anthony, this is Ginger down at *Ginger Snips.* Good,

good, how are you? Yes, please . . . a large cheese . . . thin crust, yep . . . and an order of cheese bread. No, for Ruby-Jane . . . I know, she's a carb addict."

"I am not."

"Sure, one of us will come down to get it." Hanging up, Ginger slipped her phone back into her pocket. "Let's just take the money from petty cash."

As the words left her lips, the bells hanging from the front door clattered against the glass as a customer pushed in.

Glancing around, she rested her roller on the paint tray. Ginger sucked in a breath. *Tom Wells Jr.*

Her skin flamed as she adjusted the dark orange scarf tighter around her neck. She'd rather face Tracie Blue's paparazzi than Tom Wells.

"Well, look who it is. My, my, Tom Wells Jr." Ruby-Jane crossed over and gave him a big hug. "What brings you to town? Ginger, look what the cat dragged in." RJ sort of shoved Tom further into the shop.

"I see."

"Ruby-Jane, hey, good to see you. Ginger . . . it-it's been a long time." He ran his hand over his long, wavy hair as his blue gaze flipped from Ruby-Jane to Ginger who wobbled, powerless in his presence. "Are

165

y'all open? Is Maggie around? I was hoping for a quick haircut."

Ruby-Jane smiled, patting him on the shoulder. "Good ole Maggie Boyd retired." She shoved him forward again, indicating behind his back that Ginger should *talk* to him.

"So Maggie finally took that trip to Ireland? I wondered why the sign said Ginger Snips."

"S-she's in Ireland as we speak. I-I own this place now." Ginger's voice faded, weak under the thunder of her heartbeat. She reached for her brush handle and faced the wall. *Get a hold of yourself. Remember what he did to you.* If she had any gumption at all, she'd roll him with paint.

"Remember we studied calculus together, Ginger?"

"I remember." She cut him a glance, trying so hard to be cool, but Tom Wells, with those blue eyes and mammoth shoulders, was standing in *her* shop.

Ruby-Jane stepped around him, still communicating to Ginger with glances and expressions. "It's been a long time, Tom. Since you left town our senior year. What brings you back?"

"Yeah it's been awhile. I-I'm back . . . for the wedding. Bridgett and Eric's." He seemed reserved, almost shy. Definitely a lot more humble. "I'm the best man."

Ginger pressed the roller brush against the wall. What? He was one of Eric's groomsmen? She'd be around him all weekend?

"I hear it's going to be the wedding of the decade." Ruby-Jane flicked her hand toward Ginger. "She's the stylist for the whole she-bang."

"Really?" Despite his expression, Tom sounded impressed. "Not surprised. You were always good with hair, if I remember right." He brushed his hand over his thick hair again, glancing around. "As you can see, I'm in desperate need of a haircut. But looks like you're not open."

His smile darn near skewered Ginger to the wall. *Simmer down, he's just passing through . . . do not feel for him.*

"Sorry but we're painting today. You can go to the new shopping plaza south of town if you need a cut."

"The roads are horrible," Tom said, stepping close enough for his subtle fragrance to slip beneath the paint fumes and settle on her. "Big backup on Highway 21."

"You know how it is in the South," Ruby-Jane said. "We can't drive in a rainstorm, let alone ice or snow."

167

Tom laughed, shaking his head. "Very true." He raised his gaze to Ginger. "So is it possible to get a cut here? This is the only time I —"

"Absolutely." Ruby-Jane set her paint-brush down and kicked the visqueen aside, leading Tom to a chair across the room. "Ginger, does this station work?" She mouthed some sort of pinched-lipped command, gesturing toward Tom. "You ready?"

It was then Ginger noticed her arm, peeking out from under the cloak, her scars exposed. And he'd been looking right at her. Could the floor just open up and swallow her whole? She lowered her brush to the tray and tugged her sleeve down, stretching it to the tips of her fingers.

Tom Wells . . . in *her* shop. In her chair . . . waiting for her to touch his hair. The very notion made her feel like she might fly apart.

"Listen, if Ginger doesn't want to —" He tried to get up, but Ruby-Jane shoved him back down.

"She does. She'll be right with you. Ginger, can you show me where we keep the petty cash? I'll run and get the pizza." RJ snatched her by the arm and led her to the back room.

"What is wrong with you?" RJ, who knew perfectly well where the petty cash was

168

located, took a painting of a pasture off the wall, revealing the safe, and spun the dial. "Tom Wells . . . hello!" She reached in for the petty cash bag. "If he's not better looking than he was in high school, I'll eat the pizza and the box. And sweet. He seems so sweet. How unfair, you know? Men get better-looking with age and women just *sag.*"

"What's wrong with me?" Ginger kept her voice low but intense. "I'll tell you what's wrong with me. He was the only guy I've ever loved, who ever paid one lick of attention to me, and he dumped me before our first date."

Ruby-Jane took out a twenty, then closed up the money bag in the safe. "His family *moooved,* remember?" She slipped from her paint cloak, dropping it over the back of a chair.

"But he didn't tell me he was leaving. How hard is it to pick up the phone. 'Uh, Ging, can't make it. Dad says we're moving.' Then afterward, he never called or e-mailed."

"So go in there and botch his haircut if you want, get him back for it. But girlie-girl," Ruby-Jane wiggled her eyebrows, "it's Tom Wells. *The* Tom Wells. Besides, that was twelve years ago. Don't tell me you still hold a grudge."

Tom Wells, a two-named brand which meant gorgeous, athletic, smoldering, knee-weakening, kissable —

Ginger grabbed RJ. "Don't leave me alone with him. Stay here. I'll be done in ten minutes."

"Forget it. The pizza will be cold." RJ smirked and walked around Ginger into the shop. "Say Tom, we ordered too much pizza. Want to hang around for a slice?"

Note to self: fire Ruby-Jane.

The front door bells rang out as RJ left, waving at Ginger through the glass. *No worry, RJ. What goes around comes around.*

"Ginger," Tom said, rising from the chair. "I'm not going to force you to cut my hair."

Their eyes locked for a moment and her pulse throbbed in her throat. From the corner of her eye, she could see the small white swirl of snow drifting over them. Even if she turned him out, she'd have to see him at the wedding. Might as well cut his hair, then she could ignore him this weekend.

"It's fine." She motioned toward the wash bowls, removing the cloak she wore for painting and tying on a clean *Ginger Snips* apron. "Take the one on the right."

Tom situated himself in the black chair as Ginger rested his head against the bowl.

"H-how are you?" he said as she sprayed his head with warm water.

"Good." She hesitated, then raked her fingers through his luscious hair. In high school, she'd daydreamed of cutting Tom's dark, heavy locks. Then when Mr. Bickle paired them as calculus study partners, she darn near thought she'd died and gone to heaven.

The fragrance of his cologne subtly floated through her senses and she exhaled, trying to rein in her adrenaline, but one touch of his soft curls and her veins became a highway for her desires.

This is nothing. Just another client . . . just another client.

Ginger peeked at Tom's face, a best-of composite from the Hollywood's Golden Age leading men. Cary Grant's sophistication with Gregory Peck's smolder all tied together with Jimmy Stewart's lovable, everyday man.

Steady . . . She pumped a palmful of shampoo and lathered his hair, catching her reflection in one of the mirrors.

Her scarf had slipped, exposing her frightful scar, which beamed red with her embarrassment. Ginger pinched the scarf back into place before Tom could look up and see her.

171

She'd never get used to it. Never. The ugliness. The memory of the fire, of the day she realized she was marked for life. Of lying in bed, tears slipping down her cheeks and knowing no one would ever want her. Even at twelve, the truth trumpeted through her mind.

No one . . . no one . . . no one . . .

CHAPTER TWO

Reclined against the shampoo sink with Ginger's hands moving through his hair, massaging his scalp, driving his pulse, Tom regretted his fine idea to step out on this snowy day for a quick haircut.

Had he realized Maggie sold the place to Ginger, he'd have braved the slick roads and traffic boondoggle to try the new salon on the other side of town.

Yes, he knew he'd have to see her sooner or later — the latter being optimal — but not his first full day back in Rosebud. Not lying back in her sink with her hands in his hair.

He'd thought to leave as soon as Ginger said they were closed but then Ruby-Jane pushed in and, well, here he sat.

"Ginger," he began, clearing his throat. "How long have you —"

"Sit up, please." She pushed lightly on his shoulder. When he sat forward, she draped a towel over his head and dried his hair, stirring his dawning emotions. "Take a seat." She motioned to the station where Ruby-Jane had deposited him.

He peeked at her in the mirror as she removed the towel and snapped a cape around his neck. "How long have you been back in Rosebud? And six months ago I hear you were on the road with Tracie Blue?"

She angled in front of him, taking up her shears and comb. "And yes, I was."

Brrr. He figured it was warmer outside than inside the shop.

Raising the height of the chair, Ginger combed through his hair, her subtle fragrance sinking into him. She smelled romantic, if he could claim romance as a scent, like a melting, sweet Alabama summer evening. The fragrance gathered in the hollow place between his heart and ribs.

"Trim the sides? A little off the top?" she said.

"Yea, sure, buzz the sides a bit. Don't like it creeping down my neck and on my ears . . ." When she stepped to one side, the paint fumes swooshed in, replacing her perfume and bringing him back to reality. He had come in for a haircut, not a rendezvous with an almost romance of his past.

Besides, she didn't even seem to care that

he drifted into her shop quite by accident. Maybe she didn't remember the affection between them, how he flirted with her, seeking a sign, a hint, of her interest in him.

He'd just invited her to the movies when Dad announced they were moving. Leaving town in the middle of the night. Tom didn't have a chance to say good-bye to anyone, let alone Ginger Winters.

"Tip your head down, please."

He dropped his chin to his chest, inhaling a long breath for himself, then exhaling one for her.

Should he just open with, "I'm sorry?" Or just let the past be the past?

She must have had boyfriends since high school. After all, she toured with Tracie Blue, seeing the world, meeting all kinds of people. Maybe she had a boyfriend now. Or a fiancé. He watched her left hand in the mirror. No ring.

"So you never said. How long have you owned the shop?" Small talk. Maybe he could get her to open up.

"Six months." She exchanged her shears for the clippers.

"Are you glad to be back in Rosebud?" He relaxed, attempting a smile, trying to catch her gaze.

"Yes." She tilted his head to one side and

175

buzzed around his ears.

"Good . . . good . . . Me, too."

She snapped off the clippers and reached again for her shears, twirling them between her fingers, a trick he'd like to see again.

Either she was having a bad day or she really loathed him. Yes, he stood her up . . . twelve years ago. Surely she understood, considering the circumstances.

"Pretty rare to see snow in Rosebud."

"Very . . ."

"I'm back too. In Rosebud." He shifted in his seat. "For more than the wedding."

She slowed, glancing up, peering at him through the glass. "G-good." She faced him toward the mirror, checking the sides of his hair for an even cut.

"It's pretty nice about Bridgett and Eric, no?" All of Alabama knew the governor's son, a former Crimson Tide star tailback, was getting married.

"Yes, it is." The conversation stalled as she blasted the blow-dryer over his head, then pumped a drop of gel into the palm of her hand and ran it through his hair, inspiring a race of chills over his skin.

She snapped off the cape, dusting the final hair clippings from his ears and neck. "Do you like it?" Her words came at him but not her gaze as she turned away, draping the cape over another chair.

"I do, thank you." He leaned toward the mirror. "The rumors were right. You're good."

"Thanks." She waited for him at the reception desk and he wished she'd smile or laugh, or kick him in the knee. Then the ice would be broken. "That'll be twenty dollars."

"Twenty?" He opened his wallet. "That's all?"

"It's Rosebud."

He grinned, slipping a ten and a twenty from his wallet, regarding her for a moment. "I'm sorry, Ginger." The confession came without much thought, without an agenda. He was free to flow where the moment took them.

She froze, reaching for his money, glancing up at him with gleaming hazel eyes. "You're sorry?"

The front door pushed open and Ruby-Jane rushed in with the cold breeze, a large pizza box and three sodas in her arms, the aroma of hot tomato sauce and baked dough mingling with the paint fumes.

"I'm home, kids. Lunch in the back room. Tom, dude, awesome cut. Isn't Ging the best?"

"She's the maestro." He smiled at Ginger,

willing her to receive his apology.

"I told Anthony you were here in town and he said he'd heard you were starting a church. Is that true?" Ruby-Jane disappeared in the back room, emerging a moment later with a soft-looking cheesy bread stick. "Come on, y'all. It's nice and hot. Help yourself, Tom."

"Thank you, but I can't stay." Tom motioned to the front door, taking a step back. Besides, if Ginger's stiff posture was any indication, he was not wanted. "I have a meeting. And yes, I'm back in town and starting a church. First service is a week from Sunday at the old First United Church on Mercy Road, northwest of town. You know the place." He stepped toward the door. "Ginger, thanks for taking the time to cut my hair. I appreciate it. See you this weekend?"

She nodded. Once. "Guess so."

As the door eased closed behind him, Tom stepped down the sidewalk and into the icy breeze. What was it about Ginger that awakened a longing in him? The ache to be her friend, to laugh with her, to share his heart, to listen to hers, to touch her scars and tell her everything would be all right?

To tell her she was beautiful.

But how could he *ever* be in a romantic

relationship with her? What would his parents say?

Shake it off. He didn't come back to Rosebud to win Ginger's heart. He came to start work, to follow God's call, and perhaps restore his family's reputation and legacy. Not to remind people of his father's failing. That he'd packed up his family and exited in the dark of night amid possible scandal, abandoning his church, his reputation, and for a brief moment, his faith.

Tom had to be more than aboveboard. In all of his dealings. For his new church plant to bloom.

But heaven help him, Ginger Winters was as beautiful as ever, if not as raw and wounded as when he last saw her. And as crazy as it sounded, somewhere deep inside him, beneath all the layers of propriety, beneath any trepidation, Tom longed to be the man in her life.

Just like he did the first time he laid eyes on her.

CHAPTER THREE

She felt bad treating him like toilet paper stuck to the bottom of her shoe, but Tom Wells? She'd have been more prepared for the Man in the Moon to walk in asking for a close buzz than him.

After Tom left the shop, Ginger sat up to the back room table, sorting out her feelings, eating pizza while Ruby-Jane talked. "Dang, I might have to recommit myself to Jesus and go to Tom's church. I mean, mercy a-might girl, he's gorgeous and a man of God —"

"Ruby-Jane, please, do not be bamboozled. You remember how the whole family snuck out of town, a scandal chasing after them?" Ginger took a small bite of pizza, her appetite a bit frosted by her own attitude toward Tom. "Like father, like son."

"What was that all about, anyway?" Ruby-Jane said.

"Who knows? Who cares?" Ginger didn't.

At least she liked to think she didn't. What kind of sane woman still carried pain about a boy standing her up over a decade ago?

"I care. My future husband *might* be Rosebud's next big preacher." Ruby-Jane slapped another slice of pizza on her plate. "Come on, don't tell me you're still mad at him for leaving town without telling you."

"He didn't just leave. He vanished."

"Ging, they didn't vanish. We heard they moved to Atlanta."

"But not from him directly. I thought we were friends, you know? But not a peep out of him until twenty minutes ago when he walked in here." Ginger pushed away from the table, sad she'd lost her appetite for Antony's pizza. "Can we get back to painting?"

"So you *are* still mad." Ruby-Jane wiped the corners of her mouth with a wadded-up napkin. "It was twelve years ago."

"I'm not mad." But she was and it bothered her to her core. "Come on, let's get back to work. I want to get at least one wall painted before I leave on Friday."

"You know he's Eric's best man. He's going to be around *allll* weekend at this Maynard-James wedding extravaganza."

"I heard. I was standing here when he said it. So what's your point?"

181

"I think you're into him. Still. And you're mad at him. Still."

"You've inhaled too many paint fumes. I'm *not* into him. I'm *not* mad at him." Ginger headed into the shop, removing her apron and reaching for the slightly paint-stained cloak.

Yet, the thumping of her pulse and the anxious flutter in her chest told her otherwise. She was hurt, really. Worse, she *might* still be into him. Seeing him kicked open a door she thought she'd bolted and barred.

"You know what, Ginger?" Ruby-Jane said, entering the shop behind her, carrying a piece of pizza and her painting cloak. "Not everything is about your past, growing up in the trailer park, or your scars."

Ginger took up her roller brush. "I never said it was."

"When I see you cold and stiff with Tom, being brusque, I know you have feelings for him. *Still.* But you see yourself as that trailer park girl with the burn scars, not good enough for anyone."

"I *am* that trailer park girl." Ginger pushed back her sleeve. "And I'm still very scarred. Look, he's a dude who came in for a haircut. End of story."

"A dude who came in for a haircut?" Ruby-Jane laughed, her mouth bulging with pizza, her brown eyes sparkling. "Ginger, you should've seen your face when I said he might be my future husband. You went pale, then pink, then green."

"You are such a storyteller." Ginger aimed her roller toward the ceiling, rising up on her tiptoes to cover as much of the wall as she could without a ladder. She'd have to get the stepladder from the shed out back to cut in at the top. "Did you check with Michele and Casey to make sure they can handle the appointments for this weekend?"

"Talked to them yesterday, boss. And you know I'll be around to help out." Ruby-Jane took up her own paintbrush. "Don't fall back into high school, Ginger, okay? I like the confident salon owner who knows she's a fabulous stylist." RJ tugged on Ginger's scarf. "Even though you still hide behind this kind of getup."

Ginger moved away from RJ's touch, settling the scarf back into place, concealing the rough, puckered texture of her skin. "Some things will never change."

But other things could. Like the interior of this shop. Like her reputation as a swag shop owner in Rosebud's revitalized downtown, the hometown of Alabama's governor.

Like not letting men like Tom Wells Jr., preacher or otherwise, get to her. Men like him married waif-like blondes with God-kissed, sculpted faces, diamondesque smiles, and pristine, *smooth* skin.

"You know, Ginger, since I've known you, you've hidden behind long sleeves and scarves. I get it." Ruby-Jane eased the roller up and down the wall. "You aren't comfortable with your burn wounds. Just be sure you don't cover up too much and keep a man like Tom Wells out of your life. You never know, he might be your passion's flame."

Oh Ruby-Jane. Didn't she understand? Longing for *that* kind of flame, the flame of love and passion, was the most terrifying fire of all.

Wednesday afternoon, Tom swept the rough, wide boards of the old sanctuary floor with a wide straw broom he'd found in the storeroom. Like most of the church's furnishings, the broom was probably from the 1950s. Starting a new church with only enough funds to pay his meager salary meant he was janitor and secretary as well as pastor, preacher, and counselor.

Dust drifted up from the floor and swirled in the dappled sunlight falling through the transom over the stained glass windows.

He hummed a song from last night's worship practice, his chest vibrating with the melody, the lyrics skimming through his spirit.

. . . you fascinate us with your love.

He'd thought he might have to add worship leader to his duties — with his elementary guitar skills — until a talented young woman, Alisha Powell, volunteered for the job.

Last night Tom sat in the back of the sanctuary observing her first band practice and nearly wept with gratitude, sitting in the presence of God, feeling for the tenth time since he arrived in Rosebud that he'd returned home by the inspiration of the Almighty.

"Well, I see you found the most important tool."

Tom glanced toward the back of the sanctuary. Pop. He leaned on the broom, smiling as his grandfather sauntered down the center aisle.

"Did you come to make sure I worked the broom right?" Tom extended his hand toward Pop.

The old man waved him off and drew Tom into his embrace. "I reckon you can handle sweeping up well enough. But glad to know you can sweep as well as you preach." Pop eased down on the front pew, taking in the altar and pulpit, raising his gaze to the ceiling, then fixing his eyes on Tom. "Preached my first sermon here when I was nineteen." He pointed to the pulpit. "I think that old thing was here way back then."

Tom sat next to him, resting the broom against his leg. "What'd you preach on, Pop?"

"Walking worthy of His calling. Fulfilling every desire for goodness and the work of faith with power."

"Second Thessalonians."

"Good," Pop slapped his thighs and pushed to his feet. "Number one job of a preacher. Know the Word. Live it, pray it, sing it. So, Edward Frizz worked a deal for this old place?" He stepped up and moved behind the pulpit.

"He did me a solid. Found this place for sale, cheap, right before we signed a big, expensive lease on . . ." Tom paused, about to stir up painful memories.

"Your dad's old church?" Pop said it for him.

Tom dashed the broom bristles against the floor as he stood. "That building was in good shape. Way more modern than this place, but expensive. And, I don't know, I didn't want to —"

"Be in his shadow?" Pop leaned over the

brown, thirsty wood pulpit. "Remind folks of what happened?"

"I just want to walk my own path. You and I both know Rosebud is populated with a lot of people who attended Dad's church. They know he left under suspicious circumstances. I only found out recently what happened and why we left town in the middle of the night. But I can guarantee there's a boatload of folks with their own ideas. I came here because the Lord directed me. Not to drag up the past and its suspicions." Tom pointed the broom handle at the ancient pipe organ behind the baptismal. "I want a fresh start. Even if we have to do it in this old place. With that big, old organ in place."

Pop came down the platform steps. "Your daddy did the right thing leaving the way he did. Cutting ties. Not taking anything but his family and the necessities."

"Didn't seem so at the time."

Pop made a face. "No, but you turned out all right."

"After a wild detour in college and too many drunken fraternity nights."

"Which led you to say, 'Okay God, I'm Yours,' after waking up week after week with your face in the toilet bowl."

Tom laughed, shaking his head, grateful

to be in his grandfather's presence, finding comfort in the old man's wisdom and spirit of peace. "Looking back, I can see God's hand in my life, even in the family's sudden departure from Rosebud, but at the time?" Tom ran the broom lightly over the dry hardwood. "I was convinced Dad and God had ruined my life.

"So, you think anyone under the age of fifty will come here next Sunday morning? Walking over from the parsonage this morning, I realized the church looks and feels so old. White clapboard exterior, steeple, narrow foyer, long, rectangular sanctuary, stained-glass windows."

"You just be faithful to your calling and to the Lord. Let Him do the drawing and choosing."

Tom leaned against the side of a pew. The light had shifted and a kaleidoscope of colors moved across the white plaster. "Think I can do this?"

"Does it matter what I think?" Pop took a seat again and sat back, hands on his knees, his plaid shirt smooth against his lean chest. "It only matters what He thinks, and that you're confident in His love for you and His leadership."

"Guess that's the trick for everyone who wants to follow Jesus."

"Best thing I can tell you is love Him with all your heart, mind, soul, and strength. You do that and you won't have time for any other kind of hanky-panky."

Speaking of hanky-panky . . . "I ran into Ginger Winters this morning."

Pop furrowed his brow. "Not sure I recall —"

"She's the daughter of the woman —"

"Ah," Pop nodded with realization. "I see."

"She owns a salon on Main Street now. Where Maggie's used to be. I went in to get a haircut for Eric's wedding this weekend and found Ginger there instead of ole Maggie."

"I'd heard she'd retired. But news travels slow out to the farm." Pop peered at Tom with a twinkle. "What's with this Ginger gal? Other than being the daughter of —"

"Right . . . Well, we were friends, starting to get close when everything went down. I didn't even know her mom and Dad *knew* each other."

He never got to ask Ginger how she felt about him. School had just started. They had a couple of study sessions together but not much more. But when he was around her, his heart felt things new and wonderful. He wanted to be a better person.

189

She, on the other hand, was hard to read. She kept her feelings close.

"Did you break her heart?"

"I don't know. We were supposed to go to the movies the night Dad had me packing my stuff." Tom shook his head, staring past Pop at the choir door. "I never called her. I felt too embarrassed. I didn't know what to tell her. 'We're sneaking out of town. My dad's a jerk.' So I just left it. Never wrote to her. Never called."

"Twelve years is a long time, Tom. I hardly think she's holding a grudge because a high school boy didn't pick her up for pizza and a movie. She might know the whole story since her mama was involved." Pop rubbed his chin. "Though Tom Senior did manage to keep it all so very quiet."

"I don't know what she knows except I stood her up." The Thursday afternoon he had asked her out, after school, he'd almost kissed her as they stood by his car. But Eric and Edward dashed onto the scene, out of nowhere, rabble rousing, full of pre-football practice mischief, and spoiled the whole mood.

Then, seeing her today? He felt like some dangling part of his heart had been put back into place. Ginger was all right. Doing well. And still beautiful. "Well, anyway," Tom said, glancing down, sweeping the floor. "She went on to do some pretty great things. She was a stylist to Tracie Blue. She's a major country music —"

"I know Tracie Blue," Pop said, smiling. "Very impressive for Ginger."

Tom laughed. "And how does an old evangelist like you know about Tracie Blue?"

"Facebook."

"Facebook?"

Pop nodded. "Your Aunt Marlee hooked me up."

"I'm not even on Facebook, Pop." Tom laughed and stamped the broom against the floor.

"Well, get Marlee to set up your profile thingy." But Pop sobered. "Tom, best advice? Don't stew on this Ginger business. Make it right if you think something is amiss, but don't stew. Don't assign thoughts and emotions to her based on what you think and feel. That's how the world gets messed up."

Pop, such a well of wisdom and truth. "She'll be at the wedding. Guess I could find a moment to speak to her."

"Just don't try to make her some sort of project." Pop leaned forward, tapping Tom on the arm. "Let God see to her eternal soul. You point her to Him, not to yourself."

"Yeah, yeah, I hear you. Dad's given me the same speech."

"He should. Because that's what messed him up. Taking on people projects. Feeling responsible. Letting others see *him* instead of Jesus. He always struggled with his pride. I busted him many a time on it. But God redeems. God heals," Pop said. "However, you, dear boy, must remember why you returned to Rosebud. It wasn't just because Edward Frizz called asking you to start a new church."

"And *not* just because I want to see Dad's name and reputation restored."

"No." Pop's laugh barreled from his chest. "You best let that part go. You start worrying about reputations and you'll be sunk before you even start." He pointed to the ceiling. "Gaze at Him, not yourself, your family, the name Wells, *or* the past. You know King Saul's downfall? He cared more about what men thought than what God thought."

Tom listened, mulling, thinking, trying to connect the gnawing in his gut over Ginger Winters with his thoughts, with what Pop was saying, with the truth.

"You know," Pop said, pushing to his feet. "If you want to really help this girl, win her to Jesus."

"Isn't that making her a project?"

Pop grunted. "No, it's showing her love. Everything else is lust or pride. Leading her to Truth, at the risk of your own heart and reputation, is love. How about we finish this over lunch? I'm starved."

Tom anchored the broom against the side of the pew and went to his office for his jacket. *Win her to Jesus?* Was she in need of winning? *How do I relate to her? What do I say?* He muttered in prayer as he returned to the sanctuary, meeting Pop in the middle of the aisle.

A simple but sweet answer to his questions rose up and lingered in his heart.

Tell her she's beautiful.

CHAPTER FOUR

The rain started the moment Ginger left Rosebud city limits on Friday evening. Blasting the radio, she was exhausted.

She'd painted late into the evening Wednesday — the one wall took forever and still needed another coat — then filled Thursday and Friday with her regular and snow-day appointments.

In between clients, she answered frantic, last-minute texts from Bridgett suggesting "one more thing" or wondering if "there's time to perm Aunt Carol's hair"?

So now as she drove south toward the Maynards' Magnolia plantation on the southwest corner of the county, the winter light masked by rain-weighted clouds, she wanted nothing more than a long, hot bath and her bed.

Bridgett informed her she was sharing a room with one of the bridesmaids, Miranda Shoemaker. Ginger didn't mind as long as she had her own bed.

To be her charming, make-them-beautiful self, all she required was a good night's sleep. The bridal party wouldn't need her tonight, so she hoped to excuse herself after introductions and slip off to her room.

Tracie Blue always knew that about her. *Ginger needs her sleep.* She made sure she had her own space on the touring buses.

Now, driving the twenty miles down a desolate highway through a frigid, icy monsoon, Ginger exhaled the day's tension, and Tom drifted across her mind.

He was back in town.

Ginger gripped the steering wheel a bit tighter, shifted in her seat, and adjusted the seat belt of her '69 VW Bug.

How could that fact make her heart smile after twelve years? Years in which he'd not once contacted her.

Nevertheless, his presence changed everything about this weekend. She'd signed on as the stylist, to be a person behind the scenes, detached from the wedding, the guests, and the celebration. That was fine with her. She'd perfected that persona while working for Tracie.

But now, a small part of her wanted to be a woman, not just a servant, and to be seen by *him.* She had visions of participating in the wedding festivities, and they disturbed her. Rattled her well-built, well-structured emotional barriers.

She'd only felt this way one other time in her life. In high school. When Tom Wells Jr. was her calculus study partner. *Grrr,* this whole thing irritated her, making her feel like an emotionally trapped seventeen-year-old.

Around the next bend, between the skinny pines and live oaks, Ginger spotted the golden lights of the plantation house, glowing like a low moon rising on the thin, wet, dark horizon.

She pulled around the curved driveway, parked, and dashed to the veranda, the rain easing off as the storm clouds inhaled for a second breath.

She was a professional. Just the stylist. Detached and aloof, a hired hand.

Shivering in the dewy, cold air, Ginger rang the doorbell, fixing on a smile when an older woman in a maid's uniform answered the door.

"Hey, I'm Ginger Winters. The stylist."

The maid stood aside. "They're in the drawing room."

"Thank you." Ginger stepped inside, offering her hand. "And you are?"

"Eleanor."

"Eleanor. Nice to meet you."

The woman's stern expression softened. "Yes, you too. This way." She led Ginger through a small, formal living room and a massive library, then down a short corridor where laughing male and female voices collided.

Eleanor paused at a set of double doors. "Tonight's dinner is buffet, on the sideboard. Help yourself."

"Thank you." Ginger hesitated as she stepped from the marble hallway onto the plush emerald-and-gold carpet, scanning the room. No one noticed her. But that wasn't unusual.

A pale glow from the teardrop chandelier hovered above the room as if too good for the thick, heavier gold light emanating from the wall sconces and table lamps. On the farthest wall, deep-red curtains framed a working white stone fireplace. Despite its size, the drawing room was warm and cozy, inviting.

Come on in. Even you, Ginger Winters.

Several women sat reclined on a matching set of white sofas by the fireplace, wine glasses in hand. The fire crackled and popped, the flames stretching into the flue.

But the sofas by the fire were not for her. The beauty of the fireplace aside, Ginger avoided flames of any kind. From bonfires to matches, lighters, and sparklers, to men who made her heart feel like kindling.

Speaking of men, she'd not spotted Tom yet. To her right, she saw the groom, Eric, with several others watching ESPN on a large flat screen.

To her left was Bridgett and a mix of folks talking at the wet bar. There was Edward Frizz and Brandi Heinly, one of Bridgett's friends from high school. They were all part of the beautiful and bold to which Ginger had no admittance.

Since no one saw her, should she just walk in? *Hey y'all?* The aroma of roast beef and something cheesy whetted her appetite. She'd snatched a slice of cold pizza for breakfast but had eaten nothing since.

But first, she needed to connect with Bridgett, let her know she'd arrived. Then beginning tomorrow morning, she'd start washing and setting hair for the mothers at nine o'clock.

Ginger inched across the room, arms stiff at her sides. "Bridgett, hey, I'm here."

"Ginger!" A beaming and bright Bridgett wrapped her in a happy hug and walked her to the center of the room. "Girls, this is Ginger Winters, the one I was telling you about, Miss Marvelous. Her straight iron is a magic wand."

Ginger smiled and waved toward the women on the sofa. "Nice to see y'all."

One of the women rose up on her knees, leaning on the back of the sofa. "Did you really tour with Tracie Blue?"

"I did, yes. Three years." One lingering benefit of working for a superstar? A great conversation piece.

"Oh my gosh, I can't believe it. She is my favorite singer." This from Sarah Alvarez, another bridesmaid and Rosebud High alum. "How exciting. What dirt can you give us on her?" Sarah wiggled her eyebrows as she joined the other women on the sofa.

"None I'm afraid. I signed a confidentiality agreement. She could sue me for more money than I'll make in three lifetimes."

Sarah made a face, shrugged and turned away, rejoining the conversation around the fire.

"Never mind her," Bridgett said, slipping her arm through Ginger's. Her burned one, but she didn't pull free. Her sweater was thick enough to hide the scars. And Bridgett wasn't holding on too tight. "Come over here. You remember my handsome groom, Eric."

He glanced around, pulling away from SportsCenter long enough for a, "Nice to see you again."

"You remember Edward and oh, look, there's Tom Wells —"

Ginger pulled away from Bridgett as Tom entered through a doorway across the room. A low, creeping shiver started in her bones. "H-hello everyone." She tried for a sweeping glance past the men but her gaze clashed with Tom's.

He watched her with those blue fireballs he used for eyes. One look and she felt engulfed, aching to be with him.

He terrified her more than the man-made flames across the room. Those flames she understood and could avoid. But the kind Tom Wells ignited seemed impossible to predict, avert, or extinguish.

"So, that's everyone," Bridgett said. "Help yourself to the buffet. There's wine and beer, but if you don't drink, the fridge is full of water, soda, and tea. We're just hanging out, talking wedding. Can you believe I'm getting married?" Bridgett squeezed Ginger's arm, giggling, effervescing.

"I'm happy for you." Ginger smoothed her hand down her sweater, tugging at the end of the sleeve to make sure her scarred hand was covered. "It's exciting. Rosebud High's prom king and queen and most likely to marry . . ."

"I know, what are the odds? We're actually getting married. After eight years apart I never thought I'd see him again, let alone marry him." Bridgett leaned over the chair where Eric sat, roping him in her arms, and kissed his cheek. "But, well, love's arrow doesn't miss, does it?"

Oh yeah it does. By a county mile.

"So . . ." Bridgett turned around with a clap of her hands. "Fill your plate and join us girls on the sofa. We can talk hair."

Ginger looked back at the cluster of bridesmaids. By the fire. A sliver of panic cut through her delicate confidence.

"It's easier to eat sitting at the counter." Tom's bass declaration offered a welcomed truth, drawing Bridgett's attention.

"Guess you're right, *Reverend* Tom." Bridgett wrinkled her nose at him. "All right, Ginger, grab a bite but don't let this scoundrel keep you too long. Lindy and Kyle want to talk to you about their hair ideas for tomorrow."

"Looking forward to it," Ginger said, turning to the buffet with a backward glance at Tom. How did he know?

She filled her plate and set it on the counter two seats down from Tom, who nursed a frosty root beer. "Are there any more of those?"

"At your service." He hopped up, rounded the bar, and pulled a cold soda bottle from the fridge. He twisted off the top and slid it toward her. "On the house."

She laughed, covering her mouth with her smooth left hand.

"Wow, I got a laugh out of you." Tom came around the bar and took the stool next to her, relaxing with his elbows on the bar. "Don't act so surprised."

"But I am. I didn't know I possessed the power."

"Very funny." She lifted the soda bottle and took a hearty swig of sweetness. "Sorry about the other day . . ."

"I get it. Caught you off guard."

Making sure her sweater sleeve covered her hand, Ginger split apart a fluffy yeast roll, the kind her Gram used to make when she was a kid. She popped a steaming piece in her mouth.

"What? No butter?"

She smiled, shaking her head, relaxing a bit. Whether she wanted to admit it or not, Tom Wells made her comfortable. He made her want to be a better person. "My grandma made rolls like these for holiday dinners and birthdays when I was growing up. They were so good they didn't need butter. We'd eat them plain or maybe with homemade black raspberry jelly." Her voice faded. Those times ended right after Ginger turned thirteen. A year after the fire. An aneurysm claimed Gram's life when she was only sixty.

"My grandma made dumplings." Tom shook his head, humming. "Best thing you ever put in your mouth." He peered at her. "But the same thing happened to us. She died and so did the tradition."

"I keep telling myself I'll learn how to do it but —"

"Life gets in the way."

Ginger set her roll down and reached for her napkin. "Thank you." She nodded toward the sofa and fireplace. "For that."

"Bridgett can be a little obtuse."

"Apparently you're . . . What's the opposite of obtuse?"

"Bright, smart, intelligent, handsome, sexy."

Ginger choked, wheezing a laugh, pressing the back of her hand against her lips. She finished swallowing her roll, washing it down with a nip of root beer. "Someone doesn't think well of himself."

He grinned. "I like hearing you laugh."

"Yeah, well . . ." Ginger shifted around in her stool and adjusted her scarf, making sure it was in place, covering her flaw.

Under the heat of his gaze, she felt exposed and transparent, as if he could see the things she longed to hide.

"They've been talking about you." Tom gestured to the women on the sofa with his root beer bottle. "Apparently Bridgett hired some world-renowned photographer for the weekend and they are counting on you to work your wonders."

"Women like to feel beautiful. Especially in photos. Double especially for a wedding."

"You say that like you're not one of *them*."

His words and the tenor of his voice confirmed her suspicion. He read her, saw through her. Ginger tore another corner bite from her roll. "I say it like it's true. Don't read anything into it. Women like to be beautiful and men prefer them that way."

"I suppose so." He turned his root beer bottle with his fingers, glancing toward her. "But there's two kinds of beautiful."

"Only two?" She peeked at him and forced a relaxing exhale. *He's just being nice, Ginger.*

"Touché." His soft laugh tapped a buried memory of sitting in the library, trying to get him to study calc problems for a quiz instead of doodling caricatures of Mr. Bickle. "I was thinking of outside beauty and inside beauty."

"What of all the layers and nuances in

between?"

"Touché again." He tapped his bottle to hers.

"Either way, I have a big weekend ahead, doing my thing, making women beautiful."

"Do you enjoy it?"

"I do." She nodded with a strange wash of rising, hot tears. She hid them with a dab of her napkin. "Ruby-Jane says it's my superpower."

"It's good to do something you're good at and that you love."

"I think so." But how could she give words to the underlying truth? That she ached to do it for herself. How she envied women with smooth skin who wore sleeveless tops in the summer with low v-necks.

On her days off, when she cleaned her apartment, she wore a tank top and scooped her hair into a ponytail, feeling free.

"I was thinking maybe you could come to church next week. See me off on my inaugural Sunday." He pushed his hand through the air as if sailing.

"Church?" She cut a bite of roast beef. Funny how talking with him encouraged her appetite. But church? "I don't think so."

"Didn't you go for awhile? When we were in high school?"

"Until my mother suddenly *stopped* going

and started working Sunday mornings." She shrugged. "Wasn't sure I liked it all that much anyway."

She bought the message about a loving God. She really did. But when she tried to reckon with Him about the night she was trapped in the trailer fire, about the pain and agony of second- and third-degree burns, she couldn't find love in any of it.

If God delivered those young guys out of the fire in the Old Testament, Daniel's friends, why didn't He do it for her? Did He love them more? She'd concluded that He must.

"Why didn't you go on your own?" Tom said as a commotion arose from the sofas.

A shrill, "I can't believe you're here!" shot through the room before Ginger could answer. One of the bridesmaids, Miranda, launched from the couch and into the arms of a man standing just inside the drawing room doors.

"I told you I'd make it, baby." He swept her up, kissing her, wanting her.

Ginger turned back to her plate, feeling every movement, every emotion of the couple at the door through the ugly lens of jealousy.

She would never have that . . . never. Even if some man did want her, one look, one touch at her relief-map skin and he'd turn away. Experience was her truth.

"Cameron, you made it." Eric broke his trance with SportsCenter and football highlights, coming around to greet the most recent guest.

"Cameron Bourcher," Tom whispered toward Ginger. "I met him at the bachelor party. He's a Wall Street dude, comes from money, almost engaged to Miranda. Or at least she thinks so."

Ginger glanced toward the door, at the cuddling couple surrounded by the wedding party. "Looks to me like she might be right."

Cameron bent down, giving Miranda another kiss, holding her close, his arm about her waist. Her smooth-skinned waist.

"Now we're all here." Bridgett beamed, wrapping her arms around Eric. "What an amazing weekend. Our wedding, darling. So far, so perfect. Except, oh —" Bridgett turned to the bar. To Ginger. "Ginger, I'm sorry. Now there's no room for you. Cam will be sharing with Mandy."

Everyone stared at her. Even the chandelier light seemed to brighten and angle Ginger's way, spotlighting her embarrassment.

"Oh, okay, n-no problem." But yes, a huge

problem. *Floor, open up, let me in.* The slight comfort and ease she'd allowed herself, sitting with Tom, vanished under the hot stares of the beautiful people.

"What? No." Tom slipped from his stool. "Don't kick her out. Cameron can bunk with me and Eric."

Cameron laughed. "No offense, Tom, but I didn't fly a thousand miles to *bunk* with you and the groom."

"Of course, of course," Bridgett said, moving between Tom and Cameron, batting down the contention. "I'm sorry, I should've planned better. Oh, bother, we don't have any more rooms in the house. Lindy could share, but she's such a light sleeper and I promised her a private room. The rest of the family arrives in the morning and will need their rooms to rest and get ready. I'd hate for the staff to have to redo them . . . Oh, I know. Ginger," Bridgett crossed over to her, eyes wide with her pending solution. "You can stay out at the homestead tonight." The bride peered at the others, satisfied with her quick solution.

"The homestead?" Tom said. "That place at the end of the property? It's like a mile away."

Ginger snatched Tom's arm. What was he, reverend attorney? She didn't need his defense. "Tom, it's okay. Don't make more out of the situation than necessary."

"Thank you, Ginger. Yes, Tom, it's a bit far but it's very nice. Daddy's been fixing it up. Ginger, you'll love it. It's right on the edge of the woods."

"Is there a road to this homestead?" Tom insisted on defending her. "Last time I was here, the old road had been busted up. You had to cross a field to get there."

"Yes, Tom," Bridgett said with a sigh. "There's a road, sort of, a *path* really."

"Is it safe?"

"Of course." Bridgett laughed, but not in a fun way. More of an aghast way.

"Look," he said, stepping forward, addressing the entire wedding party like a jury. *Tom, please shut up.* But Ginger couldn't release the words. Speaking out would only draw more attention to this humiliating situation. "Let Ginger stay in my room. I'll go out there."

"Kind of need you here, man," Eric said, securing his arm around Bridgett, holding her close. "You're my best man."

Enough. Ginger hopped off her stool. "Bridgett, thank you for dinner." She mined every ounce of cheer and joviality. "I've not unloaded my things yet so I can easily move.

Point me in the direction of the old homestead."

"Perfect." Bridgett walked Ginger through the clustered bridal party, and *guest,* Cameron Bourcher, out of the drawing room, down the hall, their footsteps echoing with fading ooohs and ahhhs over Cameron, who apparently arrived via his private jet.

"Really, Ginger, the old homestead is lovely." Bridgett walked with her onto the veranda, into the rain-soaked night. Bridgett's instructions to the homestead billowed in the frosty air.

"Go to the end of this driveway . . ." she circled her hand in the air. "Turn left like you're going back to the main road. About twenty yards down . . ." She leaned toward Eric, who had just joined them. "Wouldn't you say about twenty yards?"

"Roughly. Just look for the sign."

"Right, the sign. It's on your left. It says 'Homestead.' Can't miss it. Turn there and just keep going straight until you run into the old place. A one-story ranch."

"Do I need a key or anything?"

"Nope, Daddy keeps it unlocked."

"Then how can you say it's safe?" Tom's voice boomed over Ginger's left shoulder.

"Because it's a mile out that way . . . because the plantation is gated." Bridgett swatted at Tom. "Stop being a killjoy. The homestead is safe, Ginger."

"The woods aren't gated." Tom moved to the edge of the veranda, staring into the darkness.

"And what's back there?" Bridgett demanded. "Nothing but deer and wildlife."

"Maybe a bear or two."

"Now you're just making stuff up."

Ginger stepped forward, unwilling to be an object in their debate, tugging her keys from her jeans pocket. "Turn left at the sign?"

"You can't miss it." Bridgett smiled. "See you in the morning. Come early for breakfast. Oh, Ginger, tomorrow's my big day."

"I'll be here at eight to set up." Ginger took one step down. "You're going to be beautiful." If she was banished to the outer regions of the Maynard plantation, she was going to do it with grace. "I'm bringing my A-game tomorrow."

"I knew you would. I showed you the look I wanted, right? The one on Tracie's last album. That was your handiwork?"

"It was, and I'm all set to make you even more beautiful than Tracie." *Now, let's forget this mess and move on.* Ginger moved down the steps, through the freezing rain, keys gripped in her hand.

If she was known only for making others beautiful, if that was her life's signature, wouldn't that be enough?

Slipping behind the VW's wheel, Ginger slammed the door and fought a surprise wash of tears. No, it wasn't enough. The heart wants what it wants. And Ginger's heart wanted love and freedom from her scars.

But for now, she was tired, and mulling this over would only make her sad and she didn't want to be sad. It took too much energy.

Ginger started the engine and shifted into first, willing her thumping heart to settle down. She'd promised Bridgett her A-game. And being tired and sad was not part of her strategy.

Glancing in the rearview mirror, she saw the rest of the guests had come out to the veranda. They huddled together, laughing, being the bold and beautiful.

Easing off the clutch, she cut the wheel to move around a giant truck with mud on the tires and undercarriage when the passenger door jerked open and a wet, shivering Tom Wells dropped in.

"Excuse me? What are you doing?"

"I'm going with you." He reached for the center dash sliders. "Got any heat in this old thing?"

"Tom, no, you don't have to come with me." Ginger moved the silver slider to the right, powering up the heat. *Hear that, heart? You don't need him.*

"It's raining, freezing, dark, with an obscure path. Shoot, *I'd* want someone to go with me. Besides, I heard Eric ask if the power had been turned on and Bridgett didn't know. There's a power box on the side of the house."

"Tom, you still don't have to come with me. I'll figure it out." Wasn't that the way she lived life? On her own, figuring it out?

He glared at her through the muted light of the dash and their visual exchange did something to her. Something scary and wild. Like making her want to touch him.

But she'd never touched a man other than to wash his hair.

"Really," she said with a wide, forced smile. "I'm fine." Ginger patted his knee, once, oh so lightly, but she felt a plump of muscle beneath her fingertips.

"Too bad." He caught her hand, giving it a tender squeeze. "I'm riding along. Now, let's get moving."

CHAPTER FIVE

The night rain poured from celestial buckets. Tom rode silently alongside Ginger, debating with himself why he'd forced her to accept his help.

So he could apologize for the past? So he could be near her? All of the above?

Watching the overgrown and rutted road through the VW's bouncing headlights, it was hard to see exactly where they were going. Man, it was dark and wet out. For this alone, he was glad he nudged in.

"Careful, Ginger, there's a big —" Tom braced as the nose of the VW Bug crashed into a rain-gutted rut. "Rut." Did Bridgett sincerely mean to send Ginger out in this gully-washer alone?

"Sorry." She jerked the wheel right, then left, down shifting, trying to maneuver through the pitted path.

"This is crazy. We're a mile from a marble and crystal plantation with three stories.

Couldn't you have slept in one of the many parlors or living rooms?"

"Tom, don't, please."

Fine. He could tell his ranting only wounded her more. But it just burned him that Bridgett had so casually booted Ginger from the house.

" 'With slaughterous sons of thunder rolled the flood,' " he said.

She clutched, shifted, jerked the wheel, voice tense when she said, "So you read Tennyson?"

"Just that one line. He claimed to have written that line when he was eight."

"You don't believe him?"

"I suppose I have to." The VW slowed, wheels spinning in mud, then shot forward, and continued down the so-called road. "I can't challenge him on it, can I?"

She laughed softly. "No, you can't. Do you read a lot?"

"As I have time. Some poetry. Novels. Theology books. Memoirs."

"I love books. Novels, poetry, memoirs, no theology though."

"I remember you as the math whiz." He liked the gentle turn of the conversation.

"I like math, but I read a lot when I was recovering from . . ." She hit another deep rut. Muddy water shot in front of the headlights. "Ah, this is no man's land."

"I'm sure Bridgett didn't realize —"

"Don't say a word to her." Ginger released the wheel long enough to scold him with a wagging finger. "It's bad enough she announced there was no room for me in front of everyone. It's another thing if you go to her complaining on my behalf."

"She should know," Tom said, his voice metered with the bumping and swaying of the VW — which was rapidly losing the rutted field versus small car battle.

"Then speak for yourself. Leave my name out of it. I mean it. I'll be gone soon enough."

He cut a glance her way. The dash lights accented the smooth angles of her face and set off the highlights of her sable-colored eyes.

"Can I at least pay for you to drive this little beast through a car wash?"

Ginger laughed, the engine moaning as she gently eased the car through a hungry puddle and nearly stalled. "Where *is* this homestead she spoke of so highly?"

"Keep going." Tom squinted through the rain. "It's so dark out here."

Another rut and the Beetle Bug's engine whined, stuttered, knocked. Ginger patted the dash. "Almost there, Matilda. Come on, baby."

"Yeah, come on Matilda." Tom ran his hand over the metal dash. "Good girl, you can do it."

The VW splashed through a large puddle, then found traction on a patch of solid ground. Ginger gaped at him, shifting into a higher gear. "Seems even Matilda is subject to your charms."

"Even Matilda? I'm not sure my so-called charms work on any of the ladies."

"Ha, right. Weren't you the one who made sure you had a date every Saturday night?"

"Is there anything your elephant brain doesn't remember?"

"Yes, like why I agreed to do this *wedding.*" Ginger groaned as the VW nosed into another pothole and ground to a stop, jerking the two of them forward.

She clutched and shifted, urging the car onward. But the Bug moaned and rattled, and the tires spun without traction.

"Reverse," Tom said. "See if we can back out." Nothing doing. More tire spinning and slipping, more engine lamenting. "Cut the wheel left, then hit the gas."

But the ground was too drenched and the revving engine lacked the horsepower to heave the little car out of the mire.

"Ginger?"

"What?" She stared straight ahead, letting out a heavy sigh.

"We're stuck."

"I'm *so* glad you came with me, Tom. Otherwise I'd sit here wondering all night what happened."

He liked being with her one-on-one, liked when she shed her shyness and timidity. "Fine, I'm Captain Obvious. It's the way I roll." Tom peered through the dash to the edge of the headlights. If there was a homestead on the horizon, he couldn't see it through the rain. Rubbing his hands together to warm them, he glanced back to see if the big house was in view. Might be easier to turn around than go forward. But it wasn't. "So what's your plan?"

"Can we call someone? Who owns that big monster truck? Can they get us out?"

"Scott Ellis owns the truck. I don't have his number but I can try Eric or Edward, have them send him out." Tom tugged his phone from his jeans pocket, calling Edward first, then Eric. No answer with either one. "Guess we're on our own."

"Let me try Bridgett." Ginger reached behind her seat, pulled her bag around, and dug out her phone. Her effort netted the same result as Tom. No answer.

Guess there was only one thing to do. He reached for his door handle. "I'll push. Stay in first gear. When I say go, gently, and I do mean gently, let off the clutch and give it a little gas." Tom cracked the door open, letting in the wet and the cold. "Cut the wheel to the left, and try to find the most solid ground you can."

"What do you think I've been doing?" She motioned to the door. "You're seriously going to push?"

"Unless you want the honors."

She hesitated, then unsnapped her seat belt. "Yes, of course, I should push. It *is* my car."

Tom snatched her arm before she could open her door. "Do you want my manly-man card too? Please, I'll never live it down with the guys if they hear you pushed. Let me do this. You're the driver of this team." Beneath the wooly knit of her sweater, he could feel the rough, ribbed skin of her arm. He'd always wanted to ask her about how it all happened. He'd only heard bits and pieces of a trailer fire. How painful it must have been. Then to live with the constant reminder . . .

"We're not a team." She slipped her arm from his touch.

"Okay . . . we are for now. Unless you

want to sit here all night." He jostled her shoulder, also coarse and jagged beneath her sweater. "Come on, if I can't push us out of this, I'll hand in my man *and* Marine cards."

She reared back. "You were a Marine?"

"Yes, and still am, I guess. *Hoorah.* Just no longer on active duty. Ready?" Popping open his door, Tom's first step sank into a pool of icy water, filling his shoe with ooze. Nice. He sloshed around to the back of the car, the rain soaking his hair and jacket, slipping down his collar, trickling down his neck and back.

At the back of the old Beetle, Tom anchored his backside against the car, hooking his hands under the fender as he tried to find good footing. He'd bet his ruined Nikes that the temperature had dropped a southern, damp, frigid degree or two in the past fifteen minutes.

"Ginger?" he called, glancing around, the rain water draining into his eyes and the crevasses of his face. "Ready?"

The engine whirred, coming to life. Tom ducked into place. "Okay, go!"

He pushed, his feet anchored against nothing but ooze, as Ginger fed the Bug a bit of gas.

But all combined, their efforts produced

nothing but spinning tires and spewing mud. Extracting his feet from the sucking mud, Tom sloshed over to Ginger's window and tapped on the glass. She inched it open.

"Hey, Tom, I think we're still stuck."

He laughed. "Now you're Captain Obvious. I'm going to rock the car a bit. You didn't eat a lot of food at the buffet, did you?"

"Such a funny man you are." She shut the window and faced forward, a slight, happy curve on her lips.

Yeah, she wasn't as hard and defensive as she let on. Tom rounded back to the VW, the rain still thick and heavy. If it took *this* to get to know her, to break down the barriers, he'd do it again. And again.

"Okay, Ginger, give this Beetle Bug some juice!"

The engine rumbled as she let off the clutch. Tom rocked the car, straining to dislodge it, adding his Marine muscles to the German horsepower.

Come on . . . He'd dealt with worse in Afghanistan. *Lord, can You get us out of this?*

The car lurched free, dropping a shivering, soaked-to-the-bone Tom into the mud. The red taillights beamed five feet ahead. Ginger tooted the horn in celebration.

Thanks, Lord.

Pushing out of the mud, Tom scrambled for the passenger door. But Ginger stuck out her hand as he started to sit.

"I just had the car detailed."

"W-what?"

"And these are leather seats."

"Y-you're joking." Meanwhile, rain slithered down his face, into his ears, and pooled at the base of his neck.

"Yeah, I'm joking. Get in here. You're letting in the cold air." Her laugh warmed his soul.

"You're a regular riot, Alice." He dropped into the seat with a squishy *slosh.* "Where's a hero's welcome when he deserves one?"

"You're right. Thank you. Very much. The stallion of Rosebud to my rescue." She shoved the heat slider to high and eased the Bug forward.

"Boy, you *do* remember everything. The stallions of Rosebud . . . I haven't thought of that nickname in a long time." He ran his hands though his drenched hair but there was no place to dry his cold, wet hands. "Sorry about this mess."

"When you don't have a life, you pay close attention to others." She chuckled softly. "I can still see you, Eric, Edward, and Kirk Vaughn strutting down the school halls, three abreast, patting your chests on football

Fridays, rapping some stallions of Rosebud song."

Tom laughed. "Yep, 'We're the stallions . . . of Rosebud High . . . fear the name, we're what we claim, when you're not looking, we're gonna crush ya . . .'" He drummed the rhythm on the dash. "Ole Kirk, I miss him." Kirk had gone pro but died in a small aircraft crash while doing mission work during the off season.

At his funeral, Tom's heart first stirred toward full-time ministry. Something he swore he'd never do. He'd watched his father and wanted nothing of that life.

"Such a senseless death."

"I can still hear Eric's voice when he called to tell me . . . I couldn't believe it." Tom glanced at her. "But Kirk died doing something he believed in. At his funeral, I stood in the back of Brotherhood Community Center — there had to be a thousand people crammed in there — and bawled like a baby. That day changed me."

"How did that day change you?" The VW nosed down again. Ginger urged the car with a bit more gas, trying to move quickly through the rut.

"I just knew. No more fooling around with God. I had to get serious."

"Serious with God? Were you not serious?

The preacher's kid?"

"I was the opposite of serious." The car hit another water patch and fishtailed sideways before listing to port, finding another rut and sinking. The engine gurgled and died with a tired sigh.

"No, no, no," Ginger rocked in her seat, trying to reignite the engine. But the rain, ruts, and mud had won. "Matilda, we were almost there." She pointed to a small light on the distant horizon before turning to Tom. "See if you can push."

"Ginger, face it. Elements one, VW Bug with humans, zero." Tom leaned out his door, looking under the car. "The back left is buried." He ducked back inside. "We're going to have to walk."

"Walk? In this?" Ginger angled over the wheel, peering at the rain. "Maybe we can wait it out."

As if the heavens heard, the clouds rumbled, lightning flickered, and the rain fell in double-time. The car sank a bit lower.

Tom offered her his hand. "I say we run for it. You with me? Do you have a flashlight?"

"Dear diary, Bridgett Maynard's wedding was a blast. I got to run in the rain and mud." Ginger popped open the glove box, producing a flashlight, then slipped the keys from the ignition and reached around behind the seat for her purse and small duffle bag. "I can't believe this."

"I was on a patrol like this one night in Afghanistan."

"In a VW?" Ginger clicked on the flashlight, shot open her door, and stepped out. "Oh, wow, it's cold. And muddy. Ew, I'm sinking."

"No, in a Humvee. And hold on." He sloshed his way around to her and without hesitating or pausing to see if she'd care, he slipped his hand into hers and pulled her past the car onto a piece of solid ground. "Better?"

"Better." She exhaled, glancing up at him, shining the flashlight between them. "Thanks for coming with me."

He curled his hand into a fist, resisting the urge to wipe the rain from her cheek. "Wouldn't have missed it." This was ten times better than sitting around with a bunch of guys, wondering if she was all right.

"Well . . ." She turned toward the small light beaming through the rain. "I say the last one there is a monkey's uncle." With a rebel yell, Ginger launched into a full-on sprint, the beam of the light bouncing about the darkness.

"What? Wait —" Dang, the girl had wheels. He caught her in a few strides and was about to swoop her into his arms when Ginger disappeared, face first, into a slop of mud, the flashlight sinking with her hand while her purse and duffle floated beside her like useless life preservers.

"Ginger?" He bent for her, swallowing his laugh. It really wasn't funny. No . . . it was hilarious. "Are you all right?" He looped her bags over his head, settling the straps on his shoulder. What was another ounce of mud or two sinking into his shirt? "Here, let me help you." He offered his hand but she refused.

"Mud. I hate mud." Ginger pushed to her feet, bringing up the flashlight, letting loose a blended laugh-cry. She shook her fist at the storm. "You can't beat me."

"Come on, Scarlett O'Hara, let's get to the house. We can argue with the storm from the other side of warm, dry walls." He took her left hand, striding forward. But a dozen steps in, Ginger went down again.

"That's it. Sorry, Ginger, but —" Tom swung her duffle bag to one side as he ducked down and hoisted her over his shoulder in one swift move.

"Whoa, wait a minute, what are you doing?" She hammered her fist against his back, kicking.

"Simmer down." He picked up his pace, his feet chomping through the water and thick, sucking mud. "I want to get to the house without you falling into the mud every five feet. Hey, can you pass me the flashlight?"

She was light, an easy load. One he wouldn't mind shouldering for, well, the rest of his life. But the history . . . Not between them, but their parents. Did she even know?

"Nothing doing. I hand you the light and you drop me, leaving me out here all night."

Tom jogged on, double-timing it. "I just picked you up. Do you seriously think I'd leave you out here?"

"Well, you do have a reputation for leaving a girl without so much as a by-your-leave or kiss-my-grits. Now, really, put me down." She kicked, pushing on his shoulders, trying to get free. "I don't need to be rescued."

"Really?" Without a by-your-leave, kiss-my-grits? So, she did remember the night they were supposed to eat pizza and watch a movie. Tom had wanted to call her that night but he'd spent the time battling with his dad, refusing to pack his suitcase until his baby sister came out of her room, hysterical with tears. *Stop it! Stop fighting.*

"Tom, put . . . me . . . down."

"Seems to me you were losing that battle with the mud." She struggled against him but he hung on. "If you keep squirming, I'm going to drop you."

"Good, do it. Better than being carted around like a sack of seed."

He should've let second-thoughts surface before releasing her but she seemed so intent on her demand. So . . . he let go, sending Ginger to the ground. She plopped into a soggy puddle and bobbled for balance while Tom continued on, plowing through the rain and muck.

"Hey!" Her call bounced through the raindrops. "What's the big idea?"

He turned, walking backward, seeing nothing but the white glow of her flashlight. "You said, 'Put me down.' "

"And you believed me?" Her sloshing and complaining trailed after him, the white light bobbing, until she finally caught up, whapping him on the back of his head.

He laughed, feigning a yelp, and caught her around the waist, spinning her around. "My mama taught me to respect women's wishes."

"You think she intended you to dump a girl to the cold, muddy ground?"

"Yes, if that's what she demanded." Slowly he set her down, her lean frame against him, shivering and soaked. Her breath mingled with his, their heartbeats in sync. Even with the flashing light aimed behind him, he could see every inch of her face. "Ginger —"

"Tom, I-I'm —" She gently freed herself from his embrace, from whatever his heart was about to confess. "Freezing. We'd better get to the house." Ginger aimed the light ahead, spotlighting the old ranch homestead.

"About another thirty meters." Tom took her hand and the flashlight, not caring if she protested, and led the way, holding her steady, instructing her around the ruts and puddles.

The yellow dot fifteen minutes ago was now a full-blown porch light. Tom jumped the veranda steps, the cold starting to sink in, bringing Ginger along with him.

She tried the door handle. "Locked," she said, shaking. "She sent me to a locked house? What happened to 'Daddy never locks the house'?"

"Hold on." Tom tried the windows by the door. Also locked.

"So, when were you a Marine?" Ginger said, following him.

"Between semesters." All of the front windows were bolted. "Stay here, let me scout out the place."

"Between semesters? Like on your school breaks? You ran down to Paris Island and said, 'Hey, I'm here.' "

He smiled back at her. "Something like that." Tom hurdled the veranda rail and jogged to the back of the house. He didn't care about Ginger's wagging finger; Bridgett was going to hear about this. It was one thing to be the caught-up bride but another to be so self-focused she disregarded her guest's well-being.

On the back deck, Tom tried the knob on the French doors, grateful when they gave way to his gentle push.

Stepping inside, he found a switch and with one click, a set of recessed lights over the fireplace beamed on. Excellent. The power was on. He started to step forward but the slosh of his shoes drew him back. With a sweeping glance Tom checked out the place. The work of Mr. Maynard was evident. He kicked off his shoes. Can't track mud across the hardwood.

Crossing the spacious room with its vaulted ceilings and crown molding, he flicked on the end-table lamps.

At the front door, he opened up and stood

aside for Ginger to enter, dropping her bags from his shoulder to the floor. "Please, enter your humble abode."

"So, like, the power was on?" She huddled by the door, a muddy mess as she glanced around. "Wow. *This* is the *old* homestead?"

"Well, consider the source. Bridgett Maynard."

"It's beautiful." Ginger slipped from her shoes and wandered toward the kitchen, then back to the great room. "I think I got the better deal coming out here."

"But everyone else is at the house with food and maids. Does this place have anything to eat? Is the water on?" Tom stepped around to the kitchen, trying the faucet. Water flowed freely. "Looks like you're set then." Tom locked the French doors and picked up his shoes. "Keep the doors locked. There's homeless camps in those woods. Even in this cold."

"Thank you. For everything." She motioned to the doors unaware that the dark scarf she wore swung loose, exposing the neck she worked hard to hide.

He fought the urge to touch her, to tell her the wounds would be all right. She didn't have to hide. But that would definitely cross all of her boundaries. Real or imagined.

"Well, then, I guess I should get back." He made a face as he set down his shoes and slipped in his feet.

"Oh, Tom." She whirled toward him. "See, I knew you shouldn't have come. Now you have to go back in the rain. By yourself."

"Like I said, I've been in worse."

"It's freezing out there. You'll catch a cold or something. I don't think Bridgett and Eric will like you hacking and sneezing through their big society wedding tomorrow."

"Can't stay here, though, can I?" His gaze met hers and for a moment, he was back in high school, watching her in math class, wondering how he could work up the nerve to ask her out. She was so walled and guarded. Then and now.

"I guess not." She stepped toward him. "See you tomorrow then."

"See you tomorrow." In that moment, it felt like something passed between them. But he couldn't quite grab onto it.

"Hey, why don't you try Eric again? He did say he needed his best man tonight. He could come get you."

Tom slipped out his phone, none the worse for the muddy wear, and rang Eric. Again, no answer. He tried Edward to no avail.

He offered up his silent phone to Ginger. "Guess I'm trekking." Tom gestured to the fireplace. "I noticed firewood out back. Do you want —"

"No." She shook her head. "I'm an electric-heat-and-blankets girl all the way."

"Right, sorry." He reached for her hand, the one she didn't hide under the sleeve of her sweater, and gave it a gentle squeeze. "If I had to be out on a cold, rainy night, I'm glad it was with you." He stepped toward the door. "Good night."

"Tom?"

"Yeah?"

"Why didn't you call me? That night? To tell me you were leaving?"

With her questions, time peeled back, and he saw her waiting at her apartment for him to come. But he never did. "I didn't know I was moving until I went home. Dad announced he'd resigned from the church and we were going to Atlanta. No debate, no questions, no argument. I was seventeen years old and my father had just destroyed my world."

"Why didn't you stay with your Granddaddy? Or one of your friends?"

"Dad refused. Insisted we move as a family. The night we packed up to go, Dad and I argued so much we almost threw punches.

Then my sister came out of her room, hysterical, begging us to stop." Ginger listened with her arms wrapped about her waist, the warm light of the homestead haloing her. "It scared me, humbled me, when I saw her pain. Then I saw the angst on my father's face and I gave up my fight. I didn't understand everything that was going on, or why we were heading out of town like bandits, but it had my dad, and mom, in knots. I'd never heard them so much as raise their voices to each other, but that night, they weren't even speaking. Nevertheless, I still managed to be a major pain-in-the-backside. I barely spoke to him for two months after we moved. Though he tried really hard to make things right between us." Tom winced at his confession. "Now I realize at the worst time in his life, his family was all he had and all he wanted."

"Trust me, if you have family, you have everything." She shivered but he wasn't sure it was because of the cold, muddy water clinging to her jeans.

"I'm sorry I never called you, Ginger. Or e-mailed. You were my friend and deserved better. I thought maybe we'd become more than friends. But when we moved, I put Rosebud and everything about it behind me."

"More than friends?" Her eyes glistened. "Even if you'd stayed in Rosebud, we'd never have been anything. We were barely friends. Your *friends* would've never allowed it."

"Allowed what? For us to be friends? Or more than? My friends had no say in my relationships." He took a watery step toward her.

"Are you sure? Seemed to me they had everything to say about your relationships. Who you hung out with, when and where. Every time we had study hall together, they pestered you to skip out. They barely spoke to me when we were together, forget when we weren't."

"Ginger, I could make up my own mind. Even then. They had no say. I asked you to the movies, didn't I?"

She furrowed her brow, shrugging. "As a payback for math help." She smoothed her sandy colored hair over her shoulder, and shoved her scarf into place. "We would've never been anything more."

"If I wanted there to be more —"

A bold knock startled away the intimacy of their conversation and Tom opened to find Edward on the veranda, Scott and his four-wheel drive idling by the steps.

"We've come to rescue you." Edward

barged inside. "Passed the VW on our way . . ." He gave Tom the once over. "Man, what happened to you?"

"We tried to push the car out." Tom followed Edward's glance across the room where Ginger stood on the other side of the reading chairs.

"Ginger," Edward said.

"Edward."

"You know our boy here is starting a church?" Edward clapped Tom on the shoulder.

"So he said."

"No offense, but considering all that happened with Tom's dad, we can't be too careful. Especially around you."

"Around me?" She fiddled with her scarf, smoothing it higher up on her neck. "What are you talking about?"

"Edward, let's go." Tom tugged on his arm, reaching for the door knob.

But Edward remained planted, his smile neither warm nor pleasant. "You know what I'm talking about, Ginger. I realize time has passed and with Tom not being married the rules are different, but nevertheless, there *are* expectations. We have to protect him from scandal and gossip all the same. He needs a good start in Rosebud if the church is going to make it."

"Edward, that's enough." Tom jerked him toward the door. "Ginger, I'm sorry."

"Sorry for what? Edward, what are you talking about? 'Protect him from scandal'?" Ginger gazed at Tom, her lips pressed in defiance. *See? Your friends won't let you.*

"She doesn't know?" Edward glanced at Tom, incredulous.

"Ginger, you're freezing and muddy. We'll get out of your hair," Tom said. Ed and his big mouth. He never did have any tact. "Say . . . I'll come get you in the morning. What time?"

"Don't dismiss me, Tom Wells. What don't I know?"

"Nothing, Edward is just talking. You know, how it's probably not good for Rosebud's newest, young, single pastor to be alone on a dark and rainy night with a beautiful woman."

She snapped back, her expression sober, the sheen in her eyes a blend of confusion and what-did-you-just-say? But she stayed on task. "Edward, what are you talking about?"

"Don't you know, Ginger?" Edward stepped around the wingback chair toward her. His voice was smooth, his movements calculating.

"Edward, enough." Tom came around the

237

other side, pressing his hand into the man's chest. "Let's just go."

"Your mom was the reason Tom's dad had to leave town. Or at least she was the final blow."

Tom dropped his head with a heavy exhale. Edward had been wanting to do this since Tom agreed to start the church. He thought Tom should, "Get it out in the open."

"We don't need any gossip or scandal cropping up."

Ginger glanced between them. "Excuse me? My mom? The woman who hates church? Who . . . wouldn't . . . even . . . take me?" Her words slowed as some sort of revelation dawned. But only for a moment. "No, no, not my mama. Preachers were definitely not her type."

"Say what you will, but Shana Winters was in love with Tom Wells Sr."

"Edward!" Tom shoved him out the door. *What was wrong with him?* "Ginger," Tom paused inside the threshold. "I'll come for you in the morning."

"What are you talking about? She never even knew Tom Sr., let alone fell in love with him. My mother and your father? It's laughable." She turned away from them, disbelief tainting her expression. "My mother? She's a lot of things, but not a home wrecker."

"You're right. She wasn't a home wrecker," Tom said. He could deck Edward. Seriously. "We can talk about this later."

"No. Edward brought it up, so let's talk about it now. My mother is responsible for your family leaving town, for your father losing his church? For you never calling me again?"

"Okay, here's the truth. My *father* is responsible for losing his church, for us leaving town, and *I'm* responsible for never calling you."

"So my mother wasn't involved? Edward is lying?"

"Not exactly lying. Your mother and my father were friends —"

"He said something about love."

"Ed," Tom said. "Can you give us a moment?"

He started to protest, then turned for the door. "Hurry, it's late. Eric's waiting for us."

As the door clicked closed, Tom reached for Ginger but she stepped away. "Edward doesn't know the whole story."

Ginger exhaled, the light in her golden eyes dimming as she closed the small window she'd opened to him.

"Then what is the whole story?"

239

From beyond the door, the truck horn sounded. Tom grumbled low. Wait until he was alone with Ed.

"Tell you what," he said. "I'll pick you up and we can talk about it in the morning." He smiled, coaxing her agreement. "Go, shower, get warm. I'll see you at . . ."

"Eight. But is there any truth to what he said?" she said after a moment.

"Some." He peered at her, gaze holding gaze.

She sighed, sinking down to the chair, then standing back up, remembering she was wet and muddy. "Even more reason now."

"Reason for what?"

"That we can't be more than friends. I told you your friends won't let you."

"And I told you, my friends have no say. See you in the morning, Ginger. And please, do not worry about this. Trust me." The door clicked closed behind him and he jogged toward the waiting truck. Climbing in, he thumped Edward in the head. "Nice going."

"She needed to know." The man showed no remorse. "But really, Tom, her? Of all the women in southern Alabama?"

Tom mulled over the challenge as Scott revved the truck toward the big house, the powerful beast undaunted by the muddy, rutted terrain.

Why not Ginger Winters? She was kind and considerate, more than the man next to him who claimed to be a Christian. Every time Tom saw her in the past few days, she caught a piece of his heart.

But could he be more than friends with the daughter of the woman who played a role in his father's demise?

Yeah, Tom had some praying to do. A conversation with God was about to go down. He'd be open, listening. But in the moment, the answer to Edward's question was a resounding, *Yeah, her. Really.*

CHAPTER SIX

She'd tossed and turned half the night, trying to piece together Edward and Tom's
story as she listened to the rain. It peeled
off around midnight as a strong wind swept
over the grounds, batting the western corner
of the homestead.

Mama and Reverend Wells? Ginger
counted a half a dozen times she'd seen
Mama talking to the senior pastor, but she
never imagined there was anything more
than a how-do between them.

Mrs. Wells, Tom's mama, was a beautiful,
well-respected woman. And nice. Not
cranky and twisted-up like her own mama,
used and spit out from too many poor
relationship choices.

Mama never listened to anyone when it
came to men. She picked her man and that
was it. The police could show her a rap
sheet a mile long but if Mama believed in
him, wanted him, she hung on like a dog

with a bone.

Dressed and ready for the day, Ginger chose a scarf from her duffle — a dark forest green — and wound it around her neck. She wanted to get her stuff from the car and get to the main house before Tom showed up. She didn't need him to rescue her.

But his defense of her last night resonated with her. He'd stood up for her. The notion warmed her with some sort of hope.

With a glance in the mirror, she secured her scarf, then headed out, slipping on her jacket and looping her purse over her head. If she learned anything as Shana Winters's daughter, it was not to mistake kindness as affection. Or love. She'd end up like Mama if she didn't watch it — bitter and used up.

She already knew no man would ever want to hold her ugly, scarred body.

Dawn had not yet kissed the meadow, so if she hurried, she'd be at the house before Tom was out of bed. Plan for the day? Avoid him as much as possible.

But when she opened the door and stepped into the crisp morning, she was confronted with a white orb of a light and Tom Wells astride a ginormous horse.

"Good morning."

Ginger stumbled back, hand over her

heart. "Good grief, you scared me. What are you doing here so early?" She pointed to the mocha-colored beast. "On that?"

"Waiting for you. Help you get your car out of the mud." He aimed the flashlight at her feet. "It's still a mess out there."

"Well then, let's go." She hammered down the steps with a manufactured bravado, shoving past him and his monstrous mount.

"Ginger, you don't have to walk." Tom chirruped to the horse, bouncing the flashlight over the grassy, muddy path still shadowed in the remainder of night.

"I'm not getting on that thing." Ginger pointed back at the horse and plodded on, jumping over the muddiest parts, grateful for Tom's light since she'd clearly forgotten hers. "What happened to Scott's truck?"

"He got stuck himself doing some midnight mudding. The Maynards' stable horses are here, so I borrowed one to come help you."

"Seriously . . . with a horse?" Ginger's next step sank into a gloppy rut hidden by a clump of wild grass.

"Have you seen this brute? He could pull a barn off its foundation. He's a worker, Ginger." Tom landed the light on her, his sweet chuckle floating down around her. But she didn't dare look up. "We hitch your

VW to his harness, he'll be like, 'What's this little thing chained to me?' " Tom's laugh traveled through the cold dawn.

Ginger stopped, glancing up at him. "You think this is funny? I have a job to do and you're making jokes."

"Then why are you being stubborn about help? Ginger, get on the horse." Tom extended his hand toward her. "You're sinking deeper as we speak."

"I've got this." The farther away she strode from the house, the softer the ground and the wetter the grass. Her feet plunged into the mud, loading down the hem of her jeans.

"You got this?" Tom dismounted and sloshed alongside her, guiding her with the flashlight's wide beam. "Mind telling me how you're going to get your car out of the mud?"

She stopped, turning around, causing him to pull up short just before she spun into his thick, sculpted chest. "I . . . have . . . no . . . idea. There, you happy?"

He stiffened, drawing back. "Wow, forgive me. I didn't know you wore bitter so well."

She stepped into him, releasing the scent of clean cotton and soapy skin. "I find out about your dad and my mama from Ed Frizz? Why didn't you tell me?"

He sighed, running his hand the length of

the horse's reins, aiming the flashlight down at his feet. "I didn't know myself until a few months ago. At the time of the move, my parents told my sister and me they had marriage issues to work on but that everything would be all right. When I told Dad I was returning to Rosebud to start a church, he gave up the rest of the story. That Shana Winters was the reason he had to leave."

"What kind of *reason*? Edward seemed to know a whole sordid bunch."

"Yeah, Ed's a blowhard. He likes playing the role of big shot but he doesn't know any more than I do."

"But he thinks he does and he's using it to tell you what to do."

"No, he's not. It's just Ed being Ed." He sighed and clicked to the horse to walk on. "Let's just get your car out of the mud, then you can drive to the house."

Ginger stopped, wrestling with the sense she was the bad guy in this scenario. Tom was the hero, literally riding up on a dark horse to save her. How then was it her fault Tom's father and her mother had been somehow involved? Which made Ed cast shadows on her?

Ginger's emotions flowed into words. "Hey, I'm not the bad guy here." She chased after him, stumbling into yet another

246

sloppy mudhole to coat the hem of her jeans. "No one said a word to me. Never heard one shred of Rosebud gossip. Come on, I'm the scarred, freak girl. Surely someone was dying to tell me how my mama toppled the county's most successful preacher."

Ginger's intensity shaved the ice from the air. The gelding raised his head, snorting, his breath billowing from his broad nose.

"I'm sorry I didn't tell you, Ginger. But between now and three days ago, when was I supposed to do that? 'Hey, I haven't seen you in a dozen years, and oh by the way, how about your mom falling in love with my dad? What a trip!' "

"Is that what happened?" Now that would be typical Mama. Always loving what she couldn't have, from cars to men to other people's daughters — the pretty, smoothed-skinned ones.

"Yes." He peered down at her. "For what it's worth, I'm sorry I left town without talking to you. And for never writing or calling. I was so mad for so long, then I didn't know what to say once I got over myself."

"T-thank you. Sorry for hating you ever since."

"Hating me?" He slapped his hand to his chest. "Really?"

"Okay, maybe not hate but really, really dislike. Strongly." She spied her poor, sinking Bug in the distance. Reaching for his arm, she raised the flashlight's beam. "There she blows."

"She looks so sad. I think she missed us."

"Do you hate her? My mom?" Ginger jumped a puddle, heading for her car. "For whatever she did?"

"There's no benefit in hating anyone. Takes too much energy and returns so little. In truth, though, my parents both say the whole situation worked for good."

"Worked for good? I find that hard to believe." Ginger glanced over at Tom, the pale light of dawn rising behind him, accenting his broad shoulders.

"It's a gift of God. Working all things for good." He muttered a low "whoa" as they approached the VW. "Easy, Clyde."

"So this is Clyde?" Ginger hesitated, reaching up to stroke his nose. Clyde shoved his head against her palm. She jumped back with a short laugh.

"He likes beautiful women," Tom said, walking the workhorse around to the front of the car.

He'd said it again. Called her beautiful. Twice in less than twelve hours. The notion warmed her down to her cold toes. But surely he didn't mean it. Not really. Perhaps in some metaphorical, symbolic way. But oh, she wanted to believe.

Kneeling by the car, Tom hooked a set of chains to the chassis, talking to Clyde in low, tender words. "Good boy . . . you can do this . . . hang with me gentle giant . . . then we'll get you home, cleaned up, with a bucket of oats for breakfast."

Emotion swelled in Ginger's chest. No one had ever spoken to her in such sweet tones except Grandpa.

Not even when she was pulled from the fire, when she lay in a hospital bed weeping from the pain, did anyone offer her kind encouragement.

"Ginger," Mama used to say. *"Stop all these tears. There's just no other way to heal but go through the treatments. Now, come on, do you want to watch* Gilmore Girls *reruns with me?"*

Tears pushed to the surface as Tom hopped up, claiming, "Ready." Ginger ducked behind the back of the car to hide her swimming eyes.

"Born ready."

"You all right?" His soft tone drifted over her shoulder and into her soul.

"Yeah, whatever, let's just do this." Ginger wiped her eyes clear and ducked behind the car, hands on the engine's hood, bracing to push, her feet sinking into the wet, cold ground.

"Ginger, you don't have to —"

"Tom, can we just get this done? I need to get cleaned up before Mrs. James comes down for her appointment."

"Okay. But you drive, I'll push." He bent over her, his nose inches from hers. She could see straight through his sea-blue eyes and into his guileless soul.

"D-drive?" She swallowed.

"Steer? Find the high ground . . ." Tom threaded Clyde's reins between the open door and the windshield.

"Yeah, right." She tugged her keys from her pocket, her heart firing. *No, you can't do this.* She squeezed her eyes shut, holding her breath, shutting down her heart's puttering. "I drive, you push."

He grinned. "Sounds like a plan. Ready?" Tom stepped back, but held a narrow gaze on Ginger. "You sure you're all right?" He angled forward. "I mean with the news and all. It's okay if you're not. We dumped a shocking truth on you last night. Did you call your mom?"

"No. And Tom, stop trying to be Mr. Fix It. Let's *goooo* already."

"Pardon me for caring." His sharp tone pierced her fragile facade. When he moved to the back of the car, Ginger sat behind the wheel.

Oh, Mama . . .

"Here we go," he called. "Clyde, chirrup. Go boy, go."

Ginger shifted into neutral and gripped the wheel as Clyde lowered his head and leaned into his harness, air clouds swelling from under his nose. Ginger turned the ignition but the wet engine sputtered and moaned. The tires spun and whirred, finding no traction.

"Push," she called.

"I'm pushing."

Tom chirruped to Clyde again and in one lunge, the grand beast freed the car from the mud. With a shout, Ginger fired up the engine by popping the clutch. The small motor sputtered to life.

Shifting into neutral, Ginger jumped out. "We did it."

But no one told Clyde his mission was complete. With an easy gait, he trotted on, the engine sputtering.

"Hey, horse, wait —" The back wheel-well grazed Ginger's leg, shoving her to the ground, face first into a very cold puddle.

"Ginger, are you all right?" Tom, trying not to laugh, extended his hand.

"Do I look all right?" She clasped her

hand in his, rising from the mud, watching as Clyde picked up his pace, gaining the feel for old Matilda, and galloped toward the plantation house, the open car door swinging from side to side, Clyde's reins slapping the Bug's interior.

"Ginger, why didn't you grab the reins?"

"B-because . . . y-you didn't tell me to grab the reins. Why didn't you grab them?" She flipped her hand at him, ignoring the flutter in her middle inspired by Tom's sparkling grin. She scooped the mud from her shirt and jeans. "Look at me . . . I'm covered." With a grumble, she adjusted her scarf and started walking, cold, muddy water slinking over the top of her ankle boots.

"Want some company?" Tom skipped alongside her.

"Only if you can keep quiet." The breeze nipped at her, and the golden warmth of the sun peeking over the edge of dawn seemed galaxies away.

She needed to think, deal with the big issue, the dark hole in the pit of her stomach. A hole formed long before she learned that her mama had liaised with a pastor, before Tom Wells Jr. ever entered her life.

This particular hole existed despite her résumé of a big-city career, successful years with Tracie Blue, or ownership of Ginger Snips in the center of Main Street.

She, Ginger Lee Winters, was stuck. In life. In her heart. In what she believed about God, herself, and Tom. Cold tears threatening, Ginger quickened her pace, avoiding the heat of Tom's gaze.

"You okay?" The tenor of Tom's voice sweetened her mood.

Ginger squinted up at him.

"Why are you being so nice to me?"

Tom evened his stride to match hers. "Maybe because I *like* you."

Ginger laughed, loud, plodding on through the long grass, combating the swirling, swooning sensation of Tom's confession. Like her? No man *liked* her. Not in the way his tone indicated.

After a moment she stopped. He was a man of God — maybe he knew the answer to her nagging question. "Does God care?"

"Yes." Sure. Without hesitation. Catching her off guard. She expected him to pause, ponder, hem-and-haw. Because how could a man really know if God cared?

"Yes? Just like that?" She snapped her fingers in the icy air.

"Yes, just like that." He didn't move his eyes from her face. And she flamed on the inside.

Ginger walked on. "Okay, yeah, I guess it's too early in the morning for a serious conversation."

"I am serious. Any time you want to talk, let me know."

She glanced over at him, saying nothing, feeling more conflicted and twisted up than before she asked the question.

If God cared, where was He when she was trapped in the fire? Where was He in the years following? She liked being mad at Him, thinking He owed her something.

But at the moment, what bothered her more than the news about Mama or that God left her in a fire, was the fact that Tom Wells Jr. looked every bit like she imagined Jesus might if she met Him in person. Warm, kind, without accusation, but with a blue-eyed intensity.

However, on this cold wedding morning, she was not ready to trust any overtures of kindness, of love. Not from Tom Wells. And especially not from God.

CHAPTER SEVEN

The atmosphere in the third-floor atrium was electric. Gone were the cold, embedded fragments of her morning in the mud with Tom and Clyde, who, by the way, nudged Ginger's shoulder after Tom unhitched him from the car as if to say, "You're welcome." She felt a rush of joy at the tenderness of the gentle giant.

However, digging out of the mud, communing with horses, cracking open her heart, even the tiniest bit, to Tom Wells, and musing over her past and the existence of God was completely out of Ginger's element.

But in a room full of women, doing hair? This was Ginger Winters's wheelhouse. And she intended to never leave. Gone were her insecurities and trepidations.

Once she and Tom arrived at the barn, where Clyde had taken the VW, Ginger accepted Tom's help to unload and haul in her crates and cases. They did so in a contemplative silence that was not quite comfortable but not at all awkward.

He bid her a quick good-bye when they were done, holding onto her gaze for a second longer than her beating heart could stand, then jogged down the hallway.

Ginger slapped her hand over her heart, willing every beating corpuscle to forget the handsome visage of one Tom Wells Jr.

Ducking into the bathroom, she'd rinsed off in a hot shower, soaping away the chill of the dawn, cleaning off the mud and sending any lingering thoughts of *him* down the drain.

Then she dug clean clothes from her bag and tugged on her spare boots, entering the atrium, her heels resounding on the tile.

By three-thirty, she'd coiffed, twisted, teased, and sprayed the hair of three grandmothers, two mothers, one great-aunt, seven bridesmaids, and two flower girls.

All the while the music was blasting everything from Michael Bublé to Jesus Culture to Beyoncé's "All the Single Ladies."

Laughter tinged along with the music, becoming a part of the melody and percussion.

Right now the bridesmaids were circling

Bridgett, turning up the music, belting out the lyrics with their heads back, arms wide. *"You call me out beyond the shore into the waves . . . You make me brave . . ."*

Ginger closed her eyes, leaning against the makeshift beauty station, breathing in the lyrics. If there was a God who cared, could He make her brave? She liked the idea of it all.

A blip of laughter from the older women chatting on the matching sofas caught her attention.

They reclined in their wedding attire, the glitter in their dresses snapping up the light draining through the high arching windows, and sipping a fruity Ginger Ale punch.

"I sure could have used a song like this on my wedding day." One of the grandmas pointed to the singing circle. "I was so nervous I could barely stand let alone belt out a song with my bridesmaids. It took all of my gumption to make it down the aisle."

"That's nothing," said the great-aunt. "At my wedding, Daddy turned to me just as the pianist started the bridal march and said, 'Lovie, you don't have to do this if you don't want.' Lord a-mercy, I liked to have crowned him right then and there."

Ginger smiled and checked her watch, picking up her own punch glass. Three forty-five. An hour and forty-five minutes until the wedding. So as soon as Bridgett was done singing about bravery, Ginger would have her in the chair.

Hair and makeup was her world. Where she was in command, captain of her destiny. But out *there,* in the everyday world, she was the poor, pitied, scarred one. And now the daughter of the woman who took down a preacher.

Which was why she'd remain hidden in her shop behind long sleeves and peacock-colored scarves. And she'd glean a little of life from the women and men who entered her shop, sat in her chair, and told her their stories.

The song ended and the girls laughed and cheered, drawing Bridgett into a hug, forming a magical bloom of beauty.

Ginger would never fit in their garden. She'd be pruned for sure.

But in the field of helping others, ushering every woman, young and old, into a realm of beauty, she'd thrive.

"Oh, Ginger, look, my hair is coming undone." Miranda broke from the circle with panic in her voice, making her way to Ginger. "Look." She patted the loose weave Ginger had given her.

"Have a seat." Ginger patted the chair,

squinting at Miranda's sandy-beach colored updo. It was perfect. And practically impossible to fall since she'd plastered it in place.

"How about some long strands . . . for curls?" Miranda said, trying to tug strands from the clips.

"Mandy, good grief, let Ginger do her job. She's the best. Your hair is perfect." Bridgett stood off to the right, beaming, wrapped in a white robe and drinking a sparkling water.

"I just like long curls over my shoulder."

"Because you always wear long curls over your shoulder. Be *brave,* do something new."

Ginger smiled at Miranda through the mirror. "Trust me, this twist works perfectly for your face. If you want curls, we'd have to start all over which means washing your hair."

Miranda made a face. "Fine, but I still think some long curls around my neck would look good." She pointed at Bridgett. "Wait until you're in this chair. You'll be bossing Ginger around all right."

"Watch me. I'm going to face away from the mirror, that's how much I trust her."

"Then here you go." Miranda stood, shaking the folds from her long gown. "Your turn to be *brave.*"

Without a word, Bridgett turned the chair

away from the mirror and sat with a glare at her friend. "Ginger, do your thing." She glanced up. "We go back a long way, don't we?"

"We do." In these moments, high school became a mythical, fun place with treasured memories, where, for a brief second in time, Ginger was a part of the sorority.

"Remember when you pulled my backside from the fire the night I tried to —" A deep red blushed Bridgett's cheeks as she stumbled over her words. "I mean, the night I tried to . . ." She swallowed, ". . . color my hair, and . . . green. Everywhere . . . green."

"It was a class A emergency." Ginger let the reference to fire pass. When she commanded her *space,* not even her dark tragedy overshadowed her.

"It was my first date with Eric and my hair was all kinds of messed up. I ran, literally, to Ginger's house, crying the whole way."

"And look at you now," Ginger said.

"Marrying" — Bridgett's voice broke — "that same man."

"Who probably would've never noticed green hair."

"True, so very true." Bridgett's laugh sweetened the room, and the bridesmaids *ahhhed.*

Ginger combed through Bridgett's slightly

curled hair, then divided it into sections, planning to fashion a light updo with tendrils drifting down the curve of her neck. Because the bride's hairstyle should tell her story, reflect her essence.

Bridgett's updo was intricate with twists and curls, but entirely and altogether elegant and rich.

Ginger teased the top of the hair, slipping into her space of contentment and peace. Because no matter how scarred or hideous she was to others, no one could take this away from her.

If she had any true courage, she might bless the tragedy that introduced her to her destiny, to her superpower.

As she twisted and pinned Bridgett's hair, the women continued talking, laughing, calming the distraught wedding planner who barged into the room announcing the flowers had not yet been delivered.

Ginger watched the drama through a covert gaze, all the while twisting, tucking, and smoothing. When Bridgett's hair was pinned and frozen in place with hair freeze, her mother called for the dress. The designer entered along with her assistant as Bridgett stood.

"Here we go." She glanced back at the mirror, then at Ginger, her eyes glistening.

"Exactly how I imagined my hair. Thank you."

Suddenly the burn of the previous night's banishment dissipated and all was right with the world.

Slipping from her white robe, Bridgett stepped into the fur-trimmed gown, fitting it on her shoulders and setting it on her slim waist, the crystal beading catching the light.

Then, like bustling elves, they straightened and buttoned, helped Bridgett with her shoes, then last, handed her veil over to Ginger.

"Will you do the honors?" her mother said.

Standing on a stool, Ginger fitted the comb at the base of Bridgett's silken poof and draped the blusher over her face.

"Oh darling . . ." Mrs. Maynard cupped her hands over her mouth, not worried about her tears streaking her makeup. "You look beautiful, simply, elegantly beautiful."

"Eric's eyes are going to pop out of his head." Miranda said.

Bridgett glided across the room to the full-length mirror and sighed. "Just like I dreamed." She turned to Ginger. "I knew you'd make me beautiful."

"I think Mother Nature took care of that for you."

Bridgett was the perfect bride, the prettiest Ginger had ever seen. And now that her job was done, she felt herself slipping from her empowered zone into the wishing well of wanting to a part of the bold and the beautiful.

But she'd never be a bride, let alone one like Bridgett. Ginger slipped out of the atrium onto the deck and leaned against the railing, breathing deep, swallowing the truth.

Ginger watched the reception from the doorway of the plantation's grand ballroom, away from the guests and the photographers ducking in and out of the shadows of the ornate plantation ballroom with a fresco ceiling and an imported tile floor.

The guests dined under the light of a handcrafted Waterford chandelier that disseminated light like golden scepters.

Candlelight flickered on linen-draped tables adorned with polished silver and custom-designed china. In the far corner of the room, a fire roared in the river-rock fireplace.

The aroma of prime rib and roasted duck lingered in the air as the best man and maid of honor toasted the bride and groom. While the guests cheered and silver tinkled against cut crystal glasses, Eric kissed Bridgett and the band started a Glenn Miller tune.

In less than a music measure, the dance floor was thick with folks juking and jiving.

Ginger sighed. Every hairdo she had sculpted today remained in perfect place. Of course . . .

Proud of a job well done, she debated now if she should just go on home. It was getting late and she was tired. And, despite her success with the grandmothers, mothers, aunts, and bridesmaids, she felt a little out of place and alone.

"Hey."

Ginger glanced around to find Tom approaching. "Hey."

"Having fun?"

"Sure."

Tom leaned against the other side of the doorway. "Word is Bridgett's stylist is nothing short of a wonderkid. You brought out the best in her. In all of them."

Ginger gestured to the beaming groom. "I think he's the one that really brings out the best in her."

Bridgett was a vision. She'd changed into a simple white satin gown for the reception, accented with a white, wintery shrug. Eric drank her in with such adoration and desire that Ginger could only watch for a moment, feeling as if she were a voyeur into his intimate, private feelings.

With a sigh, she slipped her hand into her hip pocket. Just once, she'd like a man to look at her with such admiration. Such love. To take her in his arms and move across the dance floor.

She loved dancing. Or at least she thought she did. She'd never *been* on a dance floor.

"By the way, when I was giving Clyde his oats he said to tell you hi."

She snorted a laugh, covering her lips with her fingers. He got to her way too easily. "Tell Clyde hi back."

"He said he'd like to give you a ride sometime."

"How sweet. But I don't *do* horses."

"Yeah?" His tone smiled.

"Yeah." She tried to sound fun and sexy but her shallow breath made her voice thin and weak.

"Do you like dancing?"

"I used to watch dancing videos all the time. Mama would rent them for me from Blockbuster." Ginger stood straight, pinching her lips. *Hey, no giving up secrets.*

"But have you ever danced? On a dance floor? With a man?"

"Does it matter?" She faced Tom, hesitated, then gathered a wad of courage and pulled up the sleeve of her blouse, exposing

265

the harsh terrain of her arm. She didn't dare expose her side or back. This would be enough to gross him out. "No one wants to dance with this."

"You seem to know what others think without asking them." He tried to snatch her hand but she was too quick.

"I don't need to know what they think." She shook her arm at him. "This is ugly, not fun to touch." She regretted her action, exposing herself to him. Really, she needed to get in her car and drive away. In a matter of mere days, Tom Wells had flashed his light over her heart and she was nearly ready to show him her deepest, darkest corners. "I'm a freak."

"Ginger, we're all freaks. We're all scarred. That's why Jesus came. Why He died and rose again for us."

"Yeah, that's what a girl loves when she makes herself vulnerable. A sermon. Save it for Sunday, Tom." She flashed her palm. "I'm not interested."

"Ginger, come on, your scars don't bother me." He gently took her hand in his, then, with his eyes on hers, traced the marks on her hand and wrist.

"Stop. Let go." She tried to wrench free but he held on. "Tom, don't . . ."

"Your scars don't bother me." He held

her hand a bit tighter and slid his hand along the rugged texture of her arm.

"Stop . . . please." Her whole body trembled, shaking her to her core.

The music from the bandstand changed, slowing down to a soft, melodic "Moon River."

"How did it happen?" He turned her arm over, exposing its tender but damaged underside, and traced his fingers, moving so delicately along the puckered ridges. "I never asked. You never told me."

"T-the . . . rattle trap . . . trailer . . ." Each stroke of his hand stole her breath. She tried to pull free again, but lacked strength and will to really be without his touch.

A tingling sensation crept up her arm and rode over her shoulder, and down her back. A gulp of pleasure filled her chest.

Never had she been touched by a man. Never, ever had she experienced such a feeling.

"You lived in a trailer?"

"North of town, off Highway 29. The wiring was rotten, eaten by squirrels." She should pull her arm away before she puddled at his feet. Did he realize what he was doing to her?

She swallowed, drawing a deep breath. "The place caught fire . . . I was sleeping.

Mama . . . had gone out . . . after I went to bed. I called and called her but she didn't answer. I thought she was dead. I had to find her but the only way to get out of my room was to run through the flames . . . my nightgown caught on fire."

"Ginger, that took a lot of courage." He held their hands palm-to-palm and linked his fingers with hers. "These scars don't make you a freak. They are not ugly."

"Because you don't live with them every day. You don't see the looks, hear the whispers. 'Oh, isn't it a shame?' 'Yes, yes it is.' "

"Maybe they're amazed how a girl with such obvious scars could be so beautiful." His low tone carried an intimacy that saturated her soul with the same intoxication as his touch.

"Stop, Tom." She broke free and shoved down her sleeve. "You're a preacher. You shouldn't say things that aren't true." Guests were coming out of the ballroom, so Ginger fell in line with them, heading toward the foyer. Time to go.

"What's not true?" Tom followed, intense and determined.

"That I'm beautiful."

"But you *are,* Ginger." He slipped his

hand around her arm. "Would you like to dance?"

"No. You don't have to pretend to be interested in me. To be kind." Because she'd rather have people exclaim, "Oh what a pity," than to discover Tom Wells was just being a *nice* guy.

"What if I'm not pretending?"

"To be kind?"

"To be interested."

Ginger fell against the wall, half in the light, half in the shadow and folded her arms. "After confessing to me that my mother played a part in your father's demise? How could you possibly be interested in me? What would Edward think?"

"Who cares? I don't. I like you. I think we could be *friends.*" His breath clung to "friends" for a moment longer than necessary. "Ginger, it's a wedding. Come on, one dance."

She gestured toward his tuxedo, then the couples coming down the hall. "The attire is formal. I'm wearing jeans."

"You think anyone is going to care?"

"Yes, I do. Mrs. Maynard for one. There's a governor, two senators, and a newspaper publisher in there. And a boat load of photographers."

"So what?" He slipped his hand into hers

again and the dying embers of his touch flared again.

"Tom, do you ever listen?" Her eyes welled up. He was going to make her confess it. "I'm not one of *them*. One of you." She'd pulled her hand from his. "I need to get going." Get back to her life and her world where everything was comfortable. Where her lines were clearly drawn.

"Why do you want to watch life from the shadows?"

"Did it ever occur to you I like the shadows?"

"Did it ever occur to you that you were made for so much more?"

She stared at him, her insides a hissing stick of dynamite. Once she thought she was made for more. She'd even tried for bigger things on the road with Tracie. But . . .

"Have a good evening, Tom. Good luck with your church." Ginger headed down the corridor. She needed to escape the house, escape all the love and happiness in the ballroom, escape *Tom.*

But he followed her down the hall, past the bustling kitchen, warm with the smells of roasted meat and baking bread, through the grand room toward the arching foyer with the sweeping staircase.

"Ginger, please one dance."

And risk her heart toppling over in love? She tugged open the foyer door, inhaling the sweet scent of her escape. "Good night, Tom."

CHAPTER EIGHT

By Wednesday the warmth and sunshine had returned to southern Alabama and Ginger settled back into her weekly routine of blue hair wash-and-blowouts, and the chatter of Ruby-Jane, Michele, and Casey.

She could almost forget the weird snow day, the odd wedding weekend, and Tom Wells Jr. with his probing power-blue eyes and intoxicating, tender touch.

Just the memory of his fingers running along her arm made her shiver.

"You cold?" Ruby-Jane said, walking by with an armload of clean towels.

"What? No. Loving these warm temps." Ginger put the finishing touches on Mrs. Darnell's short, teased hair.

Drat that Tom Wells. She was going to have to dump her head in one of the sinks after closing and wash that man right out of her hair.

"Well . . ." Ruby-Jane stood in the middle

of the shop. "Hump day. What are y'all do-ing this evening? Want to try that new burger place by the shopping plaza?"

"Not me," Michele said, counting out her tips. "We've got basketball tonight."

"Church for me," Casey said.

"Ging? What about you?"

She gazed at Ruby-Jane through the mir-ror. "Got plans. If you're looking for some-thing to do, you could finish painting the shop."

The place looked rather awkward with one long wall painted a smooth pinkish-beige while the other remained a putrid pea green.

"Ha, nothing doing. I'll help you if you want but I'm not staying here by myself."

"I would but I need to take care of some-thing." Ginger took command of the conver-sation, going over Thursday's appointments and deciding with her stylists which sup-plies needed to be reordered.

Then she closed the shop and picked up Chinese takeout from Wong Chow and drove across town to Mountain Brook Apartments as the winter sun drifted be-yond the edge of the earth's curve.

Pulling into a parking spot under Mama's second floor apartment, Ginger gathered the takeout bags and jogged up the steps.

"Hey, baby," Mama said, smiling, taking a

long inhale of the food as Ginger entered. "I was surprised you called."

"Well, we haven't seen each other in awhile." Ginger slipped off her sweater, straightening the long bell sleeve of her top, glancing about the small, charming apartment, decorated with Mama's artistic flair.

"I heard the wedding was lovely." Mama set the fried rice on the dining table as Ginger searched the cupboards for the plates. "Just use paper. In the cabinet by the sink."

Ginger set the plates on the table. "Bridgett was a beautiful bride. But no one expected less."

"Did you have a nice time?"

She shrugged, taking the napkins and chopsticks from the bag. "It was a job."

"Put any yearnings into your head?" Mama wiggled her eyebrows and did a jig across the linoleum. "Maybe a wedding of your own?"

"Hardly."

"And why not? You're smart, successful . . . *p-pretty.*"

That's how Mama always said it. *P-pretty.* Stumbling. Hesitating. As if she was trying to believe her own confession.

"Actually, I didn't come to talk about me." Ginger sat at the table, reaching for the beef and broccoli. "Did you know Tom Wells was in town? Starting a church?"

"What?" Mama's complexion paled, but she disguised it by jumping up. "I forgot the iced tea. I made some this afternoon."

"Tom junior, Mama. Not senior."

Her back stiffened and the pitcher of tea shimmied. "T-that boy who stood you up all those years ago?"

"Mama, I know."

"Know what?" She came to the table, chin up, gaze down. "Oh, shoot, I forgot ice. Give me your cup."

Ginger pressed her hand on Mama's. "About you and Mr. Wells. Tom Senior."

Mama snatched the cup, and her hand, from Ginger's grasp. "What in the world are you talking about?" She jammed the plastic cups under the ice dispenser. "This town is a gossip petri dish."

"Apparently not, Mama. I never heard word one about you and Pastor Wells before. Is it true? Are you the reason he left town?"

Mama pressed her forehead against the fridge, filling the cups to the brim with ice. "Certainly not. Who told you such a wild tale?" She came to the table and sat with a *harrumph,* tucking her bobbed copper hair behind her ears.

"Edward Frizz. Tom confirmed it."

"Just like that?" Mama scooped more rice than she'd ever eat onto her plate. "They walked up to you at Bridgett Maynard's wedding, of all places, and said, 'Hey, your mama ran Pastor Wells out of town?' Land sakes, that was twelve years ago. Some folks have to learn to let things go." Her hands trembled as she dumped almost all of the Moo Goo Gai Pan over her rice.

"You're seriously going to eat all the Moo Goo?"

"Oh, see what you made me do?" Mama shoveled some of it back into the container. "Ginger, I don't know what possessed —"

"Is it true? You and Pastor Wells?"

Mama set the container down, her eyes glistening, and stared toward the bright kitchen, sniffling, running her hands through her hair. "You were to never know."

"Why not?"

"How in the world did Edward Frizz find out?"

"I don't know about Edward. But Tom, of course, knows. His dad told him the whole story when he decided to return to Rosebud. Tom's starting this new church."

"I suppose . . . So, Tom's dad told him? Warned him?" Mama's eye sparked with a wild, rebellious glint. "Stay away from the Winters women?"

276

"Who knows? Probably." Ginger's stomach rumbled, asking for food, rejecting the forming rock of tension as any kind of nourishment. Tom certainly didn't heed his daddy's warning. "Did you have an affair?"

"No! No . . ." Mama broke open a set of chopsticks and swirled her chicken through a pile of fried rice but never took a bite. "Remember Parker Fox?"

"I think. Wasn't he the banker you dated?"

"I finally thought I'd found me a good one, you know? He adored you."

"If you say so." None of Mama's boyfriends ever adored Ginger.

"He wasn't a drinker or doper. He wanted a nice suburban life. Just like I wanted when I married your daddy."

"So what happened?" Ginger scooped a forkful of rice and beef into her mouth, exhaling, willing this conversation to be about truth. Maybe healing.

"He asked me about your scars."

Ginger set down her fork and wiped her mouth with her napkin. "He didn't want a stepdaughter with such ugly scars?"

"No, Ginger, why do you always assume the worst?"

"Because it's usually true."

"He wanted to know how it happened. So I told him. He was aghast. First that you were trapped in a trailer fire but mostly because I'd left you alone. I told him you were twelve and that I'd only gone down to the Wet Your Whistle for a beer and burger with a guy from work. That was too much for him and he wanted out." Mama snapped her fingers. "He didn't feel I'd be a fitting mother should we ever have kids."

Ginger shoved her food about her plate. "I'm sorry, Mama." But in a small way, she understood Mr. Fox.

"I was pretty messed up. Started having nightmares of you trapped in all sorts of fires. Only I couldn't rescue you. I'd wake up in a panic, trembling like a pup in a rainstorm."

"Where was I? How did I not know this?"

"You were sixteen, trying to figure out life for yourself. Wasn't fitting for me to dump my burden on you."

"But we were supposed to be the Gilmore Girls. Best friends and all." A bit of the sarcasm she loathed coated her response.

"Don't be impertinent, Ginger. Anyway, that's when we started attending church."

"And you hooked up with Pastor Wells?"

"I did not *hook up.* I started wondering if this God business was what I needed. *We* needed. I had a few questions and Pastor Wells agreed to meet with me. We discovered

278

we both liked nature and art. He lent me a book on John Audubon. I showed him a few of my sketches. I started attending the women's Bible Study on Tuesdays before work and I started stopping by his office before I left." Mama lifted her gaze. "He was so kind, you know? Actually listened to me. No man, not even Parker Fox, ever really listened to me before."

"So you had an affair? With a married man of God?" Ginger shuddered. Having experienced fire, she had a deathly fear of hell. And of the God, if He existed, who claimed He could send her there. Real or imagined, she tried to avoid ticking God off at all costs. So messing with His men was way off limits.

Another reason to avoid Tom Wells Jr.

"We didn't have an affair." Mama snatched up her glass of sweet tea, taking a big gulp. "But I was falling for him. Found myself thinking of him all the time." She pressed her hand over her heart. "He started living in here more than he should. I was falling in love . . . So I told someone."

"Who?"

"The leader of the women's Bible study, Janelle Holden."

Ginger had some experience with church women in the shop. Having a crush on the pastor was a big, fat no-no.

"Why would you tell *her*? Why not Aunt Carol or your buddy, Kathleen?"

"Because Janelle said she was there to help us, to guide us to Jesus. Ha, what a crock. She went from friend to foe before I even got to the end of my first sentence. Next thing I know I'm sitting before an elder board, confessing the whole story without a moment to defend Tom or speak to him privately. He didn't really do anything, Ginger. He was just sweet and nice. Maybe too sweet and nice. I don't know why they made him leave, but boy howdy, I wasn't surprised when I found out Robert Holden was the new pastor." Mama sighed. "I was so stupid and naive. At thirty-seven to boot. I was thinking I'd like to be saved, give Jesus a chance to straighten me out. Maybe He'd be able to lend you a hand too."

"Well, falling in love with a married preacher isn't the way to get straightened out. Did he say he loved you?"

"No, never." Mama's eyes swam as she rolled her gaze toward the popcorn ceiling. "But he showed signs of being interested. I thought he might have feelings for me."

"Mama, he was *married.*"

"Ginger, for crying out loud, I know." Mama slammed her glass down on the counter. "You think I wanted to fall in love with an unavailable man? Even if he became available, there'd be scandal and gossip, but I was . . ."

"Hoping?"

"Yes," she glared down at Ginger. "And what of it? Don't I have the right to a good man? One who cares, listens, understands?"

"Not when he's married to another woman. How did I not know about this? How was it not all over school? One of the most popular boys, a football star, upped and disappeared at the beginning of his senior year and no one came at me?"

"I agreed to keep quiet if they agreed to keep my name out of it for your sake. Everyone seemed more twisted up about Tom Senior and what was going on in his life than about me. I'm sure Janelle was all ready to blab if Tom didn't step down and leave. She didn't care about me. She cared about getting Tom out and her husband in."

"Then he must have had feelings for you. I mean, to leave the way he did."

"I don't know. We never spoke again. But I heard there were other issues with the church, with his wife, and I was the icing on the cake." Mama shrugged, swirling her tea, the ice clinking against the sides. "Who knows what's really true?"

"So that's why we never went to church again?"

"I figured they'd brand me with a scarlet *A* or something." She shook her head. "And I was pretty sure God didn't want to see the woman who caused His man to resign his church."

"Were you at least sorry?"

"Sorry? I was confused. And poor Tom. It seemed like such a brouhaha over something so one-sided."

"Why didn't you tell me? You knew how upset I was by Tom Junior disappearing without a word."

"Because I felt so foolish." She returned to the table, shoving her plate forward, cupping her tea in her hands. "I'd lost my friend Tom and my women's group. I didn't need you loathing me any more than you already did."

"I didn't loathe you."

"Yeah, whatever . . . So, now you know." Mama popped the table with her palm. "Aren't you proud? Oh, who am I kidding? It's just more of the same. Where was I the night of the fire? Where was I half your teen years?"

"Can we not rehash this?" Ginger spent most of her teen years and twenties forgetting the past. Trying to build a future with

282

her handicaps.

"I suppose not. You don't need further proof I failed you."

"Mama." *Sigh.* "You didn't fail me." Ginger wanted her confession to at least sound true even if she didn't believe it. Not entirely.

"Look at you, all scarred on your arm and side, across your back and that sloppy skin graft on your neck. That's what government-funded medical care will get you. And you have a sexy figure. But can you show it off? Wear a nice bikini down to the lake? No —"

"Mama, stop. I don't need an inventory. I see myself every morning in the shower. Can we talk about something else? How's your Moo Goo?"

"Cold." Mama picked up her plate for the microwave. "What's going on with you and Tom Junior?"

"Nothing." A low warmth crept across Ginger's cheeks. At least she had the treasure and memory of his touch.

"Are you sure?" Mama's tone lightened, her words lilting and teasing. "He was mighty handsome as a young man."

"Mama, no, come on." The bit of rice Ginger scooped into her mouth went down sticky and dry. "I'm no more right for him

283

than you were for his daddy. Even if Tom Senior wasn't married, Mama, you never cared about serving your own daughter let alone serving others or being a woman of faith."

"I thought you didn't want to talk about how I failed you."

"I didn't. I don't."

"Look, Ginger, just because I messed up with Tom Senior doesn't mean you can't like his son. If there's something between you, then —"

"Is it seven o'clock already?" Ginger scooted away from the table, downing the last of her tea. "I need to run. The shop's books await."

"Ginger, don't deny your heart."

She snatched up her purse, a Hermès Birkin clutch gifted to her by Tracie. Styling for celebrities had its perks. "I'm not denying my heart. Tom Wells is not for me."

If she said it enough, her heart would believe it.

"Listen to me." Mama grabbed her by the shoulders. The only touch Ginger allowed without flinching. "I ruined things with your daddy because I was young and stubborn."

"He left you, Mama."

"But he wanted to come back and I wouldn't let him. Thought I wanted something better. How did that work out for me? All these years later and I'm alone."

"No, Mama, you're not alone." Ginger drew her into a hug, resting her chin on her shoulder. "You have me."

"And that is a true gift." Mama stepped back, her eyes glistening. "Now go on, get your books done. How's that cute apartment of yours?"

"Good. I like living above the shop."

"Thanks for dinner," Mama said.

"Thanks for the truth."

Ginger made her way down the concrete steps to her car, tossing her bag into the passenger seat, glancing up to the pale light outside Mama's door.

Tonight she'd discovered a few things about her own heart. She appreciated Mama more than she realized.

And she learned to never make the same mistakes. Which meant loving the wrong man. Ginger marked an *X* on the image of Tom Wells drifting around her soul. He was officially off-limits, no matter how much she yearned for his tender touch.

On Thursday evening, Tom stepped out of the Rosebud *Gazette* office and inhaled the smooth fragrance of an Alabama winter, feeling rather pleased. His interview with

Riley Conrad had gone well.

Her questions were thought-provoking and interesting. They laughed and reminisced about Rosebud traditions, recalled old names and faces. Including his father.

"Can you tell me? Did he leave town in disgrace? Did he have an affair?" Riley said.

"No, to both counts. He did have some issues to work out and along with my grandfather and mother's wisdom and support, he resigned his church, took a job in Atlanta, at which he became very successful, and fixed the things he needed to fix in his life. Look, being a pastor doesn't have to be a lifelong call. My father came to the end of that season in his life."

"But it took an outside situation to force him to make a change."

"Doesn't it for almost everyone? You left Rosebud, Riley. Why'd you come back?"

She gave him a wicked grin. "Outside situation."

Tom paused on the corner of Main and Alabaster, the glow of a street lamp on his shoulders. Riley's piece would be this Sunday morning's feature and hopefully inspire Rosebud's citizens to check out Encounter Church.

So, now what? Tom glanced left where Alabaster curved around into Park Avenue, ending at Mead Park. To his right was Main Street and downtown.

He'd parked his car in front of Sassy's Burgers, where he'd eaten every night this week. Most of the shops were open late on Thursday and their golden light fell across the sidewalk in large squares.

Including Ginger Snips. The main window glowed with a string of white lights. Was she there? It was after seven. Tom brushed his hand over his slightly gelled hair, wishing he needed a trim. Wishing he had an excuse to stop by the shop.

But did he need one? Couldn't he pop in to say hi? He'd told Ginger he wanted to be friends.

He stepped off the curb, ducking in front of a car turning left, and took long strides to Ginger Snips before he changed his mind.

He found the front door open, paint fumes scenting the breeze.

"Well, looky what the cat dragged in again." Ruby-Jane spotted him. Tom took a cautious step over the threshold. "What brings you here on a Thursday evening, *pastor*?"

"I was down —" He paused when Ginger emerged from the back room with a paint tray and a bucket swinging from her hand, "— at the *Gazette*."

She stopped when she saw him. "Tom, what are you doing here?"

"Just saying hi. So, y'all are painting tonight?"

Ruby-Jane huffed, folding her arms. "That's what she tells me. Of course the other two, Michele and Casey, get a pass."

"Leave it alone, RJ. You know why."

"Still doesn't seem fair. Just because they have families."

Ginger set her tray down without a word or a backward glance. "We can waste time talking about it or get to work and be done with it."

Tom slipped off his jacket and draped it over the nearest chair. "Can I help?"

"No," Ginger said. "We only have two roller brushes."

Ruby-Jane shot him a sly smile. "No worry. He can have mine."

"No, he can't." Ginger rose up, steel in her words, a hard glint in her eyes. "Stop yapping and start working." She peeked at Tom. "Word of advice. Don't hire your friends to work for you."

"Duly noted." He nodded, trying to hold her gaze. *You okay?* The recessed light dripping down from the ceiling haloed her chestnut hair and reflected in her hazel eyes.

She was breathtaking. But he couldn't see

her for himself, could he? He had to see her as God's daughter. Pop's advice from before the wedding had been coming back to him all week, "If you love her, win her to Jesus," along with the whisper of the Lord, "Tell her she's beautiful."

"I meant it," he said. "I can help."

"It's okay, Tom." Ginger hoisted the big paint can, sloshing some over the side as she filled the tray. "We got it."

Tom stepped over, reaching for the handle as she tried to set it down without hitting the corner of the tray.

His fingers grazed hers. When he looked at her, she was looking at him. His pulse drummed in his ears. "Y-you can let go."

She hesitated. Then, "Ruby-Jane and I are perfectly capable of doing the job."

"I never said you weren't. But many hands make light work."

"Hey, Ging," Ruby-Jane said, walking over to Tom, offering him her roller. "I need to run. Daddy just called and Mama's made a big ole spread for the entire family." RJ held up her phone as if to prove her story. "Apparently my brother just drove into town . . . So, y'all two got this?"

"What brother? *All* your people live in town." Ginger rebuffed Ruby-Jane with a stiff lip and a firm jut of her chin. "RJ, you *can't* leave."

"Family first. Besides, I'm on salary, not an indentured servant. Tom, I hereby dub you my replacement." Tom reached for the long handle. "Do me proud." Ruby-Jane edged toward the back door. "See you in the morning, Ginger."

"RJ? RJ, wait." Ginger chased her to the back room but to no avail. When she returned, she took up her roller and slapped it against the wall, mumbling, ". . . brother who just drove into town, my eye."

"She seems to think we should spend some alone time together."

Ginger rolled, rolled, rolled on the paint. "I had enough of you last weekend, no offense."

"None taken. Now, where can I power up some tunes? Let's get this place painted and beautiful."

CHAPTER NINE

She wanted to be indifferent. Take him or leave him. Forget Tom Wells was in her shop, singing along with the music from his iPhone piped into the shop through the sound system.

She just wanted to paint, get the job done, go up to her apartment and cleanse her senses of any reference to Tom's soapy scent.

"How's it looking?" Tom pointed to his cut-in work at the top of the wall, just under the ceiling.

"Great." She gave him a thumbs up, then went back to her portion of the wall.

Actually, he irritated her. Why was he here? What did he want with her? Why did he volunteer to do the neck-breaking cut-in work, even borrowing a ladder from Fred's Grocer across the street, to do the job?

And the music? Smooth and soothing, raining down peace in the shop, watering her soul.

"*. . . you're beautiful,*" Tom sang softly with the music, to himself.

Ginger pressed her roller against the wall, squeezing out the last of the beige-rose paint.

"*. . . I can tell you've been praying.*"

"Who is this? Singing?"

"Gospel artist, Mali Music."

"Never heard of him."

"Neither had I until a few years ago. He's the real deal. I like him."

Real deal? As opposed to a fake deal? Christians and their language . . . that irritated her most. Their two-faced kindness. Their faux helpfulness. Since her discovery of truth with Mama, Ginger had grown a pound of sympathy for her mother. Shana had tried to get it right, to be honest.

Tom's low, silky bass swirled through her, leaving her with the same sensation as his touch. Squirming, squeezing his vocal notes out of her soul, Ginger glanced up at him as he cut-in under the ceiling. A singing, kind, handsome pastor? Look out. He'd have women all over him.

Desperate ones like Mama who'd surrender their hearts if he'd ease a bit of their pain.

"So, Sunday," she said, shaking off a

strange jealous wave. "You ready?"

"I think so. I've got my sermon in my head. Just need to write out my notes." The beam of his smile went to the bottom of her being and she trapped it there, not willing to let it go. She could create a trio of Tom Wells Jr. treasures — his touch, his voice, his smile.

She would never be with him, but she could remember the one man in her life who made her *feel* what it was like to be a woman.

"And just what do you hope people will encounter at Encounter Church?" She filled her roller brush in the paint tray, then pressed it against the wall, working around the blue tape protecting the trim and window frame.

"God, His emotions toward us. I hope they find love and friendship with each other." He laughed low. "Maybe a good potluck dinner now and then."

"God has emotions?"

"Absolutely. Love, peace, joy. God *is* love, First John tells us." He gazed down at her. "Love's an emotion, right? God created us with emotions. Why wouldn't He have them Himself?"

"Because emotions can be manipulated. Go bad . . ."

"Ah yes, if you're a human. But God has perfect emotions. Don't you think it's kind of cool God feels love or delight in you?"

"Me?" Ha, ha, now he talked crazy.

"Yes, you." Tom came down the ladder and toward her. "He loves you. He also likes you."

"You don't know any such thing." His gaze, the intensity of his words, set her heart on fire. "I prayed once. It didn't go well."

"Wimp."

"Excuse me?"

"You prayed once and gave up? Is that how you became the stylist to the stars? By giving up the first time 'it didn't go well'?" He took the roller from her hand and rested it against the paint tray. Then he moved over to his iPhone and started the song again. "Follow me." He led her to the center of the shop and took her in his arms, resting his hand against the small of her back.

As the music played, he turned her in a slow, swaying circle, singing softly in her ear.

. . . you're beautiful.

For a moment, she was enraptured, completely caught up in the swirl of being in his arms and the velvet texture of his voice slipping through her. But only for a moment.

"Tom, stop fooling around." She pushed

away from his warmth and into the cold space of the shop. "Don't be singing about how I'm beautiful."

"But you are."

"Don't you understand?" She gritted her teeth and tightened her hands into fists about her ears. She jerked off her scarf and gathered her hair on top of her head, exposing the botched skin graft. "Beautiful, huh?"

"Yes." He stepped toward her, hand outstretched.

But she backed away. "And this?" She turned her back to him, raised the lower hem of her top, and exposed the crimped, rough skin of her back and right side. "It's disgusting. And not desirable. So don't come up in here singing, 'you're beautiful' when it's not true."

"Who told you it's not true?"

"Me. My bathroom mirror. The men Mama dated when I was a teenager. 'Too bad about all those scars, Shana, she might have been a real looker.' "

"Most people don't see your scars. You cover them up. Just because a few foolish, lustful men projected their idea of beauty on you, you accept it? Ever think those scars protected you? Kept you from predators?"

"Also from nice men like you who might have been my high school boyfriend or taken me to the prom."

"I like your scars."

She reached down for her roller. "Now you're just being mean."

"I like that they've made you a fighter. I like your face, your eyes, your smile, your heart. I love your ability to see beauty in others and bring it out for the rest of us to see. Those are the things that make you beautiful and extraordinary."

Eyes flooding, she rolled paint onto the wall, her back to Tom. "You'd better get back to work or we'll be here all night."

"But first . . ." He rested his hand against her shoulder and turned her to him. "Tell me you're beautiful."

She refused, eyes averted, unable to contain her tears. In her ears, her pulse roared.

"Ginger." He touched her chin, turned her attention to him. "Say it. It's the first road to healing. You are beautiful."

"I'm not your project, Tom."

"Agreed. But you are my friend. And I hate to see my friends believe lies about themselves."

"I believe what's true."

"Then say it. 'I'm beautiful.' "

She dropped her roller brush and crossed the room. "You're infuriating. Why do you care? I'm the daughter of the woman who helped ruin your father's ministry. I asked her about it, by the way, and she confessed. She loved your father but nothing happened between them."

"That doesn't disqualify you from God's love, from my friendship, or from admitting you're beautiful."

"Tell that to Edward. What would he say if he saw you in here, with me?"

"Edward isn't my God or my conscience. My father and family have moved on, Ginger. Seems your mama has moved on, too. But you're stuck as the trailer fire girl. So let's put a big bucket of water on that fire by confessing your beauty."

Stuck. Isn't that what she confessed Saturday morning, standing in the muddy meadow? But she'd never give Tom the satisfaction. Ginger gestured toward the door, willing him to go and leave her be. "You can go, Tom."

"Not unless you say it." He didn't respect her space at all. He came up to her and swept his fingers over the scar on her neck. Ginger nearly buckled at his touch.

"Why do you want me to say it?" Her voice wilted as she spoke.

"Because I want you to combat the lie in your heart with truth."

"If you get the burned girl to say she's

pretty, do you earn a gold star from God?"

"Man, are you really so cynical? Ginger, I like you. I always have and I've always seen a beautiful woman —"

"Who allowed himself to be intimidated by his friends?" She used the courage he admired to push back.

"I was seventeen. Give me credit for maturing a little." He walked to the front door, flung it open. "You want me to defend you to Edward Frizz? To Rosebud?" He ran into the middle of Main Street. "Hey Rosebud, Alabama —"

Ginger dashed to the door. "Tom, no, what are you doing?"

Arms wide, head back, Tom shouted, "Ginger Winters is a beautiful woman. And I don't care about her scars! I don't care what her mama —"

"Oh my word, stop. Get in here." Ginger steamed into the middle of the street, hooked him by the arm, and dragged him to the shop. "You're making a fool of me."

"You? I was the one doing the shouting."

"You are so infuriating. I don't get this. Why does any of this matter to you?"

"Remember the end of the movie *The Proposal*? Drew says to Margaret, 'Marry me because I'd like to date you.' "

"Y-yes . . ."

"I'd like you to believe the truth about yourself, so then maybe, if you decide you can give Jesus a try, you'll let Him in, and see yourself as you really are from His perspective, incredibly beautiful."

"What does that have to do with the movie?"

"Because, then, if you'd have me, I'd like to date you."

Her tears spilled. "I can't risk my heart with you. With God." What was she doing before he started all this beautiful nonsense? Oh yes, painting. Ginger picked up the paint tray. "I think you should go."

"Say it. 'I'm beautiful.' "

"I'm not playing, Tom. Go." She walked to the back room, trembling, with barely enough strength to hold herself upright.

"Will you come to church on Sunday? Please."

"I said, go, Tom, just go."

She hid in the dark corner until she heard his footsteps echoing across the shop, then fading away out the front door.

Slowly she sank to the floor, cradling her face against the top of her knees, running her hand over her scars.

Horrid. Ugly. The opposite of beautiful. She'd cried oceans of tears mourning that reality, and no one — not God or Tom Wells Jr. — could ever convince her otherwise.

CHAPTER TEN

On Sunday morning, Tom sat in the old parsonage parlor, sunlight streaming through the window, praying through the swirl of excitement and peace in his soul.

First Sunday morning in his own church. He never, ever thought this would be his reality, his passion, but at the moment he knew he was in the right place at the right time.

For such a time as this.

His sermon was ready. His notes typed into his iPad. Alisha had the worship band prepped, arriving at nine for their pre-service rehearsal. Above all, his heart was ready.

If it was only Tom, the band, and the Holy Spirit who showed, Tom would consider the day a huge success.

If Ginger showed, he'd mark his first Sunday with a miracle.

He'd thought about her all weekend,

prayed for her, for himself. Had he crossed lines, demanding she declare she was beautiful? Was it too intimate? Too romantic when he had no freedom to pursue her?

It was one thing for a believing man to have affection for a non-believing woman. It was another thing entirely to woo her heart, defraud her, then brush her aside.

He didn't want to be that man.

If he was going to pastor this church, he had to find a wife who believed. Who could run this race with him.

He didn't care if she played the piano, led a Bible study, or managed the women's ministry. But he cared for her to be surrendered in wholehearted love to Jesus. To kick Tom's butt when he needed it.

Lord, here's my heart. My thoughts of Ginger. Have it all.

The mantel clock that came with the house ticked eight-thirty. Tom rocked out of the chair, taking his iPad from the side table. Might as well walk over to the church, get things powered up and going.

He was about to exit out the kitchen door when a loud knock sounded from the front. When he opened it, Edward stood on the other side.

"Did you see this?" He held up the Sunday *Gazette* and barged into the parsonage.

"No, not yet. I was going to read it after church."

"What in the world did you tell her?" Edward crossed into the parlor, popping open the paper and holding up the front page for Tom to see.

THE TALE OF TWO PASTORS
HOW WILL ROSEBUD FARE WITH A THIRD GENERATION WELLS PREACHER?
BY RILEY CONRAD

Tom snapped the paper from Edward. "How will Rosebud fare? What is she talking about? We discussed the church, how and why I came back to Rosebud, what I hoped to accomplish."

"Clearly she doesn't want another church in this town. Especially one headed by a Wells man. I ask again, what did you tell her?"

"Nothing."

"Doesn't read like nothing. She exposes the whole scandal." Edward walked toward the kitchen. "Got any coffee?"

"Yeah, sure, use the Keurig." Tom dropped to the rocker, iPad tucked under his arm, anxiety mounting.

Tom Wells Jr. is in Rosebud, seeking a flock of his own. With the American church becoming more of a consumer than a

303

provider of spiritual insight, one has to wonder if he isn't one of the many up-and-coming young pastors with charm and good looks aiming to do nothing but build his own kingdom on the backs and with the pockets of the Rosebud faithful.

"This is an opinion piece."

Edward returned, mug in hand, blowing on his coffee. "Yep."

A bit of backstory. Wells is the grandson of well-known, popular evangelist Porter Wells, who traveled the country holding tent revivals for twenty years before taking his message international. He eventually returned to the States to continue his ministry in large churches and on television.

The elder Wells retired back to Rosebud in the middle 2000s. His son, Tom Wells Sr., followed in his footsteps, planting a church in Rosebud and building the congregation to more than two thousand people before scandal routed him out twelve years ago.

What scandal? An affair. Not of the obvious kind but the emotional kind, which some declare more devastating than a physical affair. Pastor Wells spent too much time with a woman in need. Feeling defrauded, she confessed her feelings to a trusted friend who reported the misbehavior to the church elders and leaders.

The Wellses left town in a shroud of mystery, leaving nothing behind but questions and wounded hearts. My grandmother was one of the disappointed and questioning faithful. What happened to our beloved pastor?

Tom lowered the paper and sighed. "She's taken up her grandmother's offense."

"It's an opinion piece, bro. Of course she's got an agenda."

"I want a rebuttal."

Edward's countenance darkened. "My advice? Leave this be. The more you make of it, the more you fan the flames. Keep reading."

But he didn't want to keep reading. He wanted to toss the paper aside and go back to his place of contentment and contemplation. He wanted his heart to be soft for worship and the Word.

But he needed to know what preconceived notions would arrive with the congregants this morning.

The truth of the story was buried since the

Wellses left town so quickly, literally in the cover of night, the congregation being told only that Wells had an extraordinary opportunity in Atlanta and felt "the Lord wanted him to take it."

So the lies compounded. Rosebud rumors suggested Wells had an affair, but with whom? When? Above all, why?

Maybe he took "love your neighbor as yourself" a bit too literally.

When I realized his son was back in town, I wanted to know the rest of the story. So I did some digging. Who was the woman in the center of the Wells scandal? Why hadn't the complete story ever been told?

I found a lead with a former church member, Janelle Holden.

"I was leading the women's ministry when one of the newer members, Shana Winters, confessed to me rather out of the blue that she was in love with Pastor Wells. That he'd been counseling her, helping her, befriending her."

According to Holden, Wells admitted to counseling Winters, whose daughter Ginger Winters owns Ginger Snips, a local salon, and was tragically scarred in a trailer fire at the age of twelve.

The senior Wells denied having an affair

of any kind, but when the church board called an inquiry, he did admit to an emotional connection with Winters that went beyond propriety.

So, he abandoned his flock and fled town. Are you following my case here?

Twelve years Rosebud has rested, free from charlatans using the "Word of God" to dupe the weak and the willing.

Enough. Tom slapped the paper into Edward's open palm. "This will humiliate Ginger. She'll probably never darken the sanctuary doors now."

"Were you hoping she would?"

"Yes, Edward, I was because she needs Jesus. Frankly, I'm thinking you need a good dose of the Spirit yourself." Tom started for the door. "By the way, Ed, yeah, really, *her.* She's gorgeous, smart, caring and yeah, a bit physically flawed, but I'd take her over some . . . beauty queen any day." Tom slammed the door behind him.

"Tom!" Edward called after him. "Think of your career . . ."

But he kept on walking toward the church, the nine o'clock bells ringing for the first time in over two decades, waking up the community, waking up Tom's heart.

Come, take up your cross, and follow Me.

Ginger woke to the sound of church bells. But they didn't sound like they emanated from Bridge Street Baptist. These chimes were older, distant, coming from the west.

Climbing out of bed, she opened her front window, letting in the crisp, pristine breeze as she peered down onto Main.

You're beautiful.

Tom's voice had moved into her head and no amount of shop hustle and bustle, Tracie Blue music, or back-to-back movies on the Hallmark Channel could get him out.

You're beautiful.

Then Friday afternoon Mrs. Davenport caught her attention in the mirror as she styled her hair. "What's going on with you, Ginger? You look *different.* You're positively glowing."

You're beautiful. Then the melody of the song from Bridgett's wedding crashed over her. *"You make me brave!"*

Now she leaned against the screen, remembering, and inhaled the fragrance of the January morn as the bells chimed, seven, eight, nine.

Could she be brave? Go to church? She always said she'd go if someone invited her.

Technically, Tom had invited her.

Ginger hesitated. She liked her Sunday morning routine — a latte and muffin while reading the Sunday *Gazette*. But if she hurried, she could have her breakfast, skim the paper, and still make it to the morning service.

She closed her eyes. *Do it. Don't think.* Dashing for the shower, she actually let herself meditate on the pleasure of seeing Tom Wells again.

You're beautiful.

Peeling off her nightshirt, Ginger examined her familiar wounds, trying to see them with new eyes. She stared at her reflection.

"Y-you're beau—" She choked. It wasn't true. "Ginger, say it." She heard Tom's truth in her own voice. "Y-you are . . . you are . . ." She leaned toward the mirror. "B-beautiful."

A quick wind swept through her apartment. Through her soul.

"Ginger, you are" — she raised her voice — "beautiful."

The wind swirled around her again.

"Ginger!" She yelled, arms raised. "You are beautiful!"

Joy in the form of tears ran down her cheeks, somehow watering all the dry, barren places where truth had not flowered in a long time. If ever.

"Ginger Winters, you are beautiful!"

CHAPTER ELEVEN

Tom did his best to focus on the music, the songs, and worshipping his Lord, but felt the pressure of his inaugural Sunday morning. Along with the humiliation of bad press.

Alisha, God love her, curled her lip at the article. "Who cares? Is it true? No. Let God defend you, Tom."

Her confidence stirred his.

Now, as Alisha brought worship to an end, Tom prepared to take the pulpit. He'd not looked over his shoulder for the entire worship set so he had no idea if one or a hundred people filled the old, wooden pews.

In truth, he wanted to see one face. Well, two. Pop's and Ginger's. Mostly Ginger's. He needed to know she was okay. That the article hadn't stirred up bad memories.

The last note rang out from the keyboard and Alisha nodded to Tom. Go time. Up the platform steps, he faced the sanctuary and his heart soared.

The place was full. To the brim. Standing room only.

"Good morning. Welcome to Encounter —"

"Is it true?" A woman in the second row rose to her feet. "Your father nearly had an affair?"

Tom recognized her from the old days. Shutting off his iPad, he came around the pulpit, his eyes drifting over the people. "Is that why you all are here?"

Heads bobbed. Voices assented.

The heat of confrontation beaded along his brow. "Then let's just get it all out on the table. Some of the article is true. Dad had an inappropriate amount of affection for Shana Winters." In the back, the sanctuary doors opened and Tom halted, a cold dread slipping down his back as Ginger eased inside.

No, no, not today. But it was too late to reverse rudder and preach his prepared message. To pretend the article never appeared.

He caught her gaze and she smiled, offering a small wave before accepting a seat in the last row from an older gentleman.

She looked . . . different. Radiant.

"Riley Conrad," he said, "gave us her opinion about me and my family. She also dragged out the names of fellow, private citizens. I won't speak for them but I can promise you my devotion to Jesus is greater than my devotion to any of you. Than to this ministry. If the Lord said, 'Shut it down tomorrow,' I'd do it. I've already been a rebel, the resentful, bitter son of a preacher and by the grace of God, I don't care to go back. Come to Encounter Church if you want to encounter God's love for you. If you want to love others. If you want to share life and the Gospel with the Rosebud community. Don't come here if you're looking to gain something for yourself. If you have any sort of agenda. Come here if you love or want to love Jesus."

Tom shot a glance toward Ginger, who was on her feet, moving forward. "Can I say something?" Her voice carrying through the crowded sanctuary. Heads turned. Voices murmured.

"Are you sure?" Tom said. He could see her trembling.

"Hey, some of you know me. But for those who don't, I'm Ginger Winters." She held up a copy of the Gazette. "My mama and Tom's dad had a friendship that went too far in my mama's heart. It caused some problems for Reverend Wells, and he chose to leave. He has his reasons, and if you want

313

to know, ask him."

Tom watched, surprised, astounded. Something had happened to Ginger Winters.

"But don't hold what our parents did against Tom here. When we were in high school, and no one wanted to talk to the freaky burned girl, me, he did. This past weekend at a wedding, he treated me like I mattered when others didn't. He made me see that I expected them to treat me that way because that's how I see myself." She smiled up at him. "I guess I was listening."

"Amazing," he said, moving toward her. "Considering I talked way too much."

Ginger faced the congregation again. "He challenged me to believe the truth. That I was, am, beautiful. Scars and all. He told me Jesus loved me and while I'm not sure what all that means, I'm starting to wonder if this Gospel business isn't exactly what I need. I've never trusted any man with my heart. Shoot, I barely trusted anyone. But I'd trust Tom Wells. With every part of my being." Her voice wavered and watered. "He challenged me to tell myself I was beautiful and this morning, for the first time, I looked into the mirror, saw my hated scars, and told myself I was beautiful. Out loud." Her smile rivaled the sun peeking through the windows. "And for the first time," a bubbly laugh overflowed from within her, "I believe it."

EPILOGUE

Eight months later . . .

That January day it had snowed in Rosebud changed Ginger's life in ways she never imagined. Just goes to show, true love causes even the most closed heart to fling wide.

"Okay, the final touch." Ruby-Jane, in her maid of honor dress, a silk tea-length of royal plum, plopped an old, wooden chair next to Ginger and stepped up, holding the rhinestone clips of the Bandeau veil.

"Careful, RJ." Michele raised up on her tiptoes, pensive, wiping a bit of sweat from her brow. "That updo is two hours of work. Don't *undo* it in two seconds."

"As if. You put enough spray in her hair to withstand a hurricane." Ruby-Jane patted the top of Ginger's teased bouffant.

The air conditioner kicked on, humming as it swirled the room with cool air.

"Rubes, careful, please. It might not fall

down but it could crack." Ginger cut a glance at Michele, laughing, reaching for her hand. "Thank you. I've not seen it yet but I know your work. I'm sure it's stunning."

"No," Michele smoothed down what must have been a flyaway strand, "*you* are stunning. Ginger, I can't believe how much you've changed. I guess I shouldn't say that but —"

"It's true." Twitters and electric pulses crisscrossed Ginger's middle. She inhaled, her legs trembling, buckling a little as Ruby-Jane settled on the veil.

She had changed. She'd listened to Tom and believed she was beautiful. But it took letting Jesus have her whole heart to truly *get* it. To let the truth settle in and change her identity. Tom walked her through it all. As a friend. Then five months ago, she woke up one morning to realize she was completely in love with him.

A month later, during a pizza and movie night in her apartment, he slipped to one knee, kissed her hand, and proposed. "Will you marry me? Please?"

When he slid the diamond ring on her finger, she let go of her last tear and her heart became aflame with love.

"Yes, Tom, yes. I would love to marry you."

And now on her wedding day, because of love, she was going to expose herself to all.

Though at the moment, she tried to remember what had possessed her to be *so* daring with her gown. A sleeveless, V-neck chiffon Donna Karan. A gift from Tracie Blue.

"There." Ruby-Jane jumped down, sweeping the chair aside. "Oh, Ginger . . ." Her eyes watered as she pressed her fingers over her lips.

"Be honest, please." Ginger swept her gaze from RJ to Michele. "Am I crazy? Do I look ghastly?" She offered up her bare, scarred arm, the gold glitter in the body makeup catching the late afternoon light floating through the window. "Is it too much? The glitter?"

"It's perfect. You are going to blow Tom away."

She touched the skin patch at the base of her neck. The sleeveless gown was a surprise for him. Her gift. "I can live with my arm and back being exposed, but what about this?" She motioned to her neck.

"You're fine, Ginger," Ruby-Jane said. "Don't second-guess yourself now."

She was right. If she was going to be

brave, then be brave. Next month, Ginger had an appointment with a renowned plastic surgeon, a friend of her future father-in-law's, who had volunteered his time and skill to repair the botched graft.

But truth was, she'd already met a renowned surgeon. Jesus. Who'd healed the inner wounds no one could see. And all it took was love. His and Tom's.

A sweet laugh escaped her lips.

"What?" RJ said, smiling, leaning in, wanting to join Ginger's joy.

"Nothing." She shook her head, treasuring the moment. "I'm just happy." Ruby-Jane still insisted God watched from a distance, so any talk of *Him* would spark debate.

"Ready to see what you look like?" Michele turned Ginger toward the full-length mirror.

"Ready." Ginger closed her eyes and followed Michele's leading — one, two, three steps to the right. She'd insisted they get her ready without a mirror. In case she panicked. Believing she was beautiful was still a battle some days.

"Open your eyes."

Ginger inhaled, then opened her eyes on the exhale. The glass was filled with her image, clothed in white, her ombre hair sculpted on top of her head in a retro '60s updo, and gold glitter filling the creases of her scars.

Tears bubbled up.

"Wait, here, for the final look." Ruby-Jane dashed for Ginger's small, wired bouquet of roses and gypsophila. "Perfect, so per—" RJ's voice broke so she finished her thought with a sweet, weepy smile and a nod.

A tender knock echoed from the door. "Ready?" Maggie Boyd peeked inside. She'd returned home from Ireland two months ago, demanding to be Ginger's wedding director.

So much favor came when she accepted love. When she accepted God. And her destiny.

"Ginger, oh, Ginger," Maggie drew a deep breath, wiping her eyes. "We're going to have to pick Tom up off the floor."

"Let's hope so." Ginger grinned, winking. She had a bit of confidence because he'd seen her scars. He'd asked two days ago to see her side and back, so tonight, when they became one, she'd not fear him seeing that part of her for the first time.

He traced his fingers along every jagged, rugged crevasse of her disfigurement, whispering prayers of healing, peace, and joy.

Not only for her body but for her heart.

His tenderness and care, as he ran his hand over the damaged flesh that would become his on their wedding night, along with his weepy, whispered prayers created an emotional exchange between them that nearly overwhelmed Ginger.

She could never doubt God's love for her. She saw it manifested every day in Tom.

Tucked deep in her heart, that odd January day it snowed in Rosebud and Tom had reappeared in her life would always be one of her sweetest treasures.

"Baby, it's four-thirty." Mama popped into the room. "The sanctuary is filled to the brim." She pressed her hands to her cheeks. "I think my heart is about to burst. Ginger, sugar, you are so beautiful." She said it plainly, without stuttering.

Mama was changing too.

Ginger took one last glance in the mirror. She'd chosen a sleeveless gown because she loved it. Because it fit like a glove. Because if she didn't have wounds on her arm and back, this would be her dream dress.

Go for it . . . Tom. Always Tom. The voice of truth and courage.

"Ah, I hear the orchestra, the music is starting." Mama had worked double shifts at a diner after her city day job to earn money for a fifteen-piece orchestra. It was her way of, as she put it, "doing my part."

"RJ, maid of honor, get going." Maggie shoved Ruby-Jane toward the door. "Don't forget this." She snatched a bouquet from the nearby table.

Ruby-Jane's heels thunked against the wide hardwood. "Shifting gears from helping the bride to being maid of honor." She grinned at Ginger. "See you down there."

Michele also slipped out the door, blowing Ginger a kiss. "Going to find Alex and the kids. Go get 'em, Ginger."

"I'm proud of you." A corner tear glistened in Mama's eyes. "And I'm sorry for everything I've done to hurt you."

"Mama, no, no," Ginger soothed away Mama's tears. "Today is my wedding day. A fresh, new start. And you know what, we're going to bury all the junk of the past in the past. You're forgiven. It's all forgotten. From this day forth, we're going to create so many good, *new* memories, Mama." Her own speech made her cry. "Now, are you walking me down the aisle or not?"

"I am, yes, ma'am, I am." Mama snatched a tissue from the box by the mirror, the folds of her chocolate trumpet chiffon skirt with the lace bodice and ruffle beading flowing about her legs. "I'm sorry your daddy didn't see his way clear to make it."

"Last apology, Mama. That's on him. I still love him. It's just, well, life doesn't always turn out like we hoped but —"

Mama traced Ginger's arm. "We find ways to make it our own kind of beautiful."

"All right, I hate to break up the love fest but the orchestra is a minute into 'Unchained Melody' and we've only got another minute and a half so if you want to walk down the aisle I suggest you get a move on." Maggie gestured toward the door.

Mama offered Ginger her arm and together, they made their way to the sanctuary doors, Ginger's heart palpitating with electric excitement.

The ushers pulled the doors wide at Maggie's command. Ginger rounded to the entrance, catching her breath to see her handsome groom at the altar, waiting for her.

Mama trembled slightly as she escorted Ginger down the aisle. All eyes were on her now. Seeing her scars. What were they thinking? That she was hideous? Crazy for exposing herself? The thought shot a bolt of panic through her.

Then she saw Bridgett and Eric, their faces like beacons among the sea of guests. Smiling, Bridgett clasped her hands together in a "victory" pose. Eric gave her a vigorous thumbs-up.

Maybe, just maybe, she could join the bold and the beautiful.

Ginger continued down the aisle, shifting her gaze from the people to her groom. The man she loved so deeply and desperately. What did it matter what the guests thought? His opinion was the only one that mattered.

She met Tom's glistening gaze. He approved, she could tell by his expression and his trembling chin.

By the time she arrived at the end of the aisle and the music faded, the sanctuary echoed with feminine sniffles and masculine throat-clearing.

Tom's cheeks glistened. "Hey, babe . . ."

"Hey . . ."

Then Pop, who was officiating, stepped up and asked, "Who gives this woman to be married?"

"Yours truly," Mama said, placing Ginger's hand in Tom's. "I mean it now . . . I said it once, I'll say it again, you take care of my girl."

"Always, Shana. Always."

Taking Ginger's right arm, she expected Tom to lead her up the altar steps but instead he faced the guests.

"I didn't plan this but my heart is about to burst. I'm so proud of my beautiful bride . . . the bravest person I know. A year ago, she hid her scars beneath long sleeves and scarves. Even on the hottest summer days. But today, she —" His voice faltered. "I told you, babe, you are so beautiful."

Then the guests, one by one, rose up, applauding.

Tom's glistening blue eyes locked onto hers. "Ginger, I am so honored to be your husband."

"Husband?" She made a face, grinning. "Not yet. You better walk me up those steps to your Pop and get this thing going. Because I want to kiss you."

Tom laughed low. "Then by all means."

He walked her up the altar steps to Pop and she peered sideways at him. "You know I love you, Tom Wells."

"You know I love you, Ginger Winters."

Pop led them through their vows and when he'd pronounced them man and wife, Tom drew Ginger to him, his right hand about her waist, his left hand on her scarred arm, and he kissed her with passion, sealing their vows with the sweet brush of love.

ACKNOWLEDGMENTS

I heard the name Ginger and I knew she didn't believe she was beautiful. Then I thought of the hero, Tom, and knew his job was to make Ginger see her true beauty.

I cannot begin to expound God's faithfulness to me in the winter of 2014. Dropping this idea in the midst of crying out for help and ideas for another book is only one example.

I turned in the novel and went to a writers' retreat where I helped mentor eighteen aspiring authors. When the week was over, Susan May Warren, Beth Vogt, and Alena Tauriainen brainstormed *A Brush with Love* with me, beginning, middle, and end. I actually had enough story for a big novel! Their help and friendship was a blessing to the core of my soul. Another example of God's faithfulness.

To my editor, Becky Philpott, you are a dream. A friend. A champion and cheerleader. Thank you for your partnership with not only this novella, but my writing journey. You're a treasure.

To Daisy Hutton, publisher extraordinaire, I love the honest conversations we've had and how you champion your authors. Thank you for giving me opportunities to do what I love!

Katie Bond, Elizabeth Hutton, and Karli Jackson, for being a fabulous marketing and editorial team. It's such a feeling of contentment to know I can e-mail any of you, any time, and get a response. Katie, we've been together a lot of years now and it's more an honor day by day.

To the rest of the HarperCollins Christian Publishing team, let's keep writing and publishing for Him. You all are the best.

To my husband who lives with a writer. He is my hero. God knew what He was doing when He paired us together. I love you, babe!

To my canine writing partner, Lola, thanks for making me get up out of my chair from time to time. Ha!

To my writing partner, Susan May Warren, ten years we've been doing this biz together. Sometimes face-to-face but mostly phone call to phone call. I shake my head in wonder at how blessed I am to have you in my life. XO.

To my hair dresser, Michele Lacy, who's kept me looking beautiful and young for over twenty-three years. Thanks for your help on this one.

To my line editor, Jean Bloom, thank you for your time, insight, and help.

To all of the readers who take the time to curl up with a book I've written, thank you! It means more than you'll ever know. Be blessed!

DISCUSSION QUESTIONS

1. Ginger suffered a tragedy that marked her inside and out. Everyone reacts differently to life events. Was there an event in your life that marked you in some way? Do you relate to how Ginger feels?
2. Tom's family, while Christians, are flawed. He wants to make amends for his father's mistake. But it's not always possible to undo what's been done. What's the best way to show forgiveness for a wrong? Or to seek redemption?
3. Bridgett seems all about herself, doesn't she? But in the end of the book, she's at the wedding cheering Ginger on. How do you see this? Did Ginger misunderstand her friendship with Bridgett?
4. We often see ourselves through our own wounds. We think that's how others see us. Does Ginger do this when she's around the bold and the beautiful people? Around Bridgett?

5. Tom is influenced by Edward, a man responsible for bringing him back to town to start a church. Does he allow Edward too much influence? How do we walk in love with one another when we disagree?
6. Ginger's mama, Shana, was looking for help in the church. But her trust was misplaced. How can we love people who confess secrets to us? How can we bring them to truth without making them feel condemned?
7. I loved when Ginger was bold enough to walk down the aisle in her dream dress even though it exposed her scars. I actually cried writing that scene. What happened to her that she could brave such a thing?
8. Be honest, do you really believe God can change your negative emotions? Because He can. We don't have to be locked in darkness, despair, depression, and fears. How can you change your thinking to believe you are who He says you are? Ginger did it by confessing she was beautiful.
9. What aspects of Christ does Tom demonstrate to Ginger? How can you do the same toward your friends and family?
10. If you have scars, inside or out, list one thing you can do to overcome.

ABOUT THE AUTHOR

Rachel Hauck is an award winning, best-selling author. Her book, The *Wedding Dress,* was named Inspirational Novel of the Year by *Romantic Times,* and *Once Upon a Prince* was a Christy Award finalist. Rachel lives in central Florida with her husband and two pets and writes from her ivory tower.

Visit her website at www.rachelhauck.com
Twitter: RachelHauck
Facebook: rachelhauck

■ ■ ■ ■

Serving Up a Sweetheart

Cheryl Wyatt

■ ■ ■ ■

To Mom. Decades ago you endured a Valentine's Day labor of love to usher me into this world. You have not stopped encouraging me since. I'm convinced I have the most kindhearted, loving mother in the world. Thank you for always believing in me.

But with you there is forgiveness, so that we can, with reverence, serve you.

PSALM 130:4

CHAPTER ONE

The sky blew crystal kisses to the earth, the snow patterning Meadow Larson's window in white filigree flakes. That would've been fine if it weren't for Niagara Falls pouring down double-paned glass and drenching her in-home catering kitchen.

Worse, on the one day her business partner, Del, called in sick.

The leak around the window intensified, streaming wet rivulets over live outlets and onto the plethora of towels she had already placed on the counter and floor.

Mind awhirl with what to do next, Meadow rushed to shut off breakers, then snatched her phone off one of her only dry counters and dialed her sister Flora while sloshing back toward the awful mess.

"Meadow, you're panting. What's wrong?"

"I have four caters over the next week, and my place is flooding under massive snow melt." Realizing every towel she owned was now soaked, Meadow turned to grab blankets from her hall closet.

She heard an ominous creaking sound behind her. Turning back, she looked up . . . and lost her breath.

As if in slow motion, her ceiling bowed and then crashed to the floor in a thundering pile of icy lumber and tile. Her countertops and best catering supplies disappeared under a destructive mishmash of winter's white frosting and debris.

Scrambling backward, Meadow dropped the phone. Stared in fascinated horror at the cave-in that covered her kitchen in a heap of unprecedented February snow. Her dream-since-childhood business squashed by a southern Illinois blizzard. A "once-in-a-lifetime event," this morning's weatherman had called it, right after he'd informed viewers the groundhog had seen his shadow.

How could her demanding schedule survive six more weeks of winter?

Moreover, how could she fulfill contracts with clients when her workspace and best catering supplies were pulverized?

"*What* was that racket? Meadow, everything okay?"

Meadow became aware of the voice on the floor. She picked up her phone — the face of which now resembled how she felt inside:

cracked in all directions. "No. Could you please come over? My kitchen ceiling collapsed."

"You kidding me?"

"Wish I were." Meadow fought tears. She hadn't cried in ten years and wasn't about to now. Fearing more collapse, Meadow fled for cover outside. Ironic.

She'd always loved wintertime, with its beautiful diamond glisten and the enchanting allure of hoarfrost.

Not. Today.

Meadow threw on a coat from the front hall closet, and the storm door slammed in her wake as she left to pace the front yard.

Midway between her red Tudor cottage door and the street, she passed a knight-white snowman standing sentry over her sidewalk. She didn't know who had built him since no children lived near her, but she paused, glared at it, and decided the majestic ice imp was mocking her.

With a less-than-ladylike growl, she hauled her leg back and kicked.

Ploof!

Her entire foot and ankle disappeared into the snowman's torso. "I hate you, and I hate that stupid groundhog!"

Groundhog? Colin McGrath set his box

back on the passenger seat and rounded his truck to get a better look at the animated face issuing the words he'd just heard. He watched the woman across the street with interest. She had evidently just assaulted the snowman in her yard.

Stuck in an awkward stance resembling a frozen flamingo in a badly posed karate move, she whipped her arms around like a hostile windmill. Balance righted, she yanked her leg out of the snowman and raised her foot. Colin grew amused to find it shoeless.

The astonished glare she sent the snowman could've gone viral on YouTube. As she sputtered something about it being a wretched, shoe-thieving traitor, Colin burst out laughing.

Until he saw her tears.

The brunette swiped madly at them before dropping to her knees. Concern coursed through him as she started scooping out wads of snow.

Her distress drew him quickly across the street.

Recalling the strength of her kick, he approached cautiously. "Bad day, I take it?"

Frosty's would-be assassin shrieked, stood, and whirled. Hair swept from widening honey eyes, she looked familiar. But he'd been gone ten years. Colin fought to place her.

"Didn't mean to startle you" — he eyed her barren ring finger — "miss."

Her face plumed the color of cranberries on a cold winter day . . . like today. She slid back to the frozen ground and dug, probably for her MIA shoe. To no avail. Colin reached into the eviscerated snowman and yanked the footwear right out.

She stood again and snatched the loafer out of his hands. "May I help you?"

He bit his lip to block a grin. "No, ma'am, but I thought I better offer assistance."

A scowl furrowed her lovely brow. "I don't need your help."

"I was referring to Frosty. He looked in need of swift intervention." Colin could hold it in no longer. His pressure-cooked laugh released. He nodded to the snowman, then cast the pretty woman a glance he hoped would humor her. "Domestic dispute?"

Her lips thinned in a manner that made him ponder ducking. She gripped the shoe tighter and looked sorely tempted to hurl the thing at him.

He palmed the air. "Hey, kidding. In all seriousness, I noticed you seem upset. Anything I can do?"

"Unless you can fix a roof and my catering kitchen in seventy-two hours, no."

He grinned, liking her spunk. "Actually, I may be able to help. Construction's my trade. My name is —"

"I know who you are, but you obviously don't remember me." Her chin rose.

Dread hit him like a two-by-four. "Uh . . ."

Her arms locked across her chest. "You and your friends ruined my life. At least my high school experience." Arms dropped, she shook her head and started to turn.

It all flooded back for Colin, who she was and everything she'd endured. He swallowed fiery lumps remembering: his part in inviting her to the lake, then his friends driving off without her. Terror and betrayal clouding her eyes as she stumbled after them.

He reached for her arm. "Oh wow, Meadow. Sorry. I didn't recognize you."

"You didn't back then, either." She shrugged. "I am just as I was, overlooked and easily forgettable." A frustrated glower flooded her expressive face.

His chest tightened with a marbling of remorse and remembrance, acknowledgment and empathy. Things he should've felt back then . . . but didn't. Not really.

"I'm truly sorry."

He meant it. From the depths of his heart, did he ever.

She rolled her eyes. "I bet. Anyway, it doesn't matter now."

Actually, it did. If the splinter still festered a decade later, it mattered a whole lot. He couldn't let this go. Could not walk away from the distress in her eyes.

Gorgeous eyes. Hair the color of polished mahogany, too, deep shine included.

He had to make the past up to her somehow. "Let me help you, Meadow. Please."

Her fortitude ran sturdy as she shook her head. "You? Help me? Not on your life, Colin McGrath. You hurt me once. I'm not giving you a chance to do it twice."

Chapter Two

Her words hit like hacksaws, driving Colin's ego to its knees. Oh well. Better place for it anyway. Pride was never a bad thing to lose. Not knowing what to say next and rendered wordless for just about the first time in his life, Colin clamped his mouth shut.

Retort would only convince her she was right about him.

Irish temper blessedly absent, Colin tipped his ball cap to her. "Good day to you then, ma'am." He resisted the urge to bid the snowman good-bye before turning to cross the street. Meadow's hilarious tirade had somehow humanized the thing.

He'd forgotten how fickle southern Illinois weather could be. Last week it was seventy degrees. This week Havenbrook's sky dumped historic amounts of icy snow. He crunched over it walking back to his new house. The movers were finishing the last load.

Colin drew in a breath of fresh air, home-town nostalgia and peace he hadn't felt in a decade. He loved Havenbrook. Meadow's welcome had been the only one not warm.

What did he expect after the way he'd treated her in high school? His gut knotted like old pine as images assaulted him. His then-girlfriend, mayor's daughter Blythe Matthews, calling Meadow a loser. Strong Meadow leaving school in tears. Blythe calling after her that she'd never be popular, never be one of the cool kids, never fit in.

Colin had stood back against the lockers feeling horrible for Meadow yet not doing one thing to stop the bullying.

Colin swallowed. Hard. No wonder Meadow wanted nothing to do with him now.

Except, that was the old him. He determined to show her the new him.

Wanting to make sure she made it in without slipping on snow-packed ice, Colin glanced back to find Meadow looking stumped as she stared at him. Surprise swept through him at that.

Swiftly readapting her caustic body language, she tromped across her yard. But her baffled-curious look had convinced him he'd made a slight positive impression.

A car pulled up next to the curb where he

stood. A harried woman plowed out of it and into him. When she pulled back, recognition flickered in her eyes, and she paused.

"Colin McGrath. Heard you were moving back."

He recognized her as one of Meadow's many siblings. "Flora. Nice to see you."

"You check on her? She all right after the cave-in?"

Her words hammered dread into him. "Cave-in?"

"She didn't tell you?" They began walking back across the street to Meadow's.

"No. Well, not in so many words." He grinned. "She mostly just told me off."

Flora glanced sideways at him. He peered across the yard, assessing where Meadow's damage was. He shrugged. "I deserved it."

Flora looked like she wanted to say something kind but stopped herself. Good. He didn't deserve the grace of accolades where Meadow Larson was concerned.

"I'm surprised you're not giving me grief over my past of taunting your family." Blunt, but he needed to have an in to apologize.

"I know your mom from Havenbrook Garden Club. My fiancé, Pete, is the attorney handling your father's will, medical directives, and business matters. I help in the office since my counseling job is part-time. You're the new CEO of your dad's company — McGrath Construction, right?"

"Oh, so you're Pete's fiancée. Good man. Yes. Dad's failing cognitive function affected his ability to make sound business decisions. Mom asked me to take over so the company doesn't lose forty years' worth of good reputation, equity, and customers. Thankfully, my Chicago home and contracting firm sold quickly." That money left him a nice nest egg and enabled the clean break to move south. He'd needed a new start anyway, after his broken engagement.

Flora nodded. "Your mom told me it means the world to her that you came home to take care of things, despite your parents not taking the best care of you growing up. She seems very sorry and says she and your dad are desperate to have the relationship with you they'd neglected before."

"I've forgiven them. To their credit, I didn't keep in close contact once deployed overseas in the military after school. Speaking of, I hope you know I'm sorry for every terrible thing I did."

"I do. I also know your mom recently made you the medical POA for your dad. Sorry to hear about his tumor. You have enough grief to contend with right now."

She smiled compassionately. "Plus, people change for the better. Pete's business dealings with you so far make me believe you have, even though Meadow may not."

That didn't sound promising.

Colin helped Flora across Meadow's icy yard, then scanned the roof. "Your sister's not gonna be happy to see me again, but I need to make sure she's not putting herself in danger going back in there."

"Yeah, well, she can be stubborn like that."

As predicted, Meadow's face swelled like an angry puffer fish at the sight of him at her door.

"Now, now . . . cool your jets, sis. He's an expert concerned about your safety. Besides, you know all other local contractors are either bad or, with other roof cave-ins I've heard about today, probably booked solid."

Meadow's countenance visibly crushed under being subjugated by circumstance into taking Colin's help.

Thumbs hooked in his pockets, he waited for the go-ahead. She finally nodded but did so like someone eating sawdust.

Once inside, it didn't take Colin long to survey the damage.

Meadow's petrified look from the hallway twisted his insides as he descended the ladder he'd brought in from her shed. He tried not to grimace as he considered how to put this to her gently.

"What's the verdict?" Flora's voice quavered.

He steered his gaze toward Meadow. "You live *and* work here?"

"Yes. My home and business are one in the same. How extensive is the damage?" Meadow's hands wrung like nervous dishrags.

"For sure, it's not safe for you to stay here while repairs are made. The entire roof is unstable with all that snow and ice, and I can't promise there won't be more damage before morning. It's starting to get dark. I can cover the hole with a tarp and reassess come daylight, but suffice it to say that kitchen's not going to be usable for a while."

Color drained from the sisters' faces. They held one another up.

"How long's a while?" Meadow's pallor elicited his empathy.

Colin aimed for delicacy of tone. "I estimate a month."

Flora wobbled. "No! My wedding's in three weeks! This is catastrophic."

Meadow rubbed Flora's arms. "Sis, I'll figure something out. Don't worry." She faced Colin. "Thanks. I'll take care of the tarp. You may go now."

He wasn't going anywhere. "Past aside, you're obviously in a fix, and I'm a fixer. My strength is renovation of structures damaged by disaster. My schedule's open. Consider letting me help you for all the trouble I caused you in high school."

Flora waved her phone. "I need to step outside and call Pete while you chat."

Meadow winced. "What's this going to cost me?"

Her question stung for the simple fact he sensed she meant cost in emotional trauma, not cash. He wanted to say it would cost nothing but knew Meadow wouldn't buy it. "We'll hammer details out later." He wasn't worried about money.

Her eyes narrowed, alerting him that she didn't trust him as far as she could toss him. An idea struck.

"I saw Meals on Wheels stickers on your catering SUV. I know of some shut-in vets in this area. Maybe after the repair, you could spare them a few meals a month for my services."

"I'd love to help veterans, but you'd be underpaid."

He needed something else. "How about this? I noticed your design degree and chef school certificate in the kitchen. Your place is gorgeously decorated. I recall you were master decorator of the school's renovation."

He and his woodshop class buddies had taken care of the outside — Meadow the inside. She'd done fantastically. Her work had earned scholarships to a premier design school he didn't think she could have afforded otherwise.

Regret slammed him over his mistreatment of her and kids like her, harassed when they should have been helped. She and her siblings had been among underprivileged outcasts made fun of by so-called privileged kids like him.

He was obviously being handed a second chance here. To Colin, part of godly sorrow meant righting the effects of wrong conduct.

"We can barter and each pay for our own materials. I fix your catering kitchen, you feed my vet buddies a few meals and help me decorate my new place, and we'll call it even. The house — and my pole barn office-slash-shop — are complete construction-wise, but the insides are drab, blank palettes of possibility."

"That doesn't solve my business dilemma. I have contracted caters." The weight of the cave-in ramifications must have set in, because she pressed her fingers to her temples. Volcanic panic was an understate-

355

ment for the expression going live on her face.

"You could work out of my pole barn kitchen until we fix yours. I have a huge space, with a comfortable new couch you could sleep on, if you like."

Visions of wedding tulle, rainbow silk flowers, satin napkins, bows and lace, fine china and crystal assaulted him. He'd seen evidence of it everywhere at her place.

He hated frilly things, food, and breakable stuff in his workspace. He shivered.

Still, he needed to man up here.

Meadow's hands fell stiffly to her sides, revealing her simultaneously hopeless and suspicious. "Why are you doing this?"

"Honest truth? I'm not sure."

Her lips pursed. "Guilt, maybe?"

"Or maybe just because it's the right thing to do and I spent too much of my life doing the wrong thing." He held her gaze with enough gravity to hopefully begin convincing her he'd changed.

She searched his eyes in earnest. Then shook her head, broke eye contact, and paced. "Flora sure is taking a long time on that call."

He suspected she stayed gone on purpose. Why, he had no clue. To help his cause?

What had swayed Flora? Knowledge of

his family struggles? Few people knew his parents had indulged him financially and materially but neglected him relationally and emotionally. Had his mom really shared that with Flora? If Meadow knew, would she have compassion for him despite all he'd done in the past?

Colin always had a tough time being vulnerable. But he'd do it if it would help Meadow forgive him.

Colin sent a mental prayer up for wisdom and right words. "You have good reason for not trusting me, Meadow. If you want, let's have Pete draw up a contract."

Her face lessened in skepticism, her arms relaxed, and she shrugged at his last suggestion. He hoped that meant she was letting down her guard. He not only wanted to fix the damage in her kitchen but wanted to repair the pain of her past and make up for the anguish he'd caused in her soul.

As a Christian, he needed to find a good local church and get involved. He was back, but he wasn't the same. Things couldn't be the same; he'd make sure of it.

First item on his Meadow Agenda: *Earn her respect and forgiveness.*

CHAPTER THREE

"Colin McGrath is the last person I want help from." Yet here she was, shoving entrees in the fridge in his pole barn, where she'd slept the past three nights. Meadow groaned.

Flora, seated at a table Colin had scooted in for them, flipped through Meadow's appetizer book without comment. Her sister's silence spoke volumes. Meadow sighed and disinfected counters she'd prepped event food on. "To be fair, Colin made me feel welcome." Linens he'd provided were so comfortable, she'd slept like a brick.

"Don't be stubborn." Flora started logging RSVPs to her and Pete's wedding.

Anxiety in her voice gave Meadow courage to set her feelings aside for the sake of her sister, understandably stressed. "You're right. Don't worry. Your wedding will be perfect." She massaged Flora's tense shoulders, then opened her wedding décor craft bin.

"Thanks. I know this is hard on you too." A baiting look entered Flora's eyes. "Colin sure went to extra specialness to make you feel at home here."

Meadow loaded a pearlescent glue stick into her hot-glue gun. Then she spread out a satin keepsake napkin. "Out of sheer guilt."

"I don't know, sis. He lingers looks your way. You're available. Word on the street is he's eligible —"

"*That* will never happen. Once a bully, always a bully."

Flora straightened suddenly. "Nice place you've got here, McGrath."

Glue gun in hand, Meadow whirled.

Ack! The object of conversation stood in the doorway, conglomeration of bags hooked on his fingers. How much did he hear? Conviction hit Meadow at what she'd said and how. But she couldn't bring herself to bend the doubt where his motives were concerned. Plus, Flora's ridiculous romantic comments were sure to rile him.

Yet his face held amusement, not derision.

Arms unfolding, he pressed off from the doorjamb. "Thanks. It's a work in progress." He stepped over, set two carryout bags on the table, and kept a third. "Like me."

Meadow's face heated.

A grin fought for leverage on his lips as he nodded toward her hand. "If you're planning to shoot me with that thing, I suggest higher-caliber ammo."

Meadow's gaze flew to her fist. Sure enough, she was aiming the glue gun right at him. She yanked up a swath of satin and continued dotting pearl-like patterns on the bride's reception napkin for an upcoming Valentine wedding, in keeping with the client's desired romantic theme.

"You brought us lunch from Favre's?" Flora beamed like the foodie she was, but Meadow recognized her exaggerated motions as a peacemaking attempt.

"Figured if you'd eaten, you could save this for another meal." A muscle worked in Colin's jaw when his eyes roved over Meadow. Regret therein sent her gaze to her lap.

Flora chattered on, entrenched in her peacekeeping mission. She'd always tried to pacify their parents' fighting. After their dad was sentenced to thirty years for felony child endangerment, abuse, and domestic battery, their mom drugged herself into a lethal coma. Meadow was twelve.

Even after the Larson children went to

live with their grandparents, Flora was always the one soothing sibling discord. An impossible feat at times since they were all close in age and raised in an atmosphere of abuse until then.

The turning point had been the night Meadow, age ten, witnessed her father shove Flora off a porch. The fall had broken Flora's arm, his words her spirit. Worse, he'd warned them not to speak of it. Flora's muffled cries of pain into her filthy pillow had shattered Meadow's soul.

She'd run to a neighbor, who reported Flora's injury to police. That neighbor had been Del, Meadow's eventual high school home economics teacher and, retired from teaching now, her catering partner. Ironically, Meadow's courage as a teen despite social stigma had eventually empowered Del to leave her own abuse system.

Reporting her dad's abuse and mom's drug use had been the hardest thing Meadow had ever done. Even as a tween, she'd hard-earned enough wisdom to know peace wasn't possible unless her parents got professional help. Horrifically, when EMTs and police arrived, Flora had tried to pretend she was okay for the sake of keeping family peace.

Meadow's insides squeezed at the realization that her unforgiveness of Colin put Flora right back in that awful place. She saw Colin first observe Flora, then her. She avoided his intrusive gaze.

A knowing entered his expression as he commenced to help Flora reach plates.

Meadow studied him in profile. He'd matured well. He had dark blond hair and deep emerald eyes that drew a person's entire soul in and an air of humility she'd not noticed before. Yet he emitted a confidence that altered the atmosphere and yielded impressions of safety and protection that made him easy to behold.

And, if she wasn't careful, easy to open up to.

Look away. Just look away now.

Colin stepped into her view. "Sleeping okay here?"

"Yes. Thank you." She met his gaze so he could see she meant it.

A slow smile transformed his chiseled face into something exquisite. Meadow had a tough time looking away. Flora's blooming smirk put an end to that.

Seriously, no man had a right to look so incredible in a simple blue work shirt. Not to mention that his trim hips and long, strong legs entirely revolutionized cargo pants. Meadow fanned herself with banquet table flowers. Too vigorously. Silk petals whirled off like little helicopters flying every which way.

Flora's grin exploded. The fiend.

A chair creaked as Colin leaned on it. "I've got building materials in the truck. Before I unload, do you ladies need anything?"

"I'm good. You, Flora?" Meadow pulled food from the bags, grateful for her sister's perceptiveness in disengaging Colin with chatter so he'd leave sooner.

Flora patted a chair seat. "Actually, Colin, why don't you join us for lunch before you get started?"

Meadow retracted her mental praise of Flora. Her sister's Sibling Support grade just plunged from an A to a D.

"If Meadow doesn't mind."

She wriggled against his question and her unwieldy conscience. Wished for once it wasn't so strong. At present, it felt like an elephant sitting on her chest, squishing her into submission. "We'd love you to join us."

He smirked bigger than Flora and riveted Meadow with a gently humorous look that told her she wasn't fooling anyone with her stiff-as-concrete statement.

Meadow stabbed her finger at his chair. "Just sit."

Still clutching his bag as he pulled out the chair to sit, he grinned full, as did Flora. Meadow narrowed eyes at both of them. If mental snickers were a thing, they'd be masters at it.

Flora leaped up. "Oh, forgot! Need to meet Pete for lunch."

"You have lunch here." Meadow panicked at thoughts of being alone with Colin and the muddy past they shared. She felt like yanking Flora back down. "Sit."

"Nah, you two enjoy yourselves. Just stick this in the fridge. Thanks, Colin!" Flora waved and dashed out the door before they could protest, plunge their bodies in her locomotive path, or beat her outside.

"Well."

"Well."

Meadow sighed. "This ranks a sturdy ten on the Awkward Moments Richter scale."

"Yeah." He pointed a fork at her plate, filled with flat-leaf parsley, red wine vinegar, romaine lettuce, tomatoes, cucumbers, capers, black olives, oregano, and onions, topped with olive oil and crumbled cheese. "Dig in. It's Greek salad. Hope you still like it."

Still? "It's one of my favorites."

"I remember. You used to bring it at lunch."

In high school.

She set down her fork. Peered at him while white-knuckling the table edge.

He was not, not, not bringing this up, was he?

He didn't meet her gaze.

Cleared his throat. Straightened his fork. Furrowed his brow. Shifted in his seat. Re-straightened his fork. Cleared his throat again. Then again.

Crud. He was either bringing it up, or he was choking to death on fear and feta cheese. Since he wasn't turning blue, she supposed he was about to bring "it" up.

"If you intend to excavate the awful past, Colin, I'd appreciate a warning first."

He looked up now and leveled her gaze with his. "Why, so you can flee?"

"I've got too much else to think about right now without dredging it up. I realize you may feel a need to hash it out, but I just can't right now."

"Understandable."

"Good." She plunged her fork into the delectable-smelling dish.

"So we'll take a rain check with this discussion."

She crunched the salad. Hard. She needed to escape the confusing way he made her feel. Half of her actually *wanted* to hear what he had to say.

The crazy half.

She inhaled several more bites, then made a show of looking at her replacement phone, provided by the cell company this morning. "Oh, the time! I should go see Del."

He finished chewing and started gathering their trash. "Del?"

Meadow didn't figure Colin knew Del by her nickname. Deloris Delafuente went by Del to friends and family. As a teacher, she'd wanted students to call her "Miss D." Colin had been in her home economics class the same time as Meadow, but to tell him Del was Miss D would resurrect a past she'd rather keep buried.

"Del's my catering partner. She wasn't feeling well last weekend, called in sick Monday — unheard of for her. Today she was admitted to the hospital after pain sent her to the ER."

"What do they think is wrong?"

"Not sure yet, but if you don't mind, I need to skip out." Relief hit that she was about to be rid of him. She poked through her phone until she found her navigation app. "Do you know the address of Havenbrook's new veterans' hospital? It only recently opened, and I haven't ventured to that end of town in years."

"It's near your old neighborhood."

Drat. His shrewd look and compassionate cadence revealed he knew she avoided that part of town because memories of her parents' house were too painful to confront.

"I'll drive you."

What? No way was she getting in his truck with him. Memories rebounded of being left at the lake by him and his friends. "Not necessary."

"Or desired? GPS will take you to a field behind the hospital. I know from experience." He displayed his thumb, which she'd noticed earlier boasted a bandage. "Nail gun incident this morning."

She couldn't stop her sharp intake of air. "On my roof?" He'd been working late, using flood lamps, then rising early to start again. Had fatigue contributed to the accident?

He looked irritated with himself for mentioning it. "Maybe."

"Colin, let me see —"

He put his hand behind his back. "It'd be easier for me to take you than direct you through confusing mazes of road construction."

"Sure, change the subject off your injury." That she was having this much compassion for the creature irked her. "Wait, you're a veteran?"

He nodded. "I was also a contractor in Afghanistan. Rebuilt schools, hospitals, orphanages, and other war-damaged buildings."

"That's incredibly brave, Colin."

She made up her mind.

"Thank you for driving."

Guilt hit him for offering since she looked so defeated. She really did not like him, enjoy his presence, or want to be positioned to need his help. His fault. However, he wasn't that hurtful person anymore. Plus, visiting her old neighborhood would be tough, and he didn't want her facing it alone. "Look, I have no agenda other than common courtesy."

"For real?"

"Yep. Just being neighborly."

"You won't bring up the past?"

"Cross my heart." He made the gesture over his chest.

Her gaze tracked his finger motion. Colin was pleased it lit on his hard-earned muscles. He wanted to smile.

The attraction was mutual, even if she didn't want it, like it, or like *him* one iota. Nothing to worry about, though. He refused to ponder any romantic relationship.

Her face still reflected skepticism over his offer to drive her.

He didn't have all day to convince her. She was up against scary deadlines and depending on him to meet them. He stood and put on his coat, then lifted hers off the back of a chair and settled it on her shoulders as she stood, like he did for his mom, aunts, and grandmas all the time.

The air cradling them supercharged. He wasn't sure whether from chemistry that came from hands atop her shoulders or from the impressive sparks of anger arcing out her eyes. Wow. High voltage. He could weld steel with those. Wanting to respect her need for space, he stepped away and resisted chivalrous urges to finish helping her on with her coat.

One of her collar lapels curled up and one angled down, which sent his OCD into overdrive, though. His fingers itched to fix it.

On the way to the hospital, she surprisingly broke the awkward silence by shifting toward him. "You may remember Del. She was a high school teacher. Went by 'Miss D.' "

Colin's ears bled. "Oh man. She's liable to stroke when she sees me."

"Why? Oh wait. I recall her chasing you

from her classroom with a metal spoon."

"It was a wooden spoon, actually. I baked the big metal one into her birthday cake for my final exam. Which I deservedly failed." He cringed. Then laughed.

"She's full of grace now. Put it this way: God got her heart but not her mouth yet."

Colin smiled. "I can imagine. I'd like to see her again. She helped me even though I didn't deserve it. Even with her temper and sharp tongue, she had a love for all kids."

"She's the reason I went to chef school after design school to diversify my business. She always said I could. I eventually believed her over all the negative voices, including mine, telling me I couldn't."

Meadow's transparent admission surprised Colin. Stopped at a red light now, he studied her lovely profile as she faced forward. His gaze dropped to that rogue lapel. It sat even more askew than before. He and his OCD couldn't stand it another second.

He reached over and smoothed it down, hoping to bypass notice.

Her atomic glare told him she noticed.

He pointed. "Your collar was crooked."

Her nuclear expression didn't change. Which meant the subject needed to.

His mind raced for something neutralizing

to say. He'd overstepped.

To be honest, he'd hoped to impart through his hands the message that he admired her dignity and resilience. No doubt she felt the blossoming care and unexpected wonder surge through the innocent contact, same as him. He guessed that, like him, she didn't know what to do with it.

The last few days of being around one another when she'd insisted on tromping up the ladder to help him with her roof had been filled with much of the same. Chemistry and their dancing around it. Trying to pretend it didn't exist was hardly working for Colin.

A blaring series of honks told him the light had turned green. Probably awhile ago. Thankfully the cacophony of horns broke the awkward moment.

Paying better attention to traffic, Colin navigated through the intersection. "Even though I gave Miss D trouble, I admired her. She was one of those teachers who tirelessly reached into the lives of troubled kids."

Meadow grew quiet. "I should know."

"As should I. My life wasn't perfect either, Meadow. There's a lot you don't know."

As Colin spoke the words, he added to his

Meadow Agenda: *Get her to open up by being transparent myself.*

CHAPTER FOUR

What about him didn't she know?

Bitter defiance was easier to contend with than this cozy camaraderie metastasizing in the truck with each mile, but his ready presence and help this week had gotten to her.

"What do you mean?" she asked.

"I made poor choices to protect the facade that my home life was perfect. I was afraid if people saw my agony over my parents' inattention, I'd be made fun of. I know you were, and I'm sorry about that. I guess I thought if I befriended or defended you, I'd be made fun of too. That rationale was wrong."

"You were young, Colin."

"Age is no excuse for cowardice. You went through so much. I wish I'd befriended instead of bullied you."

She shrugged, tempted to fake a blow-off. But Colin's confession wouldn't let her. "The stigma surrounding my family was hard. It made us who we are today, though. For all of us to have risen — even financially — above abuse, poverty, and losing our parents to their bad choices is a miracle."

"Rough road to success, though. I'm glad your siblings are all okay."

"God-loving grandparents taking us in made the difference. Plus, teachers like Del, Sunday school and church youth workers, and coaches who invested time in us."

"I always wanted siblings. One of these days, I'm gonna have a huge family."

She genuinely hoped that dream came through for him. Yet in that cushion of well-wishing plunged a pinprick of doubt. Colin hadn't been in town long. Would he revert to old patterns when he reconnected with old friends?

Construction zone looming, he decelerated and settled into silence.

God may have sabotaged her kitchen to set her on a non-negotiable path to forgiving Colin, but that didn't mean she should trust the man.

She looked up to realize that, as he'd shared earlier, they'd passed her old street. She'd memorized his profile by now but suddenly saw him anew. "You did that on purpose."

He bit his lip. "What?"

"Distracted me."

His grin escaped. "Maybe."

After a tiny mile of enjoyment seeing him squirm, she whispered, "Thank you."

His gentle nod and tender smile touched her heart despite her not wanting them to.

Once at the hospital, he offered to wait in the visitors' lounge. His contrite countenance made her regret overreacting to his innocent correction of her minor wardrobe malfunction in the truck. Yet it had also seemed a gesture of affection. Meadow didn't want to under- or overreact, but his past mistakes still screamed louder in her mind than his present acts of kindness.

Her conscience won this round.

"Colin, come visit Del. She'd be glad to see you. I doubt she's had many visitors. She's too stubborn to let people know she's in the hospital 'incarcerated by tyrants bearing sharp objects,' as she put it. She won't want us to ask how she's doing, either. If she's in pain or drowsy from meds, she'll probably just hide it."

He chuckled. "Sounds like Miss D." He pressed the elevator button. "If you're sure seeing me won't upset her."

"No, but seeing the two of us together and not one broken bone between us may send her into seizures."

He chuckled again, and the sound should not have been as pleasing to her as it proved.

"Or it may make her believe in miracles." Colin pocketed his hands.

"She already does." That Del had lived through the last decade was a miracle. Meadow didn't want to reveal Del's history of domestic abuse yet wanted to prepare Colin for her appearance.

Before reaching Del's room, Meadow halted him. "Hey, listen. She has facial scars she's self-conscious about."

"I won't mention it," he said with understanding. "Del's story is hers to tell."

And Meadow's to keep.

They'd become catering partners after forming a friendship at church. Del's ex had pressured her to quit teaching, and Meadow provided shelter after Del's escape. Then, Del insisted, Meadow had boosted her confidence by giving her a second career in catering. Only fifty, Del could recertify as a teacher, but she'd assured Meadow that creative catering was where she wanted to be.

Meadow may've been instrumental in Del thriving after divorcing her ex, but Del was instrumental in steering Meadow to hire troubled teens to assist with catering. She grinned, missing Del's daily on-the-job antics.

At Del's room now, Meadow knocked on the partially open door. "I'm here with a special visitor. You up for company?"

At Del's permission, they entered. Meadow knew Del trusted her discretion in whom to bring.

Del smacked hands to her cheeks. "My word! I think they shoved hallucinogens in my IV. I'm having a terrible time believing my eyes here, kids. The two of you didn't exactly get along in high school. You back in town for good, Colin? Furthermore, how'd you manage to sweet-talk this former rival into becoming friends?"

Meadow wanted to correct Del's notion that she and Colin were friends, even though she couldn't deny he seemed befriend-able now. Still, she'd be stupid to trust so soon.

He hadn't been as caustic as his friends and girlfriend in school, but he'd tormented her plenty. The lake exploit had been hurtful, but the birthday party prank had — pun intended — taken the cake. That incident had mortared the final brick in Meadow's wall. Remembering it made her blood pressure seem to rise.

So did the feeling that her self-fashioned

fortress suddenly felt more like a prison.

She quieted her qualms for Del's sake.

Colin leaned to hug Del. "I bought the property across the street from Meadow's."

"On purpose?" Del wiggled her eyebrows.

Colin stiffened. "I moved back after a broken engagement."

Meadow caught the sharp look that said he wasn't in the market for matchmaking. Fine. Neither was she.

She'd believe herself, too, if his obvious slight wasn't stinging. Pride. Had to be. Because she couldn't *possibly* be interested in Colin McGrath.

To Del's credit, she looked contrite instead of compelled to borrow Cupid's arrows where Meadow's love life was concerned. "Sorry to hear that."

He shifted foot to foot. "The engagement never should've happened."

Del's hand brushed her scars. "I know the feeling. What happened?"

"My ex was a fellow service member who got PTSD. I mistook sympathy for love. She figured it out and broke things off." He paused. "But I actually moved back here to help Mom with Dad's construction business."

Her respect for him ramped. Until he added, "Meadow and I are just working out a business barter. I'm sure you already know about her cave-in."

That was all their . . . arrangement meant to him? Disappointment stung until the rest of what he said came back to mind. "Is your dad okay, Colin?"

"Not really. But sometimes when things look like they're falling apart, they're actually falling into place. That's my hope, anyway. I'm glad to be back."

Meadow tried to tamp compassion but couldn't as she recalled his reveal in the truck that his upbringing wasn't as perfect as portrayed.

Del eyed her curiously. They'd become close. She could read Meadow like a one-ingredient recipe. Del wouldn't question her in front of Colin, but that didn't keep the shrewd inquiry out of her eyes. Meadow had questions of her own. When had her heart thawed to the idea of hoping for a coveted spot on Colin's friends list?

When Colin stepped out to visit the restroom, Del smirked, and Meadow hissed, "This isn't funny, Del."

"I disagree. This is the funniest thing in a century. Your life has turned into a soap opera starring Murphy's Law."

"That's not funny either. Be nice to him."

"Say that to yourself." Del whistled. "He's

a looker. Single, too, like you."

"Don't tread there, Del. We have a history that can't be —"

"What? Forgiven? Forgotten? *Renovated?*"

Meadow clamped her mouth shut. After all, she'd been the one to drag Del to church. Now here Del was, having to preach to the choir. Meadow needed to be more mindful of how she represented Jesus. Besides, was Del right? Was she unforgiving?

"Wanna know what I think?"

"Since when do you ask? You say it whether I wanna know or not."

Del's finger shot up. "True. Here's the deal, kid."

Del's eyes took on a sparkle that clanged warning bells up Meadow's spine.

"I get feelings about these things. And let me tell you, when you two walked in together, I got God-sanctioned goose bumps."

"Because it's forty degrees in this room, Del."

"Nope. It's in my knower."

Meadow sighed. Knew she should listen, but part of her was scared to hear it.

"I really sense that once you get past the hurt of what happened, God has specialness in store for you with Colin. Something more permanent than a business barter."

That ear bomb was *not* what she'd expected Del to drop.

Didn't Del see Colin's negative reaction to her Cupid conspiracy before?

"You've been relentlessly badgering me to trust my instincts, Meadow."

She grinned. "Badgering? Isn't that your territory?"

Del chuckled. "Guilty. Through your relentless *encouragement,* you finally convinced me, despite my staying in an abuse system so long, that I have the gift of discernment and need to not only use it but pay attention and trust it. So . . . can you?"

The warning bells moved to Meadow's brain. "What do you mean?"

"Despite only interacting with Colin again for a few minutes, my discernment tells me he's way different. I'm not sure you've noticed."

Unfortunately, she was starting to. Although it'd be easier not to.

"I'm just saying give the man a chance."

"Chance for what?"

"Shh. There he is."

Upon Colin's return, Meadow forced herself to look anew. Striking, how tall and filled out he'd become. He'd always been well muscled and athletic from sports. But his well-constructed demeanor was what captured her attention most.

Del was exactly right. Something about him seemed very different from before. It was dynamic and deserving of her notice. It seemed time and trial had forged his character into first-rate greatness.

Question was, could Meadow see past the boy he used to be?

Honestly, she couldn't.

Couldn't risk heartache that hoping for a friendship with him could bring.

She just needed to bide time, get through the month, and avoid him as much as possible until she could be out from under the will-softening power of his presence.

He was busy. So was she.

Avoiding him should be as easy as baking boxed pie, right?

CHAPTER FIVE

"You what?" Meadow stared Flora down Tuesday after catering an Italian wedding, an unusual event for midday on a Monday. Actually, what she'd catered was a disaster. She'd barely kept up without Del, who was still unwell, in the hospital, and deciding with her doctors what to do about the gallstones they'd found. Del had some preexisting health problems that made surgery a risk to consider.

Normally Meadow had the luxury of her dependable waitstaff, teens with troubled backgrounds who helped serve and clear meals and dishes, but they were at school during the event. Plus, they usually only helped on-site. Del was her prep and cooking help.

There'd been so many glitches, Meadow was sure the couple wouldn't recommend her despite a discount. Now her account looked grumpier than ever. Red was not becoming to a bank statement. She'd forgotten key items Del usually handled. She'd improvised so much due to her Italian-centric catering supplies being destroyed in the cave-in that *nothing* about the gig went smoothly. It had shown.

Now, after her worst cater ever, her sister dropped this bomb.

"You heard me right. Del and I decided I should hire Colin to build my wedding props."

"What possessed you, Flora?"

"Del. She's been hospitalized so long she's concerned she won't have time or feel like making my props when she gets out."

"Pete probably could've built them, so why Colin? I smell a joint Cupid conspiracy here." Meadow stirred the meat loaf gravy simmering in a stockpot. Her next wedding bride had selected meals Meadow could precook to freeze and reheat to taste just as fresh.

That saved her time to help Colin with her roof, even though he protested every time she invaded his workspace. She felt guilty otherwise. It still seemed like he had the worst end of their bargain.

Likewise, was guilt the only reason Colin was befriending her — only guilt about the past? After all, his high school history and failed relationship were proof he was prone to being led by malformed motives. The last thing Meadow wanted to be was Colin's next pity case.

She checked pizza dough rising in the window and sprinkled flour on wax paper, where she'd roll out and carve dough into heart shapes. The Valentine bride had requested veggie pizza for her rehearsal dinner. Meat loaf would be served at the wedding feast.

Her sister was too quiet. Meadow eyed her.

Flora fiddled rabidly with Meadow's heart-shaped banquet dish.

"What?" Meadow grabbed a cloth to polish her large silver chafing pan.

"I suppose I should also warn you Del invited him to church. Colin asked if you go there too." Flora's grin widened.

Meadow set the chafer aside and went for the tongs. "I could pinch your nose off with these. Del's too. I understand if he needs a home church, but hiring him? Really? Are you two desperate to torture me?"

Flora fingered gold trim on Meadow's plate rack. "You're overreacting."

Meadow felt like pulling her hair out. Flora's too.

Didn't she understand Meadow was trying to avoid Colin? Scowling, she pulled heart-shaped cookies from the oven and distributed them on cooling racks. Then she spooned meat loaf balls into deep, heart-shaped muffin pans.

Flora folded the regal fuchsia banquet table drape Meadow handcrafted for the buffet. "Wanna know Colin's reaction when I told him you go to the same church?"

"I do not." She stuck the pan in the oven, washed her hands, and then counted china place settings, annoyed that she *was* speculating about his reaction and why he asked about her. She needn't ponder it. Pondering put her nowhere but vulnerable to pain. She threw ingredients in a blender for Valentine fruit smoothies. A grinding sound rent the air until a dreadful thought hit.

Meadow shut off the blender.

"Where exactly is he building these props?"

"Here in his shop, of course." Flora's smirk sent Meadow over the edge.

"You've gone mad."

"Ladies?"

Meadow gasped. "Will you *stop* sneaking up on me, McGrath?"

Colin sauntered over with tools. "I knocked. Four times. Promise."

Flora crunched a carrot from the veggies

Meadow planned to carve into romantic food bouquets. "Meadow couldn't hear you over the shrieking tantrum of protest going on inside her head."

Colin looked from sister to sister. Meadow shot Flora a look meant to silence her for the next century.

Carrot eaten, Flora grabbed an apple. "What're these for?"

"Empanadas for the Tex-Mex rehearsal dinner." One she'd only been able to cater thanks to Colin's kindness in opening his pole barn to her. Now she'd have to share space with him. There'd be no getting around it. Every attempt to avoid him resulted in seeing him more. At least when helping him on her roof she could avoid conversation, because who could talk over construction ruckus?

The kitchen was away from the woodwork area for health reasons, so she wouldn't have to work directly by Colin. Except when she made banquet cloths. Flora had set up Meadow's sewing center near his table saw. Now Meadow knew why. She suddenly needed to be alone.

To plot her sister's timely murder.

Meadow resisted temptation to confront Flora in front of Colin. "Pardon me; I have a ton of apples to peel."

Colin took off his coat and gloves and followed. "I'll help."

Flora shoved her peeler at him. "Good idea. I'll head out, then. My pre-wedding to-do list is proliferating and I'm here procrastinating."

If Meadow wanted to hurt Flora before, she wanted to knock her into next week now. Meadow said to Colin, "Excuse us," and marched her miscreant sibling outside.

"What?" Flora blinked big dramatic eyes.

"What *indeed.* What game are you playing?" Meadow waved her hand between herself and Flora. "*We* are a team." She jabbed a finger Colin's way. "*He* is the enemy. Or have you conveniently suppressed memories of everything he and his snooty, self-important friends and girlfriend put me through in high school?"

"He was a teenager, Meadow. My instincts, training, and experience in family and relationship counseling tell me he's changed and we should give the guy a break."

Flora's words unsettled Meadow because they eerily paralleled Del's. Flora was usually right about people. Yet she had that peacemaking side that could cloud her judgment.

Maybe Flora's upcoming vows had her too

388

veiled to see reality. If Colin was prone to hurting her back then, he could be capable of it now. Especially once his old friends re-infiltrated his life. "Knock off using your sociology degree on me, Flora. It won't work to change my mind about him or his cruel friends."

"Where are they now? Is he hanging with them? No. He's hanging with you."

"Out of guilt. Once he appeases his conscience, he'll be gone."

Flora's face grew as serious as salmonella. "I don't think so, sis."

Meadow groaned. "Regardless. It's better if I stay guarded."

"Better? Or safer?"

Meadow fought for a well-reasoned refute but came up short.

Flora leaned in. "I've gotten to know him some from working with him on his family's legal needs. He truly seems a different person now. Plus, you're single pringle. He's just as single. I thought maybe —"

"Ab-so-lute-ly not."

The sisters waffled over Meadow's lack of a love life several moments before a drilling sound drew their attention.

"Surely the man has sense enough to know not to drill wood props near my food prep!"

The sisters gaped at each other before rushing back in. Once inside, they screeched to a halt, and Flora burst out laughing.

Meadow had no words.

Colin looked up from where he'd shoved a drill in the end of an apple. "What?"

Meadow felt blood drain from her face. "What are you doing?"

"Peeling apples efficiently." He turned the drill on and pressed peeler to apple. To Meadow's surprise and Flora's glee-filled squeal, the peeling spun right off.

"In seconds." Meadow didn't know whether to laud him or yell at him.

Flora grabbed her coat. "I'm outta here. Have an appointment with my tailor."

Meadow doubted that. Flora seemed intent to leave her alone with Colin. Colin had turned, and Meadow stared at his back, trying not to let its nice V-shape appeal to her. Working up a good glare, she stepped into Mr. Innovation's line of sight.

Colin looked torn between wanting to laugh his face off and run for his life. "Before you get mad, understand there are two options here."

Meadow folded her arms across her chest.

"One: You kill me — you have no help."

"And two?"

"Let me live — I'll have a bushel peeled

in minutes."

Anger and shock subsiding, Meadow fought the urge to giggle. This would teach her to turn a construction guy loose in a kitchen alone with power tools in the vicinity.

He plucked another apple from the bowl and peeled it in two seconds.

Meadow rushed him. "Gimme that." She grabbed the drill. Tried it herself.

Hip against the counter, he grinned.

"Oh. My. Starch. It actually works."

Why did the man have to be handsome *and* right?

"The drill is brand-new and the bit sterilized."

"How?"

He pointed to her stove where she'd set a pot of water to boil. The only copper one that survived the cave-in. "That's my best pot. I'm not sure whether to applaud or pummel you."

"Applaud gets my vote."

"You aren't allowed to vote when I'm thinking up means to torture you."

He grinned, and her gaze snagged on it whether or not she wanted it to.

She tried two more apples. Hands covering hers, he repositioned the drill and peeler. The peel zipped off. So did her common sense, because she found herself stalling just to be near him and continue the friendly contact. His chest to her back, his body felt warm, smelled freshly showered. She fought to de-acknowledge appreciation of his physique and voice, but deep rumbles of laughter after every apple melted her bones into caramel.

She refocused on his drill-peeling method. Its efficiency sank in, and she turned to look at him. "You've revolutionized my vegetable and fruit prep."

He nodded, looking handsome with his heroic drill.

Her mind exploded with possibilities. "Potatoes. Pears. Everything!"

"Maybe not overly ripe pears. They'd probably tear."

"Right." She plucked up an apple. "Still, what a time-saver for this." She beamed at him. "I'm impressed, for real. Your brilliance blinds me, sir."

Colin smiled slowly, and like this morning's dawn after a stormy night, the sight of it stole her breath. Staying mad at him would be so much easier if he wasn't so funny, suave, and smart. She needed distraction. Quick!

She snatched up his drill and went to town attacking more apples.

Out of the corner of her eye, she could see that he watched her curiously before plucking his jacket from a wall hook. "I'm going across to your place and get back at it."

"I feel bad not helping you."

He tapped her schedule for the next few days, which she'd written on a whiteboard on her — *his* — office wall. "You have a catering gig tomorrow. Listen, your part of the deal can wait until after spring. It looks like you've come into a busy season. No wonder you panicked when the roof fell in."

"Yeah, so thank you. Still, I feel bad, you over there renovating and me here peeling apples."

He leaned in. His cuteness became intoxicating. "Tell you what, Meadow, you let me taste test some of that great-smelling Tex-Mex food, and we'll call it even."

She smiled. "I can do that. I'll even fix you supper, if you want."

"My TV dinner tummy won't protest that. Especially since I don't cook well, unless by microwave or grill. But regarding dinner, instead of Tex-Mex tonight, would you join — ?"

Her phone chimed. She frowned. "It's the hospital." She answered the call.

"Miss Larson? This is Del's doctor. She

listed you as her emergency contact and medical power of attorney."

"Yes." A siphoning sensation numbed Meadow's arms.

"How far are you from the hospital?"

Meadow's knees weakened at the doctor's tone. "Twenty minutes maybe. Why?"

"She's had some setbacks. We're looking at surgery pretty quick here."

"What's wrong?"

"We believe infection from gallstones. She has life-threatening pancreatitis."

After he expounded, Meadow said, "Be right there." Remembering at the same time that she had left her coat at the catering event earlier, she whirled to grab her purse and ran smack into a slab of muscle. Reflexive arms came around her, surprising Meadow with their strength and sustaining power.

Colin.

He lowered his head to peer directly into her eyes. "What's going on?"

"Del —" *My goodness, breathless.* Mostly due to Del, but partly because Colin was so close. She had the strangest, strongest urge to lean in and let him shield her from the unrest exploding in her head. Worry over Del. Catering work. Obligations. Life.

"Del's having complications?"

Meadow nodded, biting her lower lip. Everything hit her at once. Del. The train wreck her business was about to be with this new time crunch. But she couldn't be selfish. Del's health took priority. Still, Del's and the teens' futures depended on Meadow's business success. Part of why Meadow pushed it so hard.

Colin moved very much inside her personal space. "Meadow?"

Panic and desperation pulverized her pride and made her want to step close to him. She dared not. She fixed eyes on the floor. No use. His nearness magnetized. Her will stretched like a mozzarella string to a point of thinness about to break. Crazy as it was, his kindness was getting to her . . . demolishing walls. He may be reconstructing her house but simultaneously deconstructing barriers she'd spent a lifetime building.

Never mind all that now.

She returned Colin's steady gaze. "I'm scared for Del."

"God's got this. But she needs you too. When's the Tex-Mex gig?"

"Rehearsal dinner's tomorrow, wedding reception the day after. Why am I getting so many weddings during the week now, when everything is such a mess? My teen helpers will be out of school in time to help some, but I'm still short a very important hand in Del. I even have that wagon wheel prop over there she only got started." She pointed with a shaky hand.

"Oh, Colin, how will I do this alone?"

CHAPTER SIX

Enormous relief settled inside Colin. She was letting herself lean on him. Big step. Big, big. "You won't do this alone. I'll help."

She blinked. "You said yourself you can't cook. Del's my only trained chef."

"Hey, I peel a pretty awesome apple."

"Colin, no offense, but . . ."

"I can handle it. Besides, you don't have time to argue with me about this. Del needs you." Not seeing her coat anywhere, he draped his jacket around her shoulders and ushered her out the door. He always had a spare coat in his truck.

"Thank you," she said after a few blocks. "I realize you don't have to do all this."

"I feel honored to. We're neighbors." And he hoped, soon, friends.

"I can't help but think you're doing this because you still feel sorry for me."

She probably assumed that because of what he'd said about the root of his relationship with his ex-fiancée. Colin only semi-regretted sharing, but was his care forged of guilt? He'd been duped by his motives before.

"I have no basis for feeling sorry for you, Meadow. You underestimate your value. You're worthy of respect. Not pity. I do feel sorry . . . but not for you. I feel sorry about you — and for me — that I couldn't see how damaging my actions, inactions, and immaturity were to you back then."

She grew so quiet he couldn't begin to read how she took that. He knew better than to ask. She had a lot to be anxious about at the moment, and he didn't want to add to it.

"What's going on with Del?"

"Gallstones led to serious pancreatitis and infected many of her organs."

"Vital ones?"

"Yes. Fluid collected as a cyst in her pancreas to a point it ruptured, causing internal bleeding. She developed low oxygen from lung damage caused by the chemical changes. Her kidneys are beginning to fail and her blood sugar is out of control."

"Can it all be fixed?" He accelerated to get there faster.

"Only with surgery, intensive post-op care, lengthy recovery, and, according to her doctor, prayer."

The gravity of Del's situation set in. He asked about Del's military service and anything else he could think of to keep Meadow from worrying over her dear friend's fate.

After pulling into a hospital parking stall, he grabbed Meadow's hand. "Father, we place Del in your hands. Guide the surgeons, keep her safe. In Jesus' name, amen."

He slid from the truck, amused at the shock he'd glimpsed freezing Meadow's face.

"What?" he said. The shock was still there when he met her on the passenger side.

"You just . . . I think you just prayed."

"That's what people of faith do." He smiled kindly and nudged her shoulder with his. "You should know, Miss Pepper-Your-Walls-with-Scripture."

"You noticed?"

"I noticed." But truth plastered to her walls was of no help if she didn't grant him access to bring down the walls inside her. They quickly navigated halls to the elevator.

"That's what's different about you," she murmured as they exited the elevator to the surgery waiting room. His chest expanded at the wonderment in her tone.

"When did you become a Christian, Colin?"

"In the military. A chaplain led me to the Lord."

She looked interested to hear more, but a nurse intercepted them. "Here for Del?"

"Yes. Can we see her?" Meadow looked close to tears.

Colin ached to comfort her.

"She just went to the OR. Doc will be with you soon as surgery's over."

"How long will that be?" Meadow clutched her purse to her middle.

Colin put a hand to her back in case the answer upset her.

The nurse flipped through papers. "At least three hours."

Meadow's face paled. That she didn't protest his comfort proved she was reeling and feeling pressure and fear over Del, plus a wedding rehearsal the next day followed by a wedding reception that she was many hours away from being prepared for. Del took priority, but Meadow needed to meet her catering obligations to her Tex-Mex bride and groom and keep the teens' paychecks coming too.

The emotional struggle played out over her expressive face. He needed to find a way to help her and keep her contracts from jeopardy. He gently steered her to a quiet corner sofa. She sat like a statue. He sat on a chair across from her. Leaned in. "Is there someone I can call?"

She blinked. "Who? There's no one."

"Flora, maybe?"

She shook her head. "She's stressed about her wedding and readying her apartment for our siblings, arriving soon. They're staying for a few weeks. They were going to be at my house, but . . ."

"Would you like me to wait here with you? Or I could go back to my place with a list from you as to what I can do to save you some time. How best can I help you, Meadow?"

She stiffened. "You've done so much already."

His heart shredded for her. She'd had to fend for herself and her siblings for so long that she'd become destructively independent. "It's always easier to help than be the one needing it."

She met his gaze. It felt like their souls connected through their eyes. She searched his with an expression that beckoned the question he was trying so hard to prove in worthy actions the answer.

Can I trust you?

Colin cradled her gaze intently in an effort to anchor his answer therein:

I promise I will never hurt you again.

There were twelve inches, then ten, then seven inches of space between them, and it still felt like seven hundred miles. It became the longest seven inches of Colin's life as he risked rejection and found the courage to reach for her. His hands spanned across the chasm of inches and years, offenses and tears of hard history between them and grasped hers.

Rather than stiffen or pull away, she held tight. "I have the hardest time accepting help from anyone, Colin, especially you. Plus, you need to spend time with your dad *and* your business. You're the CEO now . . ."

Leaned forehead to forehead, he smiled. "Will you please stop that? I see Dad every day. We get quality time. He gets tired from so much visiting. And I do have staff and crew at McGrath Construction, you know. Besides, you want to pull off this catering gig or not?" He squeezed strength into her hands with each word.

"Of course." She slipped her hands from his. Had he imagined she'd only reluctantly done so? She dug through her shiny purse until she produced pen and paper.

A yearning to recapture the closeness whittled the edges of his resistance. He forced himself to focus on how much he loved her transformation from worry to work mode. Determination fueling her movements as she quickly jotted a list made him smile.

Paper down, she pointed. "These are things I'm certain you can do."

She made a second list. "These are things I'm okay if you can't do, but if you think you can, would save me a lot of time and preparation."

She bit her lower lip, then scratched a third list. "These are things it would take a miracle for you to be able to do, but since I'm desperate and you're nuts enough to try anything, I'm turning this over too."

He chuckled, absorbing with pleasure the camaraderie, thankful for humor lifting layers of stress from her pretty amber eyes. Owlish in the sense they were so absolutely stunning and vivid on her face. He scanned the list mostly because he could get seriously lost in her eyes, but neither of them had time for that at the moment.

Or maybe ever.

Her first list mostly involved chopping food and gathering supplies. "Got it. Keep me posted on Del." He wanted to stay here with Meadow and support Del, but they needed him elsewhere more. He picked up her phone and put his number in her contacts.

She started to hand him his jacket. "I'll come help you as soon as I'm able."

He pressed the jacket back into her arms. "Keep it for now. Call when you're ready for a ride home."

"Home?"

"The pole barn." He shook his head of ardent cobwebs. Things got too crazy cozy there for a second. He needed to remember he was out to earn her forgiveness, not her forever.

Colin had worked on the lists several hours before Meadow called to say Del weathered surgery well. Thanking God, he drove to pick up Meadow, satisfied with all he'd accomplished.

"You look beat," he said as he helped her into his truck.

"Am, but can't sleep. Have to be ready." Her shoulders and eyelids drooped.

"I only have two things left on the last list and that's because I wasn't sure how to go about them." He'd never seen so many serving dishes and cutlery in all of creation.

Her neck craned. "You finished *all* but two things? You're a keeper." She smiled so brightly and her words planted such a vivid seed, he almost ran off the road.

"You're really pretty, but exceptionally so when you do that."

"What?"

"Smile." He loved being on the receiving end. Maybe they could build a close friendship after all. It took a mile for Meadow's blush to tame. The rush of red that graced her face reminded him of the showy roses in his mom's yard. His grin faded on the fleeting memory that she'd nurtured her flowers but never her family.

Once at the barn, Meadow guided them through everything else that could be done ahead of time. Under his outdoor lights as darkness fell, they loaded covered buffet servers, hot and cold drink dispensers, serving bowls, beverage bins, and gobs of catering gadgetry Colin couldn't identify. He'd been able to finish the wagon wheel display, and they loaded that into his truck since Del's vehicle was unavailable.

He carted Meadow's countertop convection oven while she hefted her portable microwave. Midway, she yelled, "Race ya!" then sped ahead. He met her mirthful challenge. Somehow she had rallied from her earlier fatigue.

By the time they reached her SUV, they were laughing hysterically and about to drop the heavy items. Just being in her presence was fun, laughing alongside her a joy. He never realized she was so funny. He severely regretted not taking time to get to know her in high school. His loss. He'd caved to selfishness and peer pressure — big-time regrets.

Peace settled between them while they loaded pan carriers, chafers, trays, condiment holders, table numbers, signs, and nonperishable food.

She playfully pinched tongs at him and said, *"En garde!"*

Colin armed himself with his own set and countered, *"Prêt!"* He grinned at her obvious delight that he knew the French word for *ready.* He was trying to remember the word for *go* when a spark lit her eyes.

"Allez!" she commanded, then lunged, making playful contact with his sleeve.

He tamped his foot several paces forward, forcing her to scramble back. Then she blocked, advanced, and — most surprising of all — giggled like a carefree little girl.

After fencing themselves into fits of laughter, they continued gathering a plethora of other catering stuff and serving ware. It was well after 1:00 a.m. when they wrapped up. Rather than feeling exhausted, he felt exhilarated.

"Thanks, Colin. You made a stressful prep a delight rather than a duty."

"My pleasure." He fought OCD-fueled urges to sweep unruly bangs from her eyes.

She pressed fingers to her temples, something he'd come to realize she did when majorly stressed — and just when he thought she'd relaxed. She let him walk her to the pole barn and up its porch steps. "Thanks, Colin, for letting me stay here. It's cozy."

"My pleasure. I like having you close."

Her eyes softened at that. He wanted to stay and chat with her, but it was cold and late; the next day would be filled with catering challenges, and he didn't want to push down too many walls at once.

Soothing forest scents, stars, and night sounds greeted them, which added an ambience of romance to the air. He tried to ignore it, but his will vaporized the instant she tilted her face up and peered shyly through her lashes. He'd already turned off the outdoor lights except for one, one that allowed him to see every facet of her lovely face.

"See you tomorrow?"

"Are you sure after lunch is soon enough for me to get there?" He drank her in as she nodded. Wanted desperately to fix the haunted look that never really ever left her eyes. How much of it had been etched there by him? Swallowing hard, he did the exact opposite thing he wanted: said good night and stepped off the porch to head to his house.

"Colin?"

Thinking she'd forgotten something, he turned his head. Conflicting emotions swirled in her face. He swiveled fully, showing her he'd listen if she was ready. She scanned his eyes before brushing the ground with hers. "Thanks. I don't know what else to say."

"No need to."

She nodded and recaptured his gaze. He loved staring into her eyes so much; he walked backward all the way to his door since he'd memorized the path. Grateful the barn was right next to his house and that his house porch light was still on so she could see him, he waved playfully once there and, okay yeah, in a flirty way.

Surprisingly, she didn't recoil, scorn, or scoff. Rather, he saw a tremendous smile on her face that surely eased tension from her eyes and lifted her shoulders from the burdening weight of Del's emergency surgery.

"Tomorrow," he called softly as a promise. Not even sure yet for what.

"Tomorrow." She met his pledge with a grin he could swear was part miracle, part maniacal. Probably thinking humorously of him and the bumbling mess he'd be in his fledgling attempt as her assistant cooking host in an actual high-risk catering event.

Peeling apples was one thing. Pulling off chef-level meals and service entirely another. It hit Colin full force what he'd actually agreed to do for her.

Lord, help me not drop an entrée pan or something equally disastrous. He really was a complete spaz in the kitchen. Of course, Meadow already knew that and had let him help her today anyway. Did that mean it was possible to earn her trust after all?

Lord, order our day. Don't let me ruin Meadow's catering reputation.

He thought about his inability to stop thinking about her or curb enjoyment of her presence. He was making strides earning her forgiveness, but after seeing her strength today and interacting with her tonight, Colin was tempted to want more.

Much more.

It was either the stupidest or the bravest struggle he'd ever owned.

He courageously added to his mental Meadow Agenda: *Earn her admiration and build a friendship forged in forgiveness.*

Once inside, he peeled his curtain back to make sure she made it safely inside. Hand pressing the window reflecting her entry into the haven of his barn's doorway, he prayed.

"You're all about renovation, Lord. Redeem the mistakes of my past and let your will prevail between us in whatever fashion pleases you."

CHAPTER SEVEN

"It's green."

Christopher, one of the teen helpers, pointed at the blob simmering in a stockpot the next afternoon. Colin grinned at him and winked at Meadow. She felt laughter bubble at Christopher's innocent observation. Joy also rose that Colin had quickly bonded with her waitstaff teens, Chris, Aimee, Abbi, and Aurora. Clearly, they adored him.

Despite her and Colin's late-night scramble to get everything done, a feat she never would've accomplished without him, Meadow wasn't tired today. Not even after dreaming restlessly of him all night and while enduring the teen girls' matchmaking efforts ever since he'd arrived. She was glad, though, that they'd had only a half day of school that morning.

Aurora sidled next to Colin and said conspiratorially, "Mr. McGrath, did she admit how much fun she had prepping and loading supplies with you yesterday?"

Colin's eyes held delight and mirth as he faced Meadow. "Why no, she didn't."

Abbi joined the teasing by adding, "Yeah, before you got here she said you make even mundane tasks adventurous."

Chris said, "Ladies, give it a rest. Seriously, why is the chili all green and stuff?"

"It's supposed to be that color," Aimee informed him. "Meadow used authentic Hatch chiles from the bride's New Mexico family homestead."

Aurora attached herself to Meadow, as usual when she was preparing something new. She was a sponge for learning. "The bride met the groom at a rodeo there."

Meadow helped Aurora measure ingredients for Spanish flan. "She's a Hispanic New Mexico native, he's a former Texas rodeo cowboy, hence their Tex-Mex wedding theme."

Colin nodded. "Nice."

Nice was the graceful symphony of sinew and strength evident in his arms as he hand-shredded a block of cheddar cheese. Took tremendous effort to peel her eyes away.

"Plus, they rescue Andalusian horses. That mission's how they met."

"Awesome. I'd love to hear more stories

about how your engaged clients met, Meadow."

The earnestness that had entered Colin's eyes made her sad his engagement hadn't worked out. That she'd begun to have his best interest at heart made her wonder when he'd seeped under her walls. There were a billion women out there. Surely if she could turn his attention to one, the teens would stop teasing them. "Colin, I'm surprised you're not dating."

She'd know if he was. Between Flora and Del, they seemed to have found out just about everything there was to know about Colin since he'd come back. Still . . . "I hope our deal isn't impeding your social life."

His expression deadpanned. "I'm spending time exactly where I want to."

Gulp. "Out of guilt? Because I'd hate to be the cause of your lack of a love life."

"My lack — ?" His head whipped up so fast he bashed it on a cabinet, then laughed. "Spending time with you" — he gestured to the organized mess around them — "and all this chaos is an honor."

"Aw. What a guy!" Abbi breathed, to which Aurora sighed and Aimee grinned. Chris rolled his eyes, clearly in solidarity with Colin.

Meadow absolutely flustered herself by realizing she no longer had any idea which side she stood on. Nevertheless, she busied herself mostly to hide how his words thrummed delight through her. "Is chaos why you're compelled to go behind me straightening utensils, arranging pots in order of size, and lining every celery stalk to microscopic degrees on trays? Yes, I noticed."

He blushed. "I'm compulsive like that. But not impulsive." He peered from where he pulled taco shells from the oven and fixed her intently with his gaze. "Regarding your dating question, maybe I haven't convinced the right one yet."

Her pulse sped, then plummeted. He hadn't said "found." He'd said "convinced."

Which meant he had someone in mind. She couldn't deny disappointment at that. And she hoped it wasn't Blythe Matthews.

"Green chili looks kinda gross, but it's actually very tasty," she said to change the subject.

Chris and Colin eyed the bubbling poblanos, onions, lean ground beef, garlic, flour-thickened sauce, and flame-roasted tomatoes with skepticism.

"If you say so," they responded at the exact same time, then laughed.

She dipped a clean spoon into the pot and drew out a spicy bite. Chris stepped back, but Colin leaned and sipped it off, suspicious expression still intact. A moment later he lolled his head back and moaned. "Amazing. Seriously."

Chris leaned in and gave the chili a second look, eyed Colin, then tried it. "Sick!"

Meadow scowled until the girls translated, "Sick means good nowadays."

"Save us a couple of bowls of that, would ya?" Colin said to Meadow.

"Glad to. I always make extra for my veteran buddies." She recalled his pleasure at discovering she hadn't forgotten his wounded friends, that she hadn't waited to fulfill that part of their bargain. He'd thanked her profusely and offered to deliver meals she cooked. That it meant so much to Colin touched her.

"I'm gonna gain ten pounds a year if you keep feeding me like this."

His statement seasoned her confidence but also stunned because his phrasing made it sound like he thought they'd be in one another's lives for the long haul.

He'd made similar statements all week. Was he trying to hint at something? Fish for feelings? She couldn't manage to bring it — or her hopes — up. She wasn't that brave.

Yet. Every day around Colin grew her courage.

Except he'd said he hadn't convinced the right one yet.

A thought materialized that he could've meant her. Impossible, right?

That would almost be tragic. Their past and her inability to let go of it was too big a barrier between them. Plus, he'd made clear his aversion to romance in light of his last relationship. Yet sometimes it seemed he liked and treated her as more than a friend.

Should she step over fear and into faith that God may have goodness cooking for her? She'd avoided getting serious with anyone because she'd been career building and waiting for the right guy.

Is this you? Dare I hope, Lord?

Her mind swayed in constant contrast, not knowing which image to grasp. Was Colin really the man he portrayed standing here? Or was he the heartbreaker she remembered from yesteryear?

The teens had been working since shortly after noon and, thanks to Colin, Meadow felt on top of things enough to excuse them until they had to be at the rehearsal dinner venue, dressed in uniform.

After the teens left, Colin gestured to loaf pans. "We stuff chili in the soapy things?"

Yeast scents permeated the air, mingled with hearty cheese, meat, and Mexican spices.

Mouth watering, Meadow giggled. "Not soap. Sopapillas. It's like Native American fry bread, and we're going to make it from scratch."

"We?"

"Since I don't have a mouse in my pocket, yes."

"Gimme a miter saw — I'm in my element. Gimme an oven mitt — I'm a misfit."

She'd started giggling, but his last word killed it. She tried to shake it off.

He was beside her in a heartbeat. "Hey, what'd I say that upset you?"

She sprinkled wax paper with flour. "It's stupid, really. Just that Blythe called me Little Miss Misfit all through school."

"And my saying the word *misfit* induced bad memories you'd forgotten."

"Yeah. Don't worry about it. It's no big deal."

Out of the corner of her eye, she could see him lowering the bread basket he'd been holding before he curled his hand over her shoulder. "It *is* a big deal."

His words froze her frame but thawed her heart. He drew close. So close. His gentle breath ruffled hairs on her neck.

417

"Words wound worse than bullets or blades. But you'll ultimately be okay." His voice resonated deep. To barren places she'd thought too fragile, too far out of reach. Yet he managed to get there, to seep words in like water through a microscopic breach, wicking through her window frame, reversing the drought that had become her soul. A tiny bead, then a trickle, then a flood. Tears. Now.

Silent, she let them flow.

Courageously not blinking the moisture away this time, she hoped like crazy what he said was true, right, and maybe even could be a promise from God. That knowledge alone would make her — and everything — okay.

"God himself will make you okay," he repeated with penetrating conviction.

That made it sound like the promise from God she'd hoped for. Dare she believe?

"What makes you say that?" she whispered, tattered soul truly needing to know.

"Because I know it's true, I know it's for you, and I know you need to hear it."

"I hope you're right, Colin, because I feel far from okay," she whispered with such frailty from a raw-honest place, unsure he'd even hear or if she was ready for him to. "This is embarrassing. I haven't cried since high school." Her famed walk of shame, actually.

"It's time then." She turned her head to look at him. He smiled, appearing to want to encourage her. "What triggered your tears?"

"The frustrating fact that I still feel like I have 'loser' tattooed on my soul."

His gorgeous emerald greens tracked every tear as though sacred jewels slipped down her cheeks. The strength of his hand multiplied into her shoulder as care magnified in his Irish eyes. "Feelings can lie to us."

Could be good or bad, Meadow decided. Especially since she was having unsettling feelings of warmth beyond friendship, care for Colin that was scary.

"Just because someone calls you a name, doesn't make it true. How much enchilada sauce did you say?"

She smiled at the drastic change in subject, dabbed at her face with a towel, and brought the can over. "Just enough to cover the pan bottom."

He drizzled sauce while she observed the crimson pouring. She envisioned heart-red streams of forgiving oil drenching down an ancient Israel cross.

Thank you, King Jesus, for dying for me.

Meadow pictured nail-pierced hands plunging through dirt, like she'd shoved fists into the snowman for her shoe. Images hit of those strong, scarred hands deep underground, closing deftly around a root. She thought of Colin's hand coming out of that snowman with her shoe and realized the symbolism.

God sent him to encourage her. *Lord, I release Colin from any wrongdoing, and I reject this bitterness. Please pull it out of me, root and all.*

"Let me guess, tortillas next?"

Colin's question drew her from the prayer, but she departed it in peace. Something felt different inside. Either the green chili was working up an inner warmth or hope had a safe place inside her to lay its head for the first time in ten years.

"Yep. Two deep, like this." Together they layered corn tortillas over the enchilada sauce, then added hamburger meat cooked with onions and garlic, then cheese.

Colin spread her clumped cheese to the edges, making her smile. "Sorry. OCD."

She grinned. "Not complaining. My enchilada pie never looked so good."

They started adding the next layers.

"We add tomatoes and lettuce after baking?"

She nodded, not complaining one bit when their hands brushed and mingled in the process. Maybe their hearts a little too?

He peered down at her. "It layers like lasagna."

She smiled. "Exactly. You're a fast learner."

"On some things."

His remorseful tone elicited compassion and an urge to comfort. She changed the subject instead.

"Del's improving."

He nodded. "She told me about her abusive ex."

"Really? When did you talk to her?"

"Went to see her this morning after my pavement therapy."

"I see you running sometimes when I walk to the lake to watch the sunrise."

Mention of the lake jarred them both. She knew without it being said that he thought of the night he and his friends left her at the other lake. His face looked stricken with sorrow as his eyes roamed every facet of her face.

She thought the hurt had been behind her. But his coming back to town and ending up as her neighbor had shaken things up and shown her she was far from healed of it. "Not the lake. I meant the little pond at the park," she found herself clarifying.

He didn't say anything for the longest time. Just continued studying her with tender, probing eyes. Then finally, "I still had workout gear on when I went to see her." As though remembering something, a grin squeezed past the remorse holding his handsome face hostage. "She told me she wouldn't be caught dead running unless someone was chasing her with a substantially sharp knife."

"Sounds like Del." Glad he'd veered off the lake subject, Meadow turned left to put a spoon in the sink the same time he turned right to grab a trivet.

"Oomph!" They collided; her face smushed in Colin's chest, his steadying arms springing up to grasp hers.

They stood like that a shocked moment before Meadow realized Colin wasn't letting go. She stalled, not knowing what to do, say, think, or what this moment meant.

Determining to be brave, if even for a blink, she let herself feel. Strong arms shielding. Tender heart beating against her cheek. Soft cotton shirt warm against her skin. His fresh waterfall scent and piney aftershave awakened her senses. For an unguarded instant, she let herself soak in not just him but all he was becoming to her.

Breaths deepening, he shifted. She thought

he was about to let go until he further encircled her, curving his arms protectively. He felt so solid, so warm, so like heaven in a hug. Every place he touched came alive, especially in her soul.

He held her like that. The tender moment couldn't last long enough if it stretched past forever. Yet she'd never been more scared in her life. He pulled her closer until there wasn't a breath between them possible. She did the craziest thing imaginable.

Meadow let herself, and all her stress, lean completely into the strength of Colin McGrath.

His arms overpowered her deadlines, her cave-in, worry over Del. He absorbed her overdrawn agenda, her overdue to-dos, her insecurities, and her inability to discern his motives and trust. She was scared. But he was harbor. He was hope. He was haven.

She was safe.

After a moment his velvet voice threaded through the benevolent fog of bliss that cocooned her within his arms. She felt stronger and sounder than she had in years. She sensed him pray as he held her, and she knew credit for her peace and strength belonged to God. But she was thankful for Colin too.

"Wish I could stay like this forever,

Meadow. Thank you for letting me in."

She nodded against him. "Thanks for making your stubbornness outlast mine."

He smiled, and they separated slowly. Rather than feeling awkward over the extended-release hug, Meadow felt exhilarated, hopeful, and free.

She eased back into meal-prep mode. "Can you hand me the medium chafing dish?"

He blinked big at the conglomeration of pans and pitched a cute but panicked look.

"Square white serving thing with the underburner and lid."

He brought it over and set it down with a grin. "It begins."

"What?" She stirred masa batter for the chile rellenos dish.

"The crash course in Catering Dish Identification."

Meadow felt a crash coming on but not with catering. It had to do with her growing dependency on Colin. That she'd begun to long for their talks. She'd shifted at some point from doing everything she could to avoid him to seeking opportunities and excuses to spend more time with him.

"What's the rest of the week look like schedule-wise?"

She was tempted to say it looked perfect

as long as he'd be in it, but tamped down the urge. She needed to get control of herself. Stay on guard. Just to be safe. "Just in case" was her go-to phrase, the way she lived life in relationship to others. Safe.

Safe meant putting distance emotionally. Walls.

Just in case he had romantic notions toward another after all.

Just in case his care and presence in her life were only meant to last a little while.

CHAPTER EIGHT

Colin wondered what thief-draped thought slithered in to steal her smile.

Lord, that hug was sublime. It was healing to her, I know it. Help her win the backlash battle of her mind trying to rip joy from her soul and steep her in doubt.

He had a fleeting thought of what to tell her. "Meadow, this'll sound odd, but I feel like I'm supposed to encourage you to leave your walls down, *just in case* you're wrong."

She paled. Blinked wide. Then seemed to compose herself and stood on tiptoes to view her calendar. "Tex-Mex rehearsal dinner tonight, wedding tomorrow. Friday night Valentine wedding rehearsal dinner. Reception Saturday, Valentine's Day. I have an engagement party to cater the Thursday evening after Valentine's Day weekend, so that's February nineteenth. Then Flora and Pete's rehearsal and wedding reception the weekend after, Friday the twentieth and

Saturday the twenty-first."

Her hands trembled as her words tumbled out on top of each other. It seemed that what he'd said both rattled and revved her.

Interesting.

Not wanting to amplify her stress by delving into it, he craned his neck to study the calendar. "Flora's wedding is the weekend after Mardi Gras?"

"Yes, that's the theme actually. Pete is from New Orleans. Attended LSU, played pro basketball there. Injury took him out, but he said it was worth it since he met Flora."

"Lemme guess, there'll be lots of royal purple and gold at their gig?"

"Yep. Plus Bengal tiger stuff since they both love Mike, the LSU mascot."

"Wait, Flora said you're one of her bridesmaids. How're you catering too?"

"My helpers will be there, plus Del's doctor said she'll be able to work by then."

"Good." He pointed at asterisks on days prior to Flora's wedding. "What's this?"

"I have to get siblings from the airport over those dates."

"If I thought they'd get in my truck with me, I'd offer to help chauffeur."

"Maybe you can help me out. I've mentioned you already. They know we're no longer rivals."

He grinned. "Say that again."

"I've talked to —"

"No, the part about us not being rivals."

She smirked. "You seem quite pleased with yourself over that."

He was sure his smirk eclipsed hers. "Very." He softened his smile. "You look exhausted."

"I am. Everything is as ready as possible now, and I probably should catch a nap before putting this food in the SUV and heading over to the venue later."

"I'll let you rest."

He decided to say one more thing before leaving. He had no idea how she'd had time that morning, but she'd begun to decorate for him.

"Thanks, Meadow," he said as he gestured toward his office. "You didn't have to do this yet."

She smiled. "I wanted to."

"Then I'm glad you did."

She curtsied and blushed, nibbling her bottom lip as she did so. His gaze dropped there. *Walk away. Don't complicate this.*

He opened the door and stepped onto the porch. "Text me when you wake up."

"Okay," she said dreamily. No missing the gentle nuances of yearning in her eyes and voice as she held his gaze through the narrowing crack before closing the door softly.

He raised his hand, knowing if he knocked, she'd open the door and he'd kiss her right then and there. Would she let him? Fist in midair, he opened his hand and brushed it down the door. Rather than break it down to go after that kiss, he prayed for her to have a restful nap and serene dreams.

He turned to get his tools from his garage, his heart warming at her special creative touches that lifted his office and would eventually grace his home. He'd never felt like he belonged anywhere growing up, but being around Meadow was beginning to feel like family. He envied her for having so many siblings. He'd longed for that all his life.

Maybe that explained why he'd gone above and beyond to give Meadow her dream kitchen. Because she'd use it not only to prepare catering food but meals for when her siblings got together. Not that she knew about this special surprise yet.

How would she take it?

She'd instructed him to order the cheapest pro-grade kitchen appliances, countertops, and flooring he could find. Instead, he'd picked Del and Flora's brains. They'd shared every detail of Meadow's dream kitchen, a luxury she didn't feel she could afford, even with an insurance check on its way. Colin was making it happen. He smiled, remembering Flora and Del both stressing how much Meadow despised stainless steel, an endearing quirk considering she was in food service.

Her fancy dream kitchen consisted of elegant Tuscan style, warm tones, custom-carved cabinetry, rich red accents, black quartz countertops, scroll designs, textured walls, recessed lighting, top-of-the-line wall ovens, marble flooring, and stunning copper trim.

Not a speck of stainless steel in sight. Not an easy feat. Even her fridge and freezer had wood accent doors. He was building a customized food warming room onto the kitchen, too, at the back of the house where she couldn't see it from his place. Plus a butler's pantry for storage so she didn't have to keep extra catering supplies in her yard shed. Sure, it was a lot of extra work for Colin, but her happiness was worth it. The hard part was keeping her out until he finished.

He'd done so by changing all of her locks and not giving her new keys. He told her he didn't want her inside yet, that it was too dangerous. She'd been too tired, busy, and stressed to argue. But that she'd given him nearly free rein in her kitchen renovation said a ton about the level of trust she'd extended. Trust he'd never take for granted as he built on it tile by tile, brick by brick.

Colin went back to work on Meadow's kitchen, and after an hour or so, he finished for the day and gathered his tools. As he passed her living room in transit to the front door, he was drawn to cross its threshold to the fireplace, emotions unraveling at every step.

He peered at photos lining her mantel, images of the Larson children, starting on the left with Meadow, the oldest. Then Lake and River — the boy and girl twins. On the right of an intricate vase sat frames bearing Flora's face, then Skye and Rayne, then a baby dressed in pink. Meadow had six siblings. Sage, he remembered now, had died in infancy.

His heart ached for the family. He brushed fingers along the photos, praying blessings over each member before heading home to shower. He'd just dressed when Meadow texted she was awake. He headed to the barn to help her.

Later he stood in a crisp white shirt and black suit jacket alongside the line of smiling teens in Havenbrook's community building kitchen for the Garcia-Salazar Tex-Mex rehearsal dinner.

"You guys all look so professional," he encouraged the spiffy bunch.

The girls blushed and giggled behind their hands, but true to form, Chris covertly elbowed him. "For a sawdust-saturated construction guy, you clean up pretty well too."

Colin grinned at Chris, loving that he was true to himself. He'd tell him so later.

Meadow whispered, "Remember, Colin. Keep thumbs out of the food when carrying plates. Serve carefully. Last thing we need is a green chili groom or Spanish flan bride."

He whispered back, "Got it."

"Questions?"

"Nope. Let's do this." They disbursed dinner to the wedding party and guests. Thankfully, it was a smaller occasion, enabling the crew to manage fine without Del.

Meadow had placed colorfully patterned cowboy boots as vases to hold bouquets of sable brown, burnt umber, turquoise, and shimmery gold flowers, the bride's colors.

Over each table hung sombreros, which he'd helped wire into Tex-Mex chandeliers. Upside-down cowboy hats held southwestern bowls of chips and salsa. The bride had gushed pleasure upon seeing the special creative touches, especially since the hats had been donated by relatives who hadn't been able to make the cross-country trip.

"I love how you incorporated their careers and love of horses," Colin said.

"Fascinating couple, aren't they?"

"Yeah. Glad I got to spend a few minutes with them before guests arrived. I loved hearing about their humanitarian efforts for horses." Even more fascinated was he when the couple disclosed that Meadow's invoice reflected a discount. In a note, she'd expressed wanting to bless them and their efforts to help the Spanish horses they loved so much.

Colin's admiration for the couple had grown when he'd learned they started a local horse therapy ranch here for special groups such as wounded veterans, differently abled children, and at-risk teens. He admired Del and Meadow for doing likewise within their catering partnership.

Joy welled in Colin as he watched the smiling teen waitstaff serve diligently and interact genuinely with guests at tables Meadow had assigned each to watch over. Stronger emotion stirred as he watched Meadow covertly direct and praise them. She was making such a profound, positive difference in their lives. She'd make a great mom someday. After learning some of the teens' home histories, he realized she was already mothering.

He felt grateful to get to come alongside her and be a part, if even for a day. He couldn't deny the draw to live a lifetime of impacting teens and their identities for better.

In her element, Meadow beamed as she refilled the taco salad bar. She obviously loved serving people. He smiled when overhearing the praise she so well deserved. He peered around, taking in more of her special touches.

Rather than number the tables, she'd named them after horse breeds. There were Shires, mustangs, Belgians, Arabians, and quarters for the adults. The tweens and kids were all seated together by their request and pleased that Meadow had not only complied but had creatively named their tables Colts and Ponies.

The engaged couple hosted table trivia after dinner to entertain guests and because family game nights were a huge part of their upbringings.

Colin had hired several food service companies for his Chicago construction firm events over the years and couldn't think of a single other caterer who'd have gone so above and beyond to make important days that much more meaningful for wedding couples.

Remembering his own broken engagement left a sour note in his heart.

He wished he could be certain his growing feelings for Meadow weren't meshed in wrong motives. Furthermore, just because she echoed his attraction didn't mean she'd give a future with him a second thought. Nor should he.

The struggle not to consider it became bigger by the day, though.

After rechecking food temps, Colin rejoined Meadow, who grinned at him.

The groom's father approached. "The party food and setup are outstanding. My compliments to the caterer."

The bride's mother joined his praise. "We're so touched you went to such effort for our beloved daughter and future son-in-law." She dabbed tears and hugged Meadow.

Meadow blushed. Had she any idea how becoming he found it?

The bride and groom complimented Meadow's work and expressed how pleased family and friends were over her authentic food and ethnic banquet decor.

Each time she accepted the praise with

humble grace and quickly pointed out she couldn't have accomplished it without her teens and Colin. She bragged on the Tex-Mex wagon wheel dessert bar he'd completed, adorned with sweet flan and Spanish lace. Meadow leaned against the chili bar next to Colin, watching the teens refill glasses and plates as guests celebrated. "I usually have more creative leeway for decorating rehearsal dinners since they tend to be more casual. Weddings are usually far more formal."

"We have to use an entirely fresh setup for tomorrow?"

"Yes. All this has to be taken down and replaced with more traditional ritz and glitz, plus a few little surprise touches I've confirmed with the couple for the wedding reception dinner. That one will be a lot more work — and, of course, at a fancier venue."

Colin knew this couple and their horse mission were special to Meadow. Yet, knowing her work ethic, he was sure she undoubtedly made every couple's wedding dinner special. He slid close, bumping her shoulder with his. "Trying to scare me off?"

Her brow arched. "Is it working?"

He smiled slowly. "Never."

"Good." Her eyes outshone the vibrant

LED lights they'd strung around the room.

Word quickly spread about Havenbrook Creative Catering being responsible for the dinner. By event's end, nearly every guest requested Meadow's business cards, both for themselves and referrals.

Colin loved hearing her hard work commended and drew pleasure from observing her mingle and work, maintain correct food temperatures, and teach him the ins and outs of catering in a flash. He'd mastered refills. That was about it. But he admired her. Big-time.

As he eyed the wagon wheel prop and her special touches to the rehearsal dinner, the strangest sensation came over him that they'd work a lot of events together. Was that the intense draw he felt toward her? That God destined their businesses to merge in this manner? Or did it encompass more? He'd be lying to himself not to acknowledge the new seed of hope.

Trust and integrity were like bombed-out buildings: easy to obliterate, hard to restore. So either way, he needed to add another item to his mental Meadow Agenda: *Renovate fully her trust in me and restore my integrity in her eyes.*

"Well done, fearless man." Meadow wondered if Colin felt as fatigued as he looked. She'd sent her teen staff home an hour earlier so they could get a decent night's sleep.

Colin pulled off his catering cap. "Thanks. You handled my mishaps with grace."

"My fault. I forgot to explain the special diet placards. No one died of a peanut allergy or got sick from consuming gluten, though, so we're good."

Colin leaned on the last table to be taken to the SUV. "Thanks, but that vegetarian was livid over being served chicken in his tacos."

She shrugged. "Poultry happens."

He chuckled and turned the table on its side. He'd removed his suit coat and rolled up his sleeves. She enjoyed watching his muscles bunch and flex as he folded the table's legs.

She supposed since it was her table, she should help instead of gawk.

"I don't think you picked up on it, Meadow, but that rodeo star was hitting on you."

Meadow whirled. "I should hope not. He's the bridegroom!"

"Not him. His best man brother." His baited grin told her he was teasing.

"Oh." Cheeks flaming, she quickly turned.

She hated to blush in front of Colin. That might give away her feelings. "I didn't realize he was a rodeo cowboy too. The groom was."

Why was Colin bringing this up?

How would he react if he knew the guy gave her his number? Furthermore, what would Colin say if he knew she'd fed it to the garbage disposal at first opportunity?

All because she had Colin on the brain. His kindness to her waitstaff had served to soften her heart toward him even more, especially when he bolstered their confidence with kind words. Maybe he really and truly had changed. Still, a small reluctance remained that wouldn't quite allow her to trust him fully. No question their bond had strengthened, though.

She'd seen Rodeo Guy give other women his number, too, or what she assumed to be. She detested the player type.

It hadn't escaped her notice that Colin seemed to have eyes and winks only for her.

He'd probably only done so to encourage her at tense moments. Like when the groom's mother danced her samba hips into the lighted punch fountain and tipped it. Colin had righted it before it crashed.

He'd also ignored the crush of curvy women trying to sidle up to him all evening.

Her insides warmed at what that could mean.

Then she remembered he'd said the only reason he wasn't dating was because he hadn't *convinced* the right one yet.

"What's that sour look about?" Colin loosened his tie and bent to study her.

Mood dissolving, she shrugged.

"Come on. Tell me."

"It's silly."

"Let me be the judge."

"No, really. It's dumb."

"Try me."

She deflated the salad bar. "Fine. You confuse me."

"How so?"

"You send mixed signals."

"Like what?" He helped her fold the inflatable salad bar.

"You say one thing with your mouth, opposite with your actions."

"Can you be more specific?"

"Sometimes it seems you flirt with me. But there's obviously someone else."

His eyebrows drew down. "Someone else?"

"As in another woman."

"What woman?" Humor entered his eyes.

He was starting to see she was jealous. Good gravy, *she* was starting to see she was jealous. Colin was the absolute last man she should like — like *this.*

Lord, help! I am in serious stew here.

Seeming intent to stir it, Colin arched his brows while awaiting her answer.

"You denying you flirt with me, McGrath?"

He grinned. "Absolutely not."

"Absolutely not what? You aren't flirting? Or you aren't denying it?"

His widening grin frustrated her. Especially since he didn't appear the least bit inclined to quickly answer. Just studied her. Mutely. Intently. An entirely new level of brightness and mirth danced in his eyes. Why'd they have to be so delicious?

"You know what? Forget it." She huffed and started to walk off.

His arm swung out like a train crossing guard, halting escape.

She lifted her chin. "What?"

His gaze roved over her face. "What, indeed."

She gritted her teeth.

"What gave you the idea there's another woman on my radar?"

"You said so. Earlier today."

He nodded, seeming to know exactly the comment she referenced.

But just in case he'd grown dense all of a

sudden, she'd remind him. And she wouldn't be nice or vague about it, either. She went ahead and let the fire she felt inside flash out of her eyes. "You said very plainly you aren't dating because you hadn't convinced the right one."

Peanut brittle! Blazing hot moisture sprang to her eyes. It gave Meadow her first full indication that somewhere along the line, despite having meticulously watched over all her walls, she'd betrayed herself and begun to harbor hope for Colin's affections.

Upon seeing her tears, Colin's face softened. His arm curled quickly, spinning her body so her cheek rested snug against his shoulder.

Holding her securely, mouth moist and hot against her ear in a heady almost-kiss, he whispered equal parts gruff and grace, "Meadow, the woman I was talking about . . . is you."

CHAPTER NINE

Doubt hammered holes through Colin's head.

It had been six tense hours this morning of working together on her roof, then prepping for this evening's wedding reception, and she still hadn't referenced his comment from last night.

Obviously his confession bewildered her. He'd wanted to curb what he'd perceived as insecurity on her part. Maybe he'd misread her developing feelings or misappropriated timing for the reveal of his. Only God knew. So that's who Colin would consult.

After Colin helped Meadow carry fancy cutlery to her catering SUV, she left to run a load to the venue and he went back to work on her kitchen. Her new cabinets got delivered, and he was excited to incorporate all the special touches she'd dreamed of. That he'd made her happiness his life's mission launched a big clue to Colin about the depth of his feelings. Ones that weren't wavering, only growing stronger.

He was falling faster than a hammer from a ladder in love with Meadow Larson.

Her earlier silence bothered him the entire time she was gone, but when he saw how stressed she looked upon returning from the venue, he decided to wait to bring up a conversation that may add to her stress. Meadow pressed her temples, so he scrambled to think of small talk since it seemed to calm her.

"How did you segue from interior design to catering?"

She pulled a stack of server ware from one of the gazillion boxes he'd carried over from her shed. "In my catering, I do both. That's why it's called Havenbrook Creative Catering. I match the tables and serving décor with the bride's theme. It saves couples from having to hire a decorator. They get two contractors for a package-deal price, and I get more business."

She'd said Del's encouragement had given her courage to try. For that he was glad. "What originally interested you in catering?"

She stiffened, and he felt walls go up. "Our parents never did birthdays, and our grandparents had enough expenses. So I got a job to be able to afford to make holidays and birthdays matter for my siblings. I learned to cook, bake, decorate, and sew fancy things. The idea for a catering business launched from there." She paused. "I always loved to entertain because I enjoy serving people and bringing them together. But no one at school knew because no one ever showed up at my gatherings."

He recalled now how he and his friends had ignored invitation after invitation. Then once Blythe fake RSVP'd on behalf of everyone, and Meadow and her grandma had prepared all that food and decorated for around fifty people — and he'd heard not a single person showed up.

It had to have been a huge financial hit for Meadow and her grandparents, who he imagined were on a very limited budget with raising the Larson grandchildren, even if Meadow did contribute income.

Colin should've been there for Meadow.

"Hey, I'm sorry about that vicious prank Blythe pulled. I know I behaved badly toward you, but if I'd known about your party, one I would have recognized as that special, I'd have been there."

"Even if that were true, you'd have been the only one."

"Maybe not. Blythe intercepted many invitations, including mine. I didn't even find out about it until the next day."

"Yeah, my big walk of shame down the high school hall as Blythe and her group of friends clapped and made sarcastic birthday girl comments." Hurt sheared across her eyes.

His heart went out to her so powerfully, he had to force himself not to reach for her. He'd confused her by his declaration yesterday. Too much too soon. He needed to tread lighter for both their sakes. Besides, he was still only marginally convinced his growing feelings for her were unrelated to guilt.

"I thought if things were decorated pretty enough, if the food tasted good enough, people would want to come. Would want to know me, maybe like me and be my friend."

"People should've wanted to come because of you, Meadow, and not because of the food or decorating or even who else was there." His mind kept going back to the Valentine decorations that had still been up on the high school walls during her humiliating walk of shame. Her devastatingly peerless party had been at the end of February, which meant Meadow had a birthday coming up soon. "I remember the hearts on the school walls, and yet I knew even then that yours was breaking. Have you ever had a birthday party?"

"No. Never have — not since that one attempt. That's why I cater them free for underprivileged kids. Our church takes a special offering to fund it. They also waive my waitstaff's church camp fees."

His heart melted. "I knew I liked that church for a reason." Meadow too.

An idea formed. He'd talk to Del, the teens, and maybe Flora and have them help him plan a big surprise party for Meadow. He knew people would show this time.

Perfect timing since her siblings were arriving soon and staying a couple of weeks.

"I'm sorry for the heartache you experienced in high school, Meadow."

"It's no big deal. They were all kids."

He shook his head, not wanting her to minimize it. "No, we were young adults. The party was in your honor, yet you were horribly dishonored." *God, I am so sorry.*

He was sorry for not having gotten to know her better then. For not having understood the seriousness of her family situation, the danger and neglect she and her siblings had lived under at home. Then for her to go to school only to have Blythe continue the nightmare . . .

She shrugged. "People had better things to do."

"Not better than to be there for you. I'm sorry I never showed up for you."

"I understand. I wasn't on your radar."

He couldn't contain the compassion. He set down the buffet pan he'd been holding and placed a brotherly hand on her shoulder, giving a supportive squeeze. "Believe me, Meadow Larson, you're on my radar now." So strongly he couldn't get her off if he tried.

She blinked a path across the floor and eased her shoulder from his touch, pulling away from his comfort . . . in essence rebuffing his apology and care.

She might reject it, but he was going to make sure she knew it. "That I overlooked you wasn't a reflection on you, Meadow. It was a reflection on me, family junk, and my deep-seated selfishness. I hope you can someday believe I'm a different person now."

She leaned against a stool and studied him carefully. "The jury's still out on that."

He nodded. "Fair enough. I at least appreciate you giving me the chance to change your mind for the better." Colin wondered from where he'd gotten the audacious hope to add *win her heart* to his Meadow Agenda.

Lord, I may not deserve her, but I'd be so honored to be more than her friend.

CHAPTER TEN

Meadow carefully watched for Colin's reaction while asking, "Have you seen her since you've been back?"

"Blythe?"

She nodded, unsure why she'd even asked. To torture herself?

"No."

"Do you want to?" Meadow waved a towel as if to dissipate her question from the air. "Sorry. Not my business."

"What if I'm starting to want it to be your business?"

Care ebbing from his eyes was doing a number on her. She hadn't been able to sleep last night because of her unfair resistance to his gestures of comfort and affection. Her mind tormented her with its meaning, his motives. And hers.

Were his actions ruled by guilt? Was she self-sabotaging?

She wanted to be stubborn. Hold on to

the hurt. But his sincerity and compassion were rendering her resentment as slippery as the Crisco he'd painted on her baking pan.

In this moment of fiercely loyal eye contact, she wanted to race to him. Embrace him for real. Things would change between them forever. Her heart would lean toward him. But then he may turn out to be the same weapon he was back then. Too big a risk.

After all, he'd been the one who'd pretended to want to strike up a friendship when his group of friends had lured her to the lake. He'd looked genuinely distressed as they were leaving her, but they'd left anyway. She didn't know what scared her more — the possibility that he'd cared or the probability that he hadn't. Same dilemma facing her now.

She'd end up just like that summer: hopeful for a friendship with him, then humiliated. Her heart pounded with painful memories. The assault of panic she'd felt running home from that lake resurfaced with the power of a lightning bolt to her brain. Feeling confined and short of breath, she set down the fondue pot she'd just picked up and grabbed her coat. "I should get some air."

Her pride tried to demand she not open herself up to him more.

But were pride and fear the true bullies here?

Colin approached with concern. She waved him back with a shaky hand gesture to give her a minute. She stumbled outside onto the barn's porch and leaned against a column, letting her face absorb refreshing coolness for many lengthy minutes. Then she moved to sit on the top step and spent several moments inhaling calming woodsy pine and clean winter air.

Hunkering down, she cleared her mind to pray and prayed to clear her mind.

"Lord, seriously, I need to get over it. The past is the past. Please help me put it back where it belongs — behind me for good. But, if I may pick a bone with you here for a minute, Lord, why does he have to be so — so — irresistibly cute? Those dimples! My goodness, they're a bigger treat than Tex-Mex cheddar cheese. And those eyes? Way more delish than awesome Native American fry bread. And that deep voice of his could charm the rattles right off a New Mexico snake."

Fingers webbed together, she fanned her face.

A throat cleared behind her.

She jerked upright. Couldn't bring herself to turn around.

"Just came to let you know the oven timer's beeping. I don't know how to stop it."

She realized he probably didn't know his oven automatically shut off at the end of the cycle, even though the timer continued to beep. She nearly giggled at the endearing quirk that he had no clue how to work his own oven. Getting to it was going to be tricky.

Her face felt hotter than jalapenos over the likelihood he'd heard her honest confession. Mission: zip past him without getting caught in his gaze.

He didn't move aside, though, which made entry awkward. In fact, she very nearly had to brush against him to get to that screeching oven. It'd help if her heart would stop thumping like a mixer with a crooked beater.

She'd almost cleared him when his arm hooked out, caging her between his chest, his minty breath, and the door frame. *Caught.* In every sense of the word. She dropped her chin. A strong fingertip slid beneath it.

"Please look at me?"

She twisted away. "No."

His thumb swept soft, wispy circles along her jawline. "Meadow, it's okay," he whispered. "There's no need to look down. You have nothing to be ashamed of."

"I'm not ashamed. I'm mad. I don't want to be feeling this way."

With gentle pressure, he lifted her face. "Not even if I feel it too?"

Now her gaze collided with his. "Not especially in that case." Breaking the hold of his arm, she went to stab the oven display until it stopped whining.

He was behind her in four steps flat. "What's this about, Meadow?"

She whirled. "Remember the lake? You led me on, let me believe you were my friend. Then you let them leave me, and you never once looked back."

His jaw hardened. Emotion, swift and fierce, swirled over his face. "You're right. All except the part about never looking back. I've been doing that for ten years straight. And every single second since seeing you again, I've looked back to that lake and drowned in its sorrow. I'll never stop regretting what we did to you. By the way, I did go back for you."

She blinked. "You did?"

"Yes, but not soon enough. I couldn't find you, so I went to the police so they could look for you. I've never been so scared in my life."

"Of getting in trouble?"

"No. Of something happening to you. 'Sorry' seems lame, but it's all I have, Meadow. I can't rewind time and erase my actions. I can do my best to make it up to you, but it's ultimately up to you to choose to forgive me. *Us.*"

Though rationally she knew he was right and forgiveness was biblical, emotionally she bristled at his sudden solidarity with his high school friends by his use of the word *us.*

"I can't hand you the power to hurt me again."

"Sorry you feel that way, especially after . . ." He shut his mouth.

His words, spoken and unspoken, carved through her as he turned toward the door.

She stood silent and wholly haunted by the flash of hurt he hadn't been quick enough to hide. The look of a person left reeling by another's words.

She didn't know from where all this mouth venom of hers was coming, but it was vicious. She'd hate herself for it, except she knew doing so would break the Lord's heart. "I'm sorry," she whispered to Jesus.

Then to Colin's retreating back, she

breathed, "I'm so sorry. I didn't mean it."

How could she so easily wound with words after being so wounded by them?

And hadn't Colin apologized a zillion times in words, looks, and actions?

Even in her angst-ridden state, Meadow felt God's peace breaking through, his assurance that the thorns she sliced with originated from a place of deep pain.

She thought she'd been fine with Colin's confession that Meadow was who he'd thought about dating. But then terror set in. It seemed the closer he got, the more she fought. No more. She ran after him.

On the porch, her courage faltered. What could she say?

Pacing, he tromped back up the steps, whisking past her without a word. The air chilled. Courage regrouped, she prayed for grace and traced his steps.

He stacked food carriers at the counter and stiffened at her approach. Back still to her, he pivoted slightly. "Tell me what to do next." His words were calm but clenched.

Even after the prickly way she'd treated him, he still put her needs over his pride. That he was still willing to help her after the way she'd thrown his past in his face like bitter pie proved he was not going to abandon his promise to help her. That spoke worlds of wealth about his integrity and character.

"You can stop pouting and look at me." She removed her coat from her shoulders.

He turned, gaze cautious but tentatively amused.

Hands on her hips, she approached. "Colin, you said you're a work in progress. Well, so am I. I'm under construction and I might be a mess for a while. So when you see me upset, it's basically best if you steer clear of my mouth. Ugliness spews from it."

His gaze dropped the few inches from her eyes to her lips. He took his time returning his gaze to her eyes, conveying that steering clear of her mouth was the absolute last thing on his mind at the moment.

He stepped toward her. She stepped back. Bumped the counter. *Trapped.*

For the first time she didn't feel like escaping.

Then Meadow felt like the densest person alive when Colin reached and rubbed something off the corner of her mouth with a dish towel and held it up. "Nacho cheese?"

"Not sure how that got there," she hedged.

"Hmm." He nodded. "You never let me finish."

"What?"

"The rest of what I need to say. You asked

457

if I wanted to see Blythe. I said no. I answered honestly."

"That may change when you see her."

"Doubtful. She mailed me her modeling pictures. I shredded them with glee. I feel nothing for her, be assured of that. Yes, we dated. I made not-so-great choices about who I spent time with."

"We've all done things we're not proud of."

"I stayed with her because I was comfortable and afraid of losing my social status."

"With her dad being mayor, your parents probably lauded the relationship," Meadow said, feeling the need to extend grace.

"Yeah. I fell into misguided motives. I wanted my parents' acceptance, even at the cost of growing unhappiness with Blythe. That's my rocky past, but I'm overcoming it. Yes, you have specific reasons not to trust me, but that was then." He slid his hand behind her neck. "And this" — he lowered his face — "is now."

She gasped as Colin pressed pure bliss to her lips, but soon gave in to the luxury of his kiss. As his delectable mouth descended on hers again and again in a sensual ebb and flow, pain — years of it — washed away. He was appetizer, entrée, and dessert all in the same moment, and she *never* wanted it to end.

He broke free of their sweet first kiss to blaze an unforgettable trail to her ear. "You said something that first day after your kitchen cave-in that has haunted me since. You said you were overlooked and easily forgettable. For the record, Meadow, I could *never* overlook you. And you are far, *far* from forgettable."

"But —"

His mouth covered hers again with exponential purpose. Every shred of protest fled as she felt the magnificent heart of this man come through the heat of his mouth on hers.

He leaned back enough that she glimpsed his boyish grin. "You were saying?"

"I have no idea." None. No idea in the world what she'd been about to say. She'd be hard-pressed to even remember her own name right now.

He pressed his mouth to the spot on her temple her fingers reserved for times of stress, and he prayed. Beautiful words, God's bountiful answer and the care behind their comfort seamed the shards of her soul. She relished the nearness.

His eyes were closed, face serene. Dimples deepened. Smile huge.

Lord, I think I love this man. Love that he

takes pleasure in me and my well-being.

Emerald eyes opened on a face so tender and bright, she couldn't look away. And still . . . no recollection of her name. Sort of.

"Meadow . . ."

"That's it."

"What?" he murmured.

"My name."

"Your name. Your name should not be Meadow Larson."

"No?"

"No. It should be Meadow McGrath."

His words slammed her into a wall of reality. He'd said Meadow McGrath.

They'd been back in one another's lives for two weeks. No way could his feelings progress so far in so little time. Right? Seriously, no. That was crazy.

Yet didn't her soul feel the same?

She'd made herself too vulnerable, and now her heart hovered over a vat of trouble.

Just like before.

And just like before, he could burn it.

Failing to fend off the fear and confusion, she scuttled away.

He reached, tugging her hand. "Meadow, wait."

She shook her head. Pondered protest. But what could she say? She'd wanted that kiss as much as he had. To pretend otherwise would dishonor him and make her dishonest.

His jaw firmed. "Don't dare let yourself regret or second-guess this."

"What did you expect me to do, enjoy it?"

He smiled broadly. "That's the general idea."

"Well . . ."

His eyebrow arched. He folded bulky arms across his broad chest in a steady, daring challenge. Could she really lie and say she hadn't enjoyed it?

"Well?" Colin pressed.

"You're lucky you kiss way, *way* better than you cook." She tugged his sleeve. "Come on. We have a reception to set up for and cater in two hours, and the venue is ten minutes of congested traffic away."

CHAPTER ELEVEN

"Heard the wedding reception was a hit," Del said the next morning when Colin arrived at the hospital with breakfast and intent to visit. She'd tolerated solid food for two days.

"Went well considering I was there and you weren't."

She chuckled. "I'm sure you did fine. How're other things coming along?"

He unfolded his breakfast biscuit packaging since Del scolded him yesterday for not eating with her. "Roof and ceiling's fixed but trim's on hold. Lumber yard owner's on vacation."

Del chewed her biscuit with ham slowly, hoping her doctor wouldn't find out what she was eating. "I meant the other renovation."

Hand paused midway to his mouth, Colin shrugged.

One good thing was that, while praying

on his morning run, God had granted peaceful assurance that Colin wasn't mismanaging his motives.

"How'd you know?"

"What, that you're falling in love with her? Colin, come on. Anyone can see how much you care about her by the way you talk about her. She talks nonstop about you too."

They were silent as they finished their biscuits, and then Colin tossed their wrappers in the trash can. "Define 'talk,' " he finally said. His confidence that Meadow reciprocated his feelings was shaky.

"Good things. Mostly," Del teased.

"I'm crazy about her. So that leads to my next question. Will you help me plan a surprise birthday party for her?"

Del clapped. "Fantastic idea! I'm glad to help."

"Sure you feel up to it?"

"Are you kidding me? Blowing Meadow's mind is just what the doctor ordered."

"You know how to reach her siblings? I guess they are staying with Flora."

"Yes. I'll invite them for you, if you want."

"I appreciate the offer, but contacting them is something I need to do." For reasons beyond a birthday party. He needed to personally apologize to each of them for his part in their sister's pain and malformed

463

identity.

A knock sounded, and then the doctor entered. "Ready to skedaddle?"

Del flipped her covers back. "Yes, and I have a chauffeur right here. Colin, you got time to drive me home?"

"Absolutely. I just have to pick up Meadow's brother at the airport later today."

"Lake? The big, muscle-bound Coast Guard captain?"

"Yep. That would be the one."

She grimaced. "Painful."

"Yeah."

An urgent text came in from his dad's secretary. A complaint with threats of litigation for a job his dad had allegedly botched. Worse, it said a very influential customer. He texted her back to ask who, then waited for the answering text while nurses provided discharge instructions to Del.

She flagged her doctor down as he passed by her room. "Don't forget to gimme all my pieces and parts, Doc."

The doctor handed Del a container of gray rocks. "I forgot. Your royal gems, madam."

Colin would laugh if he could. Only Del would want her own gallstones. He was too troubled by the new text to let humor seep in. Colin grew wearier when he recognized the address on the text.

The mayor's mansion. Blythe's house. Did she still live there? Colin hoped not.

He really could stand to go the rest of his life without seeing her again.

After settling Del in at her home, Colin checked when he had to be at the airport against the current time. Plenty of margin. He drove to Mayor Matthews's mansion.

He pulled in the circle drive and got out of his truck. Took the steps two at a time and had raised a fist to knock when the door swung open.

Blythe stood on the other side of the doorway. "Colin! Wondered when you'd stop by." She launched into his arms. He caught her simply to keep from landing in the yard. He set her down so quickly she almost landed on her caboose.

He ignored her pout. "I came to talk to your father. He home?"

"No, the golf course. Can you run me to town, darling? It's urgent and my car is in the shop."

Colin gritted his teeth at the endearment, but she said it was an emergency. Town was on the way to the airport, so he nodded curtly to his truck. "Get in."

"Where to?" he cut through her incessant self-centered chatter two miles later to ask.

"Oh, the mall. Next stoplight."

His jaw clenched. "Really, Blythe? You have an emergency at the mall?"

She raised her pinky. "Yes! Broke a nail, and I'm attending an engagement party Thursday."

Colin gripped the steering wheel tighter. "Thursday . . . evening . . . next week?"

"Yeah, my cousin's, on my mother's side. Father's hosting an after party at their home. You should come so we can catch up." He felt like the proverbial chalkboard as she raked her fingernail up his arm, and it made him no less squeamish. "*Really* catch up."

He jerked his arm away and ignored both Blythe's come-on and her famous pout. Colin's uneasy feeling about Thursday's catering event went from bad to worse.

What were the chances the two gigs were one in the same?

His gut churned with a sick feeling, thinking that Blythe could be there.

And so would Meadow.

And possibly some people who'd taken it upon themselves to torment her.

His friends. *Former* friends.

Would Meadow believe they were no longer his friends? His biggest fear with it was that she'd revert in her progress of trusting him and slam all her walls back up like an impenetrable concrete barrier between them.

Lord, protect Meadow and the special bond you're building between us.

He may never get a chance like this again in his lifetime. He was bound and determined to use it to prove to her once and for all where his loyalties lay.

With her.

Not with his old girlfriend, nor his old friends, and certainly not with his old patterns.

"Meadow, don't read into it." Flora grabbed the dash. "And stop peeling out!"

Meadow's hands trembled on the steering wheel. She saw red, and it had nothing to do with the Macy's sign she swerved around to exit Havenbrook Mall. "She was in his truck. They seemed too comfortable. There's no way this is the first time."

Silence ruled the ride until they arrived at the pole barn. Flora said, "There has to be a reasonable explanation."

Meadow let them in and set her new serving utensils by the sink to be washed. Was Colin dating Blythe? It seemed too ridiculous to ponder.

But he'd duped her before. "I've been

such a fool to —" She bit her tongue.

Flora's wedding was a week away. She didn't need the stress of Meadow's emotional breakdown. She never should've trusted her heart to Colin. Her emotions felt grated.

Her mind was going berserk with confusion. Why was he with Blythe when he'd told Meadow he didn't want to see her? What had Meadow missed?

His lies?

Was this some big elaborate joke they were all playing on her, like in high school?

Trust Colin.

The thought ushered unbidden. Then again. Stronger.

Trust him. Trust me.

The fear that she may not have the courage to do that caused her soul to sink right back in that bitter lake.

"Meadow, will you be okay?" Flora whispered.

Meadow donned a mask of strength she didn't feel and fibbed with all her heart. "Of course. I'm always okay."

You're going to be okay.

The seemingly failed words hit like a slap in the face. She fought tears.

Lord, I know I need to trust you, but seeing her in his truck left me feeling miles away from

468

okay. Colin said feelings lie. Maybe eyes do too. Please show me what to believe.

Two hours later, Flora brought up the subject again. Meadow was still fuming.

"I keep going over this in my head, and I just can't see him with her." Flora affixed gold trim on purple banquet table draping for her food riser displays.

"You saw what I saw." Meadow ripped a crooked thread out and had to start again.

"Ladies?"

Colin.

As he strode in, he assured them Lake had been picked up and safely deposited at Flora's place, but neither sister spoke, moved, breathed, or blinked.

He set gorgeous cherry wood trim near his table saw and went to work.

Meadow feigned immersion in her stitchery.

That Flora didn't leave her alone with Colin to go greet Lake before it was time for them to pick their sisters up from the airport sent ominous confirming flares through Meadow.

Or maybe it was heat radiating off the glares Flora toasted him with as he worked.

That meant Flora may be rethinking her initial good impression of Colin.

Colin never looked up, never said another

word. His tense expression and guarded body language spoke of someone harboring secrets.

Meadow should've seen this coming. But she'd let herself trust.

Meadow didn't have a good feeling about this. Not. At. All.

The man was definitely hiding something.

He wanted to tell her so badly. He couldn't. Not with Flora's wedding days away.

At least her brother, Lake, had been civil.

Colin was glad he'd opened up. If Lake and Flora trusted him, maybe Meadow could too. He couldn't kick the fear that Thursday would summon bad memories and crack the foundation of friendship he'd carefully poured with Meadow.

Colin had about worked up nerve to pull Meadow aside and discuss the potential impending disaster of Thursday's gig when Flora jumped up, displaying a text. "Let's go. Our sisters' flight landed early."

They left without comment, but the look Meadow sent over her shoulder knocked breath from his chest. Shards of pain and accusation lanced out her eyes. Why? Did she get wind of who would be at that engagement party and suspect it was a setup?

She likely felt the distance he'd just put between them. It hadn't been intentional. He was in cahoots with himself over knowing his camaraderie with Meadow was about to further upend if he wasn't careful.

Blythe's track record suggested she'd likely get mean and mouthy if she saw Meadow, and he hadn't wanted to tip Blythe off that she might have the chance by asking more questions. He needed to find a way to go to that party to protect Meadow.

Problem was, his only in was Blythe's invitation as her guest. With Del back, Meadow hadn't asked him to assist with future caters.

Lord, you knew about this cater centuries ago, maybe even arranged it. Help Meadow through what's sure to seem like her worst job ever. Things aren't always as they appear. Look out for her that day and each day after. If I may also ask, please protect her fragile trust in me. Use this gig to strengthen rather than strain our relationship.

Over the next days, Colin grieved not getting to spend time with Meadow. She was curt at church on Sunday and wouldn't answer or return his calls. Del said to give her time. Flora wasn't speaking to him either at this point, but she was likely

471

swamped silly with her siblings and nuptials looming.

As he worked on finishing Meadow's kitchen the day of the engagement party, he wondered. Had he done something wrong, something other than keeping a distance between them that day he'd seen Blythe? He strained his brain. Had she gotten the guest list and seen his name next to Blythe's? He'd explain, if he ever got ahold of Meadow.

They'd shared a beautiful kiss; one that felt like it brushed and branded their souls as well as their lips, then *wham*. Her walls went back up. Higher and more formidable than before.

"Lord, if this is my Jericho, help me bring down these walls."

CHAPTER TWELVE

"Blythe's out of control," her cousin told Colin the instant he arrived at the engagement after party. His mother had asked him last minute to take his dad to chemo. Having done so, Colin walked in late, just in time to hear Blythe's grating voice.

"You know flora's a bacterium? Oh, I forgot. Your mama mixed her meth up with her birth control pills. Had so many kids, only organic names were left."

Refusing to stand idle this time, Colin rushed to Meadow, who looked equally hurt and homicidal. Approaching her side, he whispered, "She's not worth it. Stay calm."

Blythe's smirk confirmed she was out to destroy Meadow's career and business reputation by making her lose her temper during a legally binding job. It heartened Colin to see horror reflected on faces of family and friends close enough to hear. It proved they respected Meadow more than they pledged allegiance to Blythe and her scheme. Colin hoped Meadow saw their support too. Right now she looked like all she could see was red.

Tsking, Blythe vulture-circled Meadow. "Poor Little Miss Misfit, always running away. Never could take up for herself, even when her drugged-up daddy knocked her sister into next week."

Her self-control at snap point and her body pulsing with anger, Meadow shot forward.

Colin launched in front of her, facing Blythe, pressing Meadow backward with his body. But unleashed anger imbued her with the fierceness of a freight train in transit. She turned, wrapping her arms tightly around her so she couldn't rip out Blythe's hair. Colin kissed his mouth to her ear while walking her backward into the adjacent garden room. "Let God deal with her."

Colin's heart broke at the trembling beneath him. The depths of hurt inflicted, the guilt wound Blythe's words reopened. Meadow heaved from unchecked emotion.

He hauled her against him. "It's not your fault, sweetheart. Your dad made his choices. Had he not been sent up, worse tragedy may've befallen your family, your sisters, your brother. You protected them by telling the truth about your abuse."

No wonder she felt so close to Del, such a responsibility to help her.

Meadow still quaked violently. Now he couldn't tell if it was all from emotional trauma or also from years of pent-up anger. He held her closer. After a moment, her forehead lowered against his chest.

The click-clack of heels sounded on marble tile.

"Isn't this cozy? You two look about to make a bunch of little Irish Meadows."

Colin whirled. "Enough!"

Stunned at his tone, Blythe stumbled backward. Rage surfaced. "How dare y—."

"I'm not finished." He faced Blythe down. "I should've stood up for her against you years ago, Blythe. Meadow has actually done something noble with her life. Unlike you, still spoiled and living off Daddy's wealth."

Blythe gasped, then fled the room wailing.

"I knew she'd act like a villain."

"You knew she'd be here?" Meadow blinked.

"I tried to warn you, to cushion the shock, but you rejected all my calls and refused to answer *my* door." He smiled ruefully.

"You were with Blythe at the mall."

"You saw us?"

"Yes. I thought —" Red adorned her cheeks. She groaned. Paced.

Colin chuckled. "That's why you've been avoiding me. The reason I was with —"

"It doesn't matter." Meadow ran into his open arms. "Sorry I was swift to doubt and slow to trust."

"Meadow, you can't do something bad enough to make me stop lov—" His lips clamped. He'd almost blurted his feelings.

Her dropped chin and open mouth told him she knew. "What were you about to say?"

He drew breath. Tried to say but got tongue-tied. What if she rejected him?

Face softening, she inched close, hand over his heart. "Then I'll say it. I guess you know I love you," she whispered straight from her heart to his.

"I'd hoped." He grasped her hand, still resting against his chest, then soaked in the joyous moment of deeply held dreams coming true. "I've loved you from the moment I saw you kicking that snowman."

He hugged her securely enough to assure her he was never letting her go.

"She'll never believe this, Colin." Flora glowed from a Maldives island tan and treasured time with Pete on their honeymoon. Colin couldn't wait to whisk his own bride to Komandoo. "I hope she says yes." He was terrified she wouldn't — and glad she hadn't asked questions when he called her after a catering event to say she should meet him at her house. Del and the teens had just arrived, barely ahead of Meadow's probable arrival.

"She will. Right from the ER gurney." Flora smirked.

He turned. "Why would you say that?"

"Because she's going to faint when she figures out you single-handedly fixed all this food without burning down her brand-new catering kitchen."

"Ha-ha." He heard a car pull up. Excitement surged. "Everyone hide! She's here."

Del flicked lights off in Meadow's new kitchen. The one she'd dreamed about, not the one she thought she'd settled for. Colin's home across the street could be theirs together, her cottage the catering business. *If* she said yes, that is.

Seconds later Meadow stepped through the door to a chorus of, "Surprise!"

She blinked. Teared up. Sought Colin's face. "A party? For me?"

"Yes." He met her and motioned around the room to her family and friends, teen waitstaff, design and chef school pals, business colleagues, catering clients, and even former high school classmates — all crammed into her kitchen.

"How'd you get all these people here?"

"Sent invitations."

"And they wanted to come?"

"Most people change for the better when they grow up, but you've isolated yourself so long you couldn't see it."

As the crowd moved into other parts of the house, Meadow seemed to nearly faint at the sight of her dream kitchen, understanding now why he had kept her out so long. After giving her the grand tour, time to gush over it, and a chance to greet everyone, Colin left the guests to Flora and led Meadow outside. Candles lit a path winding through her front yard.

When she saw where they ended, she burst out laughing. "You did not."

Two snow people, man and lady, stood side by side. "Colin, really? A snow couple?"

He inched her sideways. Little snow people nestled between the two larger ones. The hole she'd kicked into Frosty was patched up nicely. It had been so cold the whole month of February that he hadn't melted.

"What is this?"

"A big family. And a big hint."

He reached behind the snowman and pulled out a big wooden box. "Open it."

Meadow did so to find a nice set of Ruffoni Historia copper cookware. "Colin! These cost a fortune!"

He draped his arm around her shoulder. "Look in the little one."

She tore the packaging away and ripped off the lid. Nested inside was a pretty set of red, white, and black damask neoprene pot holders. "They're gorgeous," she breathed.

"So are you. Peek inside the smallest pot holder."

Her heart raced as she pulled the edges apart. A red velvet box greeted her gaze. She opened the container with trembling fingers. A heart-shaped solitaire winked up at her. "Oh! Oh my starch!" She held the ring under moonlight. "It sparkles like stars."

"So do you." He dropped to his knee. "Meadow —"

"I do! I do!"

He laughed. "I didn't ask yet."

"Oh, but I know you're going to!" She squealed, grabbing his face.

Smush-cheeked, he grinned. "Glad we finally established trust." He slipped the ring on her finger. "Be my Valentine forever, Meadow? Marry me and make a bunch of little snow angels?"

"I'd be honored." She received his ring, his promise, his kiss.

"Wait. Who's catering our wedding if you're in a pristine white dress?"

"Del and the teens can handle it."

"Meadow, you amaze me."

"Trust me, beloved husband-to-be, I'm just getting started."

Epilogue

"Hard to believe it's been a year since your cave-in, sis." Lake wove Meadow's arm through his at Havenbrook Church's entrance. She nodded beneath the archway Colin had carved for their wedding. The wood boasted purple and fuchsia flowers.

Speckles of snow remained from this winter, but unlike last February, flowers had cropped up in colorful echoes of an early spring. Warmth whispered through the trees, rustling the ringlets that framed her veil.

The music started. Her heart leaped. Lake grinned. "Ready?"

"Ready," she breathed.

They started the famed walk down parchment she'd seen so many other brides traverse. Today it was her. She smiled at her attendant siblings, each one grinning and glisten-eyed at her approach. Even tough-skinned Skye.

Meadow's gaze affixed on her groom.

481

Colin's eyes shone as Lake kissed her cheek and handed her off.

As they faced the pastor, Colin clutched her hand as tightly as he held her heart.

Thirty minutes and two sets of vows later, she knelt before the candle stand Colin had fashioned with his hands.

Her *husband*. Smiles erupted inside and out.

She read his special inscription. Ran her fingers across each word, knowing they stood true and would always remain.

This day, I marry my friend.

Their Valentine's Day wedding date was etched beside the words.

Their rings reflected light from an LED cross as their fingers mingled, symbolic of good things to come. Colin held her gaze before they merged the flames from two candles into one and rose.

After a kiss that sent the church into whistling, rowdy applause, the pastor announced, "I'm honored to introduce Mr. and Mrs. Colin McGrath."

Grinning, Colin led her outside to a gorgeous horse-drawn carriage.

"A fairy-tale ride?" She ran hands down the necks of each horse.

"Yes." He smiled, watching her reaction as he helped her into the plush velvet seat.

"With Andalusians."

Squealing, she hugged him, unwittingly giving him access to her neck. He planted a steamy kiss there.

Cheeks scorching, she grinned but dipped her chin.

Reins in hand, he lifted her face. "No shame, Meadow. Blushing becomes you." Lifting emerald eyes to sapphire sky, he said, "Lord, thank you for serving up the blessing of my sweetheart."

ACKNOWLEDGMENTS

Becky Philpott, sincere thanks for bringing me into this novella collection. What an honor! I'm giddy with gratitude. Skate on and keep rooting for those Tigers, even if they beat my Cardinals.☺

Becky Monds, I'm so glad for your amazing intuition and editorial guidance. I feel so blessed to get to work with you. You have a strong pulse on what it means to tell a good story. Thank you for encouraging and growing me.

Jean Kavich Bloom, thank you for your attention to line editing. My MIA serial commas, staging issues, timeline glitches, and I appreciate you!

To the entire HarperCollins Christian Publishing team, Katie, Karli, Elizabeth, Ansley, Amanda, Jodi, Daisy, and the many others who make Zondervan such an AMAZING imprint, thank you for all you do and are.

HUGE thanks to readers. Your time is so precious and valuable. That you'd spend it on our words means the world. Your readership is a tremendous blessing. Find out what's coming next by signing up for my newsletter at www.cherylwyatt.com.

Thanks to Denise Hunter and Colleen Coble for recommending me for this project. I'm grateful for your belief in me. Thanks Joel Kneedler and John Perrodin at Alive Communications for contracts and career guidance. Thanks Rachel Hauck, Denise Hunter, and Deb Raney for answering my gazillion novella-related questions.

Thanks Sally Shupe and Casey Herringshaw for beta reading this book. Thanks Preslaysa for the novella article. Thanks to my Facebook community for all the fun ideas and excitement over every story. You are awesome! I am blessed by your presence on my author page. Those who haven't visited, we'd love to have you: https://www.facebook.com/CherylWyattAuthor.

Thanks to my family for being so supportive of my deadlines and for loving frozen pizza.

Lastly, thank you, Jesus, for the gift, the grace, and the gumption to write. May every word honor you, make you smile, and make you more famous to those who don't know.

DISCUSSION QUESTIONS

1. Meadow carried emotional scars into adulthood from having been bullied as a teen. Have you or someone you loved experienced bullying? How did you cope?
2. What was your favorite scene and why?
3. Colin gave up his life in Chicago to help his parents. Have you ever needed to make drastic life changes to help a friend or relative? Would you? Why or why not?
4. To which character could you most relate? Please discuss.
5. Meadow had a tough time believing in the goodness of people because of her childhood. People like her grandparents and Del helped shape her for the better. Who in your life has had the most positive impact on the person you are today? What did they do or say that made a difference?
6. Who was your favorite character and why?
7. Colin struggled with fear of making the same mistake twice romantically. Have

you ever held back from a relationship because of poor choices or hurt in your past? Please discuss.

8. Have you been to a wedding lately? What was your favorite wedding-themed decoration, shower game, or recipe? Please share funny or inspiring stories.

ABOUT THE AUTHOR

Cheryl Wyatt writes romance with virtue. She's earned RT Top Picks, spots #1 and #4 on her debut publisher's Top 10 Most-Blogged-About-Books list, *Romantic Times* Reviewers Choice Award, Gayle Wilson Award of Excellence final, and other awards. Cheryl loves readers!

Join her newsletter at
www.CherylWyatt.com.
Facebook: CherylWyattAuthor
Twitter: @cherylwyatt